Accidental Summer

A Star Lake Novel

Sara Rath

LITTLE CREEK PRESS
MINERAL POINT, WISCONSIN

Little Creek Press.
5341 Sunny Ridge Road
Mineral Point, WI 53565

ORDERING INFORMATION
Quantity sales. Special discounts are available on quantity purchases by corporations, associations, and others. For details, contact info@littlecreekpress.com

Orders by US trade bookstores and wholesalers.
Please contact Little Creek Press or Ingram for details.

Printed in the United States of America

Cataloging-in-Publication Data
Names: Rath, Sara, author
Title: Accidental Summer / Sara Rath
Description: Mineral Point, WI: Little Creek Press, 2024
Identifiers: LCCN: 2024906536 | ISBN: 978-1-955656-72-6
Subjects: FICTION / Women
FICTION / Action & Adventure / Romance
FICTION / Historical / Mystery & Detective

Book design by Little Creek Press

Cover photo: Shutterstock

Other Works by Sara Rath

Novels

Seven Years of Grace: The Inspired Mission of Achsa Sprague

The Waters of Star Lake

Night Sisters

Star Lake Saloon and Housekeeping Cottages

Nonfiction

H. H. Bennett Photographer: His American Landscape

The Complete Pig

The Complete Cow

About Cows

Pioneer Photographer

Easy Going: Madison and Dane County

Poetry

Dancing With a Cowboy

Remembering the Wilderness

The Cosmic Virgin

Whatever Happened to Fats Domino and Other Poems

The Night You Played the Snowy Morning Blues (forthcoming)

Screenplay

Annzinetta (for Wisconsin Public Television)

In memory of my dear friend
Professor Robert E. Gard,
who published my first book.

Note to the Reader

This is a work of fiction. The literary perceptions and insights may be based on true experiences, but all names, characters, places, and incidents are either a product of the author's imagination or used fictitiously. Except for historical newspaper accounts of Northwoods debauchery, Lotta Morgan and her murder, Piano Mary, Lumberjack Ida, Irish Annie, Razorback, Maud Cassidy, and Edna Ferber, no reference to any real person is intended or should be inferred.

You must not know too much or be too precise or scientific about birds and trees and flowers and watercraft; a certain free-margin, or even vagueness—ignorance, credulity—helps your enjoyment of these things.

—Walt Whitman, *Specimen Days* (1881)

The Celestial Chain

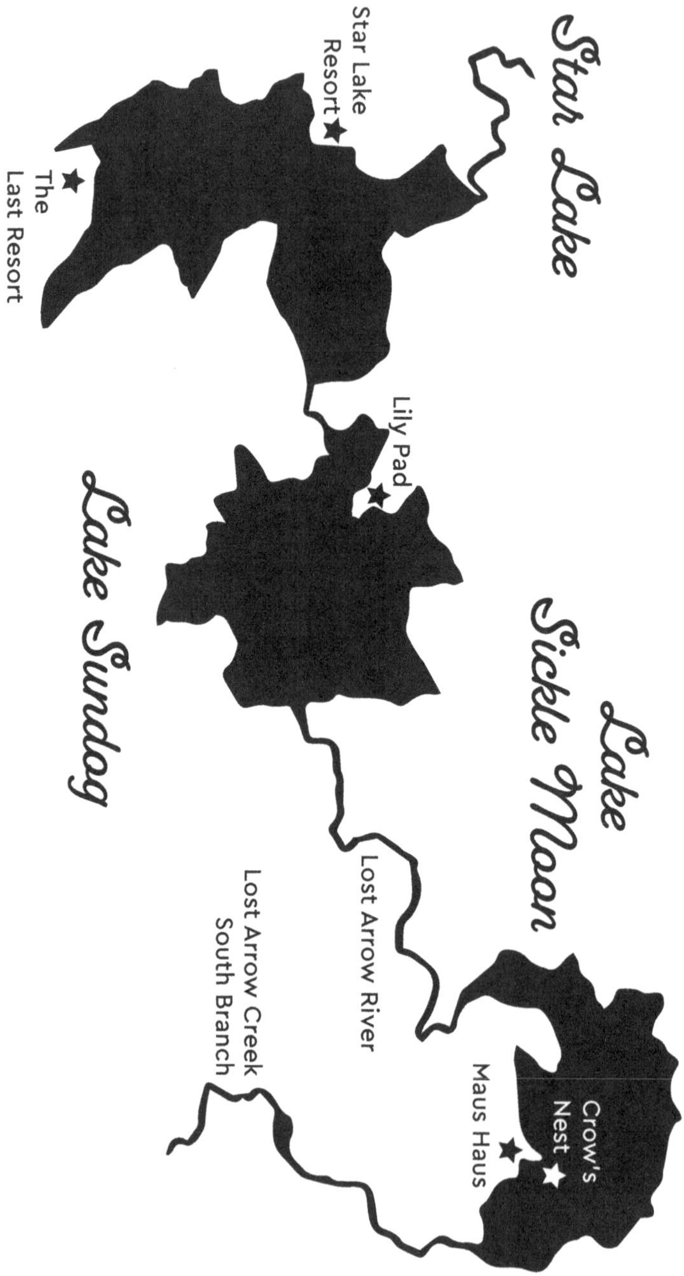

Part One

Tell me, what is it you plan to do
With your one wild and precious life?

—Mary Oliver, "The Summer Day"

One

What's on your mind, Jenny?

Where is Up North?

You know you're "up north" when you have to break out an old-fashioned map.

"Up North" is a state of mind. A feeling that once you have experienced it, it will stay with you forever.

Here you hit water if you head east or west, and if you go south, well, south is Illinois, and who in their right mind would want to waste a weekend going there?

Going "up north" is a part of the Wisconsin way of life. It's so ingrained in who we are that many take it for granted. Sometimes it takes moving away or meeting someone who didn't grow up with these experiences to make us realize just how special "up north" is to Wisconsin.

Roadside and ditch weeds like chicory, Queen Anne's Lace, spotted knapweed, and so many more. When they bloom, they're prettier than any annual to me. And lakes. I can't imagine a trip up north where the majority of it isn't spent on or near lakes.

Gravel and dirt roads. I don't care where they lead. Up north, for some reason, every road begs me to take it—the bumpier, the better. Up North roads mean possibilities and mysteries, even if there's nothing to be had on just about all of them.

⁂

On Highway 51 near Hazelhurst, just a few miles south of Minocqua, there used to be a sign: “North of the Tension Line.” I always saw this as an invitation to take a deep breath and let my worries recede. I had no idea that the “tension line” was more than an ephemeral boundary. In fact, it’s a geographic area that marks a change from one type of vegetation to another and divides Wisconsin into two major ecological regions: The oaks drop off, and you begin to see red and white pine, paper birch, and tamarack swamps. Different birds and mammals appear, like the common loon, ruffed grouse, osprey, snowshoe hare, porcupine, black bear, and timber wolf.

⁂

That Friday in late June, I looked forward to unpacking my bag and relaxing at Ada’s cottage. She’d offered her *Maus Haus* for my research as long as I wanted, although she’d warned me that the place had not been opened in at least a dozen years.

I wasn’t worried about the lack of amenities since my family had gone up north every summer to Birchwood Lodge. We always rented a cabin where the lumpy beds squeaked, and the rusty metal shower disgorged a feeble orange stream. Despite its rustic nature, I realized soothing memories from the somnolent waves that slapped the shore beneath our windows, the mystery of loons diving into the water and wondering where they’d emerge, and the joy of fishing for walleye in a rowboat with my dad. At twilight, he’d drive us to the town dump (there was no recycling then, just a place where everyone tossed garbage), and the raccoons would scatter. Other cars would quietly pull up and douse their lights. Then we all waited, windows closed, in stuffy silence for the bears to plod out of the woods and root through the trash.

I wish my daughters could have shared those simple pleasures. We lived far away when they were small, and after that marriage, I lacked the energy and resources to travel anywhere except back home to visit my parents.

As for Ada's requested research, I had some concern. I surely didn't mind a few endowed weeks in the Northwoods, but I offered an honest argument that Madison would serve just as well. I'd already checked out the Historical Society and newspapers.com to put together a modest treatise. But Ada wanted more; now she wanted a book.

⨳

There was heavy traffic heading north, normal for a weekend this time of year. Big pickups passed me with fishing boats on long trailers, SUVs with kayaks tied to their roofs and bikes to their tailgates, and motor homes that took up the space of three cars. I felt vulnerable in my Prius, despite its cherry-red exterior.

My goal was to arrive at The Star Lake Saloon in time for an early seat at their fish fry. Highly praised by Ada, she'd given me $10 and said their Friday night special would be her treat. But I was already running late when I passed Hazelhurst. Tension was building. I didn't feel relaxed at all.

"If you can hold it just a bit longer, maybe we can head straight to the Maus Haus." Dash, my black Labrador pup who'd been sleeping in his crate all the way from Madison, had begun to whimper. Yes, it had been an awkward decision to bring my new pup along. I'd had no idea when I adopted him that I'd be heading up north so soon, and I felt it would be cruel to stick him in a kennel. I'd only be away for a couple of weeks, and with Dash along I could enjoy his puppyhood.

I needed a bathroom, too. But Ada would be expecting my call from The Star Lake Saloon. Cell service at Maus Haus would be uncertain, although I was counting on some signal since I hoped to set up a hotspot there from my laptop. I'd never tried it before, but Google assured me the process was simple.

An hour later, a sign tacked to a tree declared, "THIS IS IT," followed by another that proclaimed, "THANK YOUR LUCKY STARS." My bladder felt like a snare drum. I tried to clip a leash on Dash, but he leaped out as soon as I opened his crate, and he lifted his back leg to pee on a stump. I praised him like crazy—what a good boy he was!

The day had turned oppressively humid, unusual for up north. Behind me stood the splendid new Star Lake Inn with its varnished yellow logs and majestic windows that reigned high above the property to reveal the scenic vista below, including a handful of vintage log cabins strung along the shore. I headed toward a long drooping structure next to the cabins that looked like it might slide into the water any minute. A neon beer sign sputtered "The Star Lake Saloon." This was definitely it.

Dash made his wiggly way down crude stairs of crumbling railroad ties, and I trusted him to stay while I entered a screened porch and mumbled, "Restroom...please!" I wedged past chrome dinette sets pushed against the outside wall where diners were already diving into their deep-fried perch. Above the crammed bar, a menagerie of woodland creatures gazed at thirsty patrons who waited for a table or a barstool that spun free.

Finally relieved, I was ready for a beer. I added my name to the list of loitering diners and took my beer outside to the grassy shore. Dash splashed into the lake after a stick someone threw. It was his first time in the water! I dug out my phone to make a video of this momentous event. His enthusiastic dog paddle was hilarious! The crowd cheered him on as he bounded out of the lake, delivered the stick, shook himself, and was ready to dash in the water again.

The man tossing the stick asked if I lived around there. "I wish," I replied truthfully. I already understood why Ada and Gus enjoyed this beautiful, friendly place. She said the resort was part of a chain that she and Gus could easily access by boat from their cottage.

My eyes were sore from driving and from the A/C, so I removed my sunglasses to massage my lids. I was handed the wet stick. "Your turn," the man said. "We're heading out. Take care! Looks like a stormy night."

That's when I noticed how dark the sky had suddenly become. A nauseous yellow hue illumined everything. The lake was very still. I heard someone say there was a tornado warning on TV.

"C'mon, Dash," I cried as I dumped the rest of my beer and tossed my bottle in a bin.

He was wet and slippery, but I scooped him up and carried him in my arms, squirming and wriggling, to run up the mossy staircase. I crashed into a bustling fireplug of a woman with frizzy orange hair, whom I knocked into the metal railing in my haste.

"Where the hell you trying to get to, honey?" she cried. "C'mon, you'd best take cover! Bring that pup along with you!"

Fat drops of rain fell as I elbowed my way past. I scooted Dash's tail end into the Prius and slid in after. Only a moment later, a sharp crack of thunder caused me to fall over him for protection. The door slammed from the wind.

"Sweet boy, we're going," I said, pulling Ada's hand-drawn map from behind the visor where it had been wedged. Her sketch was hard to make out in the sudden gloom, as dark as night.

Damn, I forgot to call Ada and tell her we'd come this far.

The car was hammered with a racket of hail that instantly shrouded the ground with a thick white crust.

"Hang on," I urged Dash, who still clutched his wet stick and was trying to squeeze his dripping body and the stick between my feet. "Maus Haus can't be much farther."

I could make out "THANK YOUR LUCKY" as I pressed forward blindly in lashing rain and punishing gusts that tried to force me off my path. Leaves whipped from waving branches plastered my windshield and screened my sight. I was trying to ignore the unnerving undertone rising beneath the storm's roaring worry. It resembled the proverbial freight train that victims always recognized when relating how their home had blown away.

"It's just a summer storm," I assured Dash, who cowered beneath my legs. "A summer storm," I said again to calm my galloping heart.

Then a massive fracture exploded with a jarring, numbing thud. I remember reaching for Dash. I may have seen a swish of pine needles.

There was very little I could recall after the crash.

Two

Voices. My head pulsed with pain. I tried to speak.

"Shhh, everything's all right." A man, nearby. His voice was gentle, as was his tender touch on my cheek.

It took all my strength to shape words. To open my eyes. My voice was a feeble whisper.

"What happened?"

A warm hand was placed on my forehead. "Don't try to talk," he said softly. "You're safe. We're taking care of you."

"What'd she say?" A woman now, concerned. Something soft was tucked around my shoulders and beneath my chin. "She's shivering something fierce, Brian. Took quite a hit, poor thing."

"Dash?"

"Your little pup's right down here, by your feet. I brought him a bone. Hope you don't mind. He seems to like it. Cute little guy."

"I don't...I don't..."

I felt Dash settle beside me and lick my face with his velvety tongue. Warm kisses. "Good boy," I murmured. "My good boy."

I hugged him to my side, a familiar body. I didn't even mind his needle teeth sinking into my arm.

Then I dozed off again. The next time I tried to squeeze open my eyes, the room was dark, but there seemed to be a steady glow nearby. Now a man beside the bed held my wrist. I pulled away. He said he was checking my pulse. A blood pressure cuff gripped my arm.

When I leaned on one elbow to sit, a raging bolt of pain knocked me back. I was impossibly dizzy. Everything spun.

"Can't stay..." Now my mind raced with panic. I tried to kick away the quilt that felt like a trap. "Let me go!"

The man placed a restraining hand on my shoulder. "Be still," he ordered gently but firmly. "Take a few deep breaths."

"Where in the hell am I?"

"This is The Last Resort," he said.

I paused for a moment, not certain I'd heard him clearly. "Don't fuck with me," I pleaded.

"It's not a joke," he said. "A tree fell on your car. We heard your dog, found you, and brought you here. Right now, you need to take it easy. I promise you're safe. I'll take you to the hospital as soon as we can get out."

"I'm sorry." Apparently, I'd caused this man a lot of trouble and needed to apologize. Tears squeezed from my eyes; I couldn't help it. He blotted them with a tissue.

The woman was gone, but he was there when I surfaced again. I couldn't stop shaking. An oil lamp dimly lit the room. How long had I been there? I was handed a couple of tablets with a glass of water. "Tylenol," he said. "Just take a sip. Lift your legs."

He placed a pillow beneath my knees to help with circulation and fit my arms into the soft fleece jacket that had been beneath my chin.

"Dash?" I said. "He'll need to go out and pee."

"All taken care of."

"I'm still really woozy. When I close my eyes, it feels like I'm going to fall over the side of the bed."

He lay down next to me. "I won't let you fall," he said, reaching over to squeeze my hand. "It'll be morning soon. Let's get some rest." He didn't let go. Dash wriggled himself between us and began to snore.

I inhaled the scent of pine, clean and fresh, that drifted from an open window. I heard rain dripping from the trees and thought about forest bathing, a Japanese practice—a process of relaxation. Becoming calm and quiet. Pine trees were supposed to be good for that. The natural pine fragrance had always captivated me, but now in my mind's eye, I saw broken branches, bleeding sap, and jagged stumps.

I slept until the loons' calls began to echo. An uneasy dawn slid into the room.

"I'm Jenny," I said to the man as I eased my tight grip.

"Brian," he replied. "This is my resort. Or what's left of it. I need to look around."

He swung his legs over the edge of the bed and stood.

"The Last Resort?" I inquired. "Isn't that what you called it?"

"Right," he said, bending over to inspect my wounds with a flashlight. "Not going to win any beauty contests today, I'm afraid."

I couldn't see him clearly, but I sensed a rueful smile.

"Your eyes are bruised, probably from the impact of your airbag. And a branch must've hit your face when the tree came through your windshield."

I reached up to touch my forehead. Gauze and a large bump.

"Blood vessels there are close to the skin, so those wounds bleed a lot. Nothing to worry about."

"Can I have a mirror? I need to see."

"Not a good idea right now." He pulled away. "I really have to go."

"I want a mirror!" I sat up a bit, still dizzy but fully awake.

"I used butterfly bandages," he said. "I know what I'm doing. I was a nurse practitioner in Milwaukee before I moved up here. If you end up with a scar, it'll just add character to your beautiful face."

"A goddamn mirror," I demanded so forcefully that Dash let out a yelp.

I had to know how hurt I was before my imagination pushed me over a very thin edge. I even tried to get out of bed, but Brian put a restraining hold on my arm.

"Look," he said impatiently, "you might have a mild concussion. For now, you're okay, but you need to rest. Meanwhile, I've got three cabins torn apart and three couples without a place to stay. One's bunking with a couple in my fourth cabin, and two are downstairs on the floor of the bar.

Their week is up, and they want to get out of here."

Then he got a hand mirror from what must've been the bathroom and tossed it on the bed along with a box of Kleenex.

"I want to get out of here, too," I said, my voice breaking.

"I'll send somebody up with ice chips, and later on you can have some toast. I've got to pull things together. You're not going anywhere until the road's open."

"Wait—what day is it?"

"Saturday."

"And your name?"

"Brian. Brian Cullen."

"Let me see you." He placed a hand beneath my chin and leaned close. As far as I could tell, in the early morning light, he had smiling eyes, curly reddish hair, and a trim auburn beard. I felt I could trust him.

"C'mon, Dash," he said. My pup leaped off the bed, ready for breakfast. "We'll talk later."

My eyes, black slits, sagged with bruises that spread down into my cheeks. The forehead injury was wrapped with gauze tied around my head.

Resigned to my fate (which I prayed was temporary—at least I was alive) and unable to stay awake, I faded away once more. When I awoke, a different man sat by my bed.

"Ice chips," he handed me a plastic glass with a calloused hand. "Brian says you got to stay hydrated. I'm Stumpy." He spoke quietly. "Brian's got to look after those folks downstairs, get some breakfast for 'em and make arrangements and so forth, but I'm supposed to sit here for a while. Said to tell you your car is on its way. What's left of it."

"Stumpy," I repeated.

"Some folks just say *Stump,*" he smiled, then indicated his left shirt sleeve, which was folded in half and pinned in place. "Nam," he explained. "My buddies have a good-natured time with it. I don't mind."

He wore a faded Brewers baseball cap over a long gray ponytail. A handsome man with a weatherworn face that could use a shave. He arranged my pillows so I could sit at a slight angle. The dizzy feeling had abated a bit.

"Jenny Burgess," I said.

"Nice to meet you." Stumpy shook my hand. "You'll be glad to know your pup's been running all over the place with plenty of piss and vinegar, making friends. No sign anything's wrong with him at all. We're keeping a close eye, though, 'cause he sure likes the lake. And we found your glasses and other stuff in your car."

He dug out my glasses from his shirt pocket and handed them over.

"Where's Brian's wife?" I knew I'd heard a woman's voice during the night.

"Aw, that's a sad story," Stumpy said. "Never met her; none of us did. Ellen, her name was. She passed away before Brian moved up here. Some think that's why he bought this place, to get away from losing her. It was a hellhole then and didn't cost much. Toad and I were hired to help clean it up, and we stayed on."

"Toad?"

"My buddy, Toad. You'll meet him soon enough. He's the one who's towing your car up to our parking lot. The two of us hang around here for odd jobs. Like fetching you!" he chuckled.

"I thought I heard a woman's voice."

"Oh, that'd be Ginger, without a doubt. Nosy old gal. Would you believe she hopped on an ATV to come over here in the rain in the middle of the night to see what was plugging up the road? Seems folks are trapped at the Saloon and can't get out due to your car and the downed trees. She brought you this here soft jacket that you're wearing. It says, 'Thank your lucky stars,' and I guess you should. We had a helluva time wrenching you out of that mess."

Indeed, Thank Your Lucky Stars was embroidered in a circle on the front. It was almost as ironic as finding myself at The Last Resort.

Three

When Brian helped me walk to his truck on Monday, we had to step around limbs and branches thrown everywhere. Torn roofing and glass—all kinds of debris—were mounded in a dumpster. My little red Prius was an abysmal wreck; I couldn't hold back an anguished sob.

⁂

Doctor Singh at the Cedar Springs Hospital was an old friend of Brian's from Milwaukee. I was given a CAT scan and X-rays and a bunch of other tests. Then I was free to leave under Brian's care.

"Ordinarily, we'd keep someone in your condition overnight for observation," Dr. Singh said. "But if he keeps an eye on you, that's good enough for me. Follow Brian's orders and get plenty of rest. I'll want to see you in a couple of weeks and then again later for a final checkup."

How much later, I wondered. My two weeks of tranquil repose at the Maus Haus had metamorphosed into two weeks of stark solitude at The Last Resort. My car was junk, I felt like shit, and I'd been condemned. There was no way around it.

Brian attempted to cheer me up with the promise of my prognosis, but I remained silent, angry, and depressed—a dark mood that lingered when we returned to the resort, where a silver Porsche convertible was parked by the side of the road. I heard Brian mutter "damn" under his breath. He announced, "Cynthia Curtis," as he killed the motor and pulled his cell from his shirt pocket. The flat tone of his voice should have been a clue.

The woman was already at my door to help me climb down from the cab, and although I had no idea who she was, I was enveloped in a perfumed hug. Tall, slender, platinum hair was pulled back into a careless bun, and she wore a black tank top tucked into white capris. That morning I'd grabbed some wrinkled pajama pants from my battered suitcase and a gray sweatshirt of Brian's stained with green paint. Oddly, I didn't care.

"Jennifer, oh my God!" Cynthia exclaimed. "The boys told me everything. What a horrible nightmare for you! And your poor car! What did the doctors say? Are you all right?"

Queasy from the ride, I had kept my eyes closed for most of the drive because the scenery flew past too swiftly, and the sun was too bright. Maybe it was the pain or the meds, but I'd lost my ability to process my emotions. Cynthia's profuse greeting was overwhelming.

"Brian, is she all right?" When the question received no response, I drew away from her arms to glance back at him, still behind the wheel. He was engaged with his phone in an imaginary conversation, I was certain.

Then Dash bounded up to me with his welcoming puppy dance. When he jumped to lick my face, Cynthia turned, arms up, to guard her chest. Dash saw that as an opportunity for a generous sniff of her crotch. I made a futile attempt to catch his collar.

"Brian," she shouted again over my shoulder. Then, "I'm sorry, but I'm uncomfortable around dogs." Her white capris had muddy smudges on the front. She tried to brush them off, which only made them worse.

I began apologizing, but she grabbed my hand and led me much too quickly to the porch in front of the bar. I stumbled and she slowed.

"This place looks like a bomb exploded," she exclaimed. "I can't believe it. Why weren't Brian's bar and his apartment blown away, too? Tornadoes are so erratic. Like, why were you chosen, at that exact moment, to have a tree fall on your car and change your life?"

It was a baffling thought. I'd been wondering the same thing since it happened, especially the part about *change your life*.

"So, I got an idea after I talked to the boys," she indicated Stumpy, who was playing fetch with Dash, and another man seated nearby drinking coffee, presumably Toad. "C'mon and see what we did for you. I hope you like it."

I couldn't climb the stairs as fast as Cynthia. She continued to chatter as I lagged behind and clung to the railing.

"Of course, this is the lounge here at the top of the steps, and I suppose you've spent some time here already because I can see dog fur on this cushion. And this hallway leads back to the side of the building that faces the lake, past Brian's room on the left and the bathroom on the right."

It didn't take much to figure out that Cynthia was in real estate with this ridiculous guided tour.

"But you probably weren't aware of this little hidden storeroom."

She opened a door, and I found my things, such as they were, had been moved from Brian's bedroom to a small space with a window overlooking the water. It had pale log walls and may have been a storeroom but now featured a single maple bed with a puffy pink comforter, a matching maple dresser, French lace curtains, and a colorful braided rug. Very girly. Very not my style, but Cynthia had made an ambitious gesture to please me. It was nice.

I wilted onto the bed, incredibly weary. Strong pain medicine from Dr. Singh was kicking in.

"Thank you, Cynthia. This is so kind of you."

I sincerely felt it was. "I'm just really, really tired."

"Of course you are," she said, placing both hands on my shoulders with one cheek touching mine.

"You can rest right here all you want, where it's quiet. No one will interrupt your privacy in this little room. And it's nothing, really, just a few things from my condo to help you feel cozier. The least I could do. Stump says you'll be here a while, and this way you won't be bothering Brian. The boys say he's been sleeping on a cot in his office. Now he can have his own bed back."

There was a fleeting moment when I wondered about her motives, but when she added, "I also laundered the bloody sheets," I shoved them aside. I was grateful to Brian, too, and I liked his bed. So what if she also liked Brian? And his bed. I could have died.

"Now, is there anything else I can do to make you comfortable? Tell me, and then I'll get out of here. Can I make some calls? Family, friends? I think the landline's working now."

"Ada," I offered at once with alarm. I knew my friend must be sick with concern. I gave Cynthia her number and briefly described the situation, instructing her to say my car had sustained some minor damage and I would be in touch with her about the condition of Maus Haus very soon. I stressed that Ada must absolutely not be informed of my injuries.

"Got it," Cynthia repeated. "Soft and sweet, right?"

"Sensitive," I replied. "Carefully. She's in her nineties. Can we talk more tomorrow?"

"No worries," she said as she removed my sandals and placed them neatly next to the bed. I was tucked under a fluffy fleece throw. Cynthia flashed a tearful smile and closed the door with a gentle click. A few deep breaths and a wisp of my anxiety drifted away, but then I turned to cry into a pillow and didn't stop for a very long time.

⁜

I saw little of Brian and a lot more of Cynthia over the following week as he and the boys assessed the damage with insurance adjustors before anything was greatly altered. It took him a long time to cancel the rest of the upcoming reservations for the summer.

Each day Brian checked my wounds but said very little. I knew he was preoccupied, so I was quiet, too. "You're coming along," was his only encouragement.

"How are you managing everything?" I inquired one day. I apologized for becoming yet one more responsibility and reminded him of my intention to leave as soon as possible. That drew a remorseful smile.

"You're not going anywhere, Jenny," he replied firmly. It'll be another few weeks before you're even close to normal, so you might as well enjoy the fine amenities we have to offer."

Around dinnertime, he brought up a pizza or a BLT, which I usually shared with Dash while sitting in the lounge. He never lingered, as there were usually patrons in the bar. Cynthia kept a basket of fresh fruit replenished daily.

She brought me lunch, often a sandwich or salad of some kind that she'd prepared, and later in the afternoon, a hot mug of her own herbal tea mixture, which is why, she claimed, I was healing so well. In time, we shared our stories while we sat on the ragged loveseat. The sagging plaid fabric mended with duct tape was also Dash's bed, so when we chose to sit there, I had to move his blanket to the floor, and he lay at my feet. Cynthia had become more accustomed to his presence and even reached out to pet him occasionally.

She'd never married, never had children, and (aha!) *was* involved in real estate. My brain was often too scrambled to follow everything she conveyed, but my initial resentment of her beauty and fear of potential nuisance dissipated as we became friends.

"Tell me more about Ada," she asked a few days after I'd asked her to call. "She said you were a writer, and the two of you have an agreement. Explain!"

"She wants me to write about an unsolved murder," I revealed. "A cold case from well over a hundred years ago. The murdered woman's name was Lotta Morgan."

Then Cynthia demanded to know how Ada chose me to tell the story. She took my empty mug and placed a pillow at my back. "Start at the beginning. We have all afternoon, but wait a minute until I get more tea."

I began with the end of my miserable second marriage. I figured she didn't need to know about my life up to that point because it didn't relate to who I was now, except that my twin daughters, whom I didn't see as often as I'd like, had moved to opposite coasts, and I'd sold our big house in Madison's University Heights to purchase a condo in the center of the city. For the last decade, I'd been the features editor of an alternative weekly, but the paper was recently sold to investors from Chicago who wanted to make it more web-based and focus on a younger, trendier audience. I understood completely since the city's art scene—especially music—had transitioned to something I'd been struggling to appreciate. It was a relief not to be assigned to review bands like Mother Earth Muggers, or Bless the Worry.

"Ada," I explained, "was the subject of a profile piece I wrote. A friend who was a social worker at Laurel Lodge—that's a posh retirement home—suggested her because she was the real deal: colorful, brash, and original."

I showed Cynthia a photo of Ada that I'd kept on my phone, and her reaction was expected.

"Oh my god! I love those eyelashes. Do you think they're mink? That red lipstick!"

I agreed. Ada may be ninety, but she was truly a free spirit. Her husband, Gus, told her he liked her that way. He traveled a great deal, according to her, and during that time, she entertained a variety of lovers. He didn't mind.

"Now Gus is long gone, her daughter lives in Paris, and their son was killed in Vietnam. She doesn't have many callers. I was smitten!

"One day, I was in her apartment sipping chai and finishing off the last of a bag of Milanos I'd brought when I mentioned that I'd lost my job and was pondering a move east or west to be closer to one of my daughters.

"Ada told me that sounded like giving up. I knew what she meant—my independence, my self-reliance, my unconventional lifestyle. I'd stayed in Madison when the girls left because I knew that neither Emily nor Charlotte would want me so close. How would they handle their lonely aging mother who wanted to stop in unannounced for coffee or dinner or share my woes whenever it was convenient? They may be twins, but they've always had their own lives. Both have careers and plenty of friends.

"Charlotte and her husband have a little boy, and I suppose I could offer to babysit, but they already have a live-in nanny. I'd be a burden. Besides, Charlotte's in Seattle and Emily's in Boston. Did I want to live in a big city? And how could I choose between them?

"Ada confessed she'd often dreamed of becoming a writer but lacked the discipline. I had to laugh. That was one of the things I admired about her—her lack of conformity, the effervescence of her free spirit.

"I told her I'd gladly lend a hand with her memoirs—it would be kind of fun to sort through her vivid past—but she dismissed that idea with a swat of her manicured hand and said, 'Silly garbage.'

"Then, a week later," I told Cynthia, "she called to say she'd had an appointment with her financial advisor on the Square and asked if I could meet her at the Edgewater for lunch. She said she'd Uber. Ada is definitely on trend.

"And from our table, we had a great view of the vast expanse of Lake Mendota with the University of Wisconsin campus on one side and the governor's mansion hidden in the trees on the opposite shore. I was pointing them out to her when Ada interrupted with an unexpected request.

"She said she'd underwrite my expenses for a year if I'd explore the life and death of a Hurley woman, a 'sporting girl' who was murdered in 1890."

"A lady of the evening?" Cynthia asked.

"A polite way of saying *prostitute*. I was kind of shocked, really. I mean, a year's expenses? To research...I mean, 1890? How crazy is that?

"Ada explained that she held many lucrative investments, thanks to Gus, and her daughter Susan had married well, so there was no need for a large inheritance to pass on to her. When she suggested it, Ada's financial advisor agreed it was a healthy challenge for her to take on a venture of her own, suggesting there was only a minor risk and the excitement could be entertaining."

"So, you're the risk," Cynthia said, patting my leg. "And that's why you're here."

I nodded. "Well, I'm supposed to be at Ada's Maus Haus, but I was regrettably delayed." We laughed at that. "But whenever I get there, I have Ada's credit card and the use of her cottage for free for as long as I want. I figure a couple of weeks will be enough.

"Gus bought several properties up north, and Ada apparently holds on to a couple. This is where they spent their summers with their children, on Lake Sickle Moon and the Celestial Flowage. Maus Haus can be reached from The Star Lake Resort within an hour. And Gus learned about this murdered woman, Lotta Morgan, when they mingled with the lake crowd each summer. One of his fishing buddies, an older guy, said he'd been the first to discover Lotta's gruesome body. But no one was ever charged with the crime. Gus had been fascinated by the story and tried to track down more details on his own, but the internet wasn't available back then, and Ada was still intrigued.

"For Ada, it's unfinished business and remains an open-ended wish for Gus to discover what happened to that woman. She gave me only one stipulation: when I finish my research, if it evolves into a book, the dedication must read *'To Gus Vogel with Ada's love.'*"

Cynthia wanted to know if I thought there might be a book.

I had to admit that I had no idea, but probably not. As quaint and colorful as the project may have seemed at that moment, my heart wasn't really in it anymore.

"Maybe when I get settled at Ada's Maus Haus, I'll be inspired. Who knows? I owe it to her to see what I can dig up. Right now, obviously, I can't do much.

"For now, all I can do is kill time."

Four

Then, somehow, it was Friday again. I'd been at The Last Resort for two weeks. Still suffering from balance issues, I wasn't yet in perfect form, but I had made progress, and my vision was much better.

By late morning the sun was shining, and I took my time holding on to the banister and made my way carefully downstairs to the screened porch in front of the bar, where I picked up a walking stick and ventured outdoors alone. I hoped to run into Brian. When he saw me moving around on my own, perhaps he'd be convinced I was well enough to move to Ada's cottage.

Except for brief moments before and after visits to the hospital, I hadn't had any opportunity to explore the grounds. Cleanup was still underway, and I was startled to see how complete the devastation had been. A few downed trees still cluttered the setting, their black roots exposed and reaching out like angry wraiths. Stump was working a Bobcat to haul a dented water heater to another dumpster parked near what remained of the garage. His buddy, Toad, was reducing huge branches to a manageable size with a chainsaw and heaping them into a pile. Toad was so-called due to a generous handful of warts on his face. He was also totally bald and pleasant. I responded heartily to their welcoming waves.

The bar appeared empty, so I figured it would be a good time to survey the place. Light came only from the jewel-colored jukebox and neon beer signs for Miller Light, Budweiser, and Pabst. There was the typical sour tavern smell, not entirely unpleasant. Barstools would accommodate maybe ten or twelve; I didn't count. Behind the bar, against the wall, was a glass cooler that held bottles and cans of beer. Beside that was a swinging half-door that opened to what was most likely the "kitchen" due to the electric pizza oven I spied on the counter.

Beyond the pool table, at the rear of the room, were a couple of high-top tables with scenic views of the lake and two small but clean restrooms. On my way out, I straightened a stack of brochures on the bar that summarized the place:

The Last Resort

Is an all-season family-style resort in business since 1926.
Our 4 rustic log cabins are located on beautiful Star Lake,
part of the notable Celestial Chain comprised of Star,
Sundog, Lake Sickle Moon, and the Lost Arrow River.
All cabins come complete with screened porch, shower,
heat, fully equipped kitchen, and bed linens
(please bring your own towels).
Bar serving beer and pizza.
14-foot rowboat included. Motors available for rent.
ATV and snowmobile access.
Great fishing for musky, largemouth bass,
northern pike, walleye, and panfish.
Fish cleaning house on the premises.

The Last Resort, Antler, Wisconsin

It was folded in thirds, and on the back, there was a map.

I called for Dash, who'd been tagging along with the men. He bounded over to me with that goofy sideways bounce that puppies have—he always made me smile. I hugged him profusely before we began a casual stroll. We hadn't gone far before I noticed a small granite marker in the ground engraved with "Bubba" buried near the bar. Someone's pet?

I was feeling okay physically but deeply disheartened as we skirted the wreckage of a couple of cabins on the shore. I paused at the third. A weathered sign above the door said "Bluegill." This was the one remaining cabin, its roof enclosed with a blue tarp. It resembled the rustic nature of the tavern with the same dark brown logs, and a porch on the front beckoned with its rusty screens and wicker chairs. Eager now to escape the mosquitoes and painful bites of marauding deerflies, I climbed a few steps and chose the rocking chair with a pillow on its sagging seat. Dash went out on the pier, had a quick swim, then joined me, collapsed at my feet, and fell fast asleep while I rocked.

Even with the background of grumbling motors and the flapping of the blue tarp, I grew sleepy in this serene and charming spot. A cushion of blue forget-me-nots lined the shore, and the lapping waves caused a lovely somnolent state. I closed my eyes and easily envisioned what the resort must have been like in the 1920s. Convivial and unpretentious, no doubt. The kind of place where you could take out a boat and fish whenever you felt like it or play shuffleboard for fun. Or sit on the porch like this and snooze with a good book in your lap. No excuses.

Brian had certainly suffered a profound loss. Even if he attempted to build it back up with fresh new cabins, they'd lack the patina laid down by generations of bygone lodgers.

I was musing, partly dozing, and hoping that Maus Haus would possess the same contentment when I heard, "Oh, here you are!"

It was Cynthia bringing our lunch. She joined me on the porch and agreed it was a perfect spot for a nap. I'd run out of clean clothes and was wearing a flannel shirt of Brian's with a pair of his floppy gray sweatpants. When I found enough energy—and a washing machine—I needed to tackle some laundry if I was going to hang around here for a month.

We had cheese and tomato sandwiches and sipped iced tea. I expressed my sorrow now that I'd finally witnessed the tornado's ravage.

"I hope and pray Brian doesn't sink any more cash into this place," Cynthia remarked. "It was foreclosed when he bought it, so I helped him get it as a 'short sale,' but even then, it wasn't a good investment, and I told him so. That was when I began overseeing the garden-condo development nearby, and I encouraged him to purchase a nice unit from me, but he said he wanted a place that needed work. This pathetic resort appealed to him. It was a mess.

"I was friends with Ellen, Brian's wife," Cynthia continued. "Not close friends, but before I moved to Chicago, we worked out at the same gym in Milwaukee and occasionally went out for coffee afterward. She was sweet, kind of quiet, and crazy about children. She'd started a series of daycare centers where working mothers could drop off their children, day or night. They really caught on. After she died, well, I think they faded away. Very sad."

I was hesitant to dig deeper but said, "Stumpy did say he thought Brian bought this place because he was depressed."

"She'd developed stage 4 pancreatic cancer. It moves very fast. By the time she was diagnosed, it was already too late. And despite his medical training, Brian couldn't prevent her decline. He took her to Mayos and MD Anderson in Texas, desperate to get her a transplant. It was devastating for him to feel so helpless and watch her die.

"Then, six months after her funeral, I got the commission to oversee Aspen Glen," she said, "and I asked him out of the blue—because I didn't dream he'd agree—if he'd like to take a weekend ride up north. I got a room for him at the Star Lake Inn. When he spotted the "For Sale" sign at this place, he started making inquiries. I tried my best to dissuade him, but he was determined to make an offer. Stumpy, Toad, all of us concur that he bought it out of guilt and a need to get away from his memories of Ellen's suffering and death. There was no discussion of the medical career he'd left until you came along, Jenny, and now he's practically too busy to even bother with you. He still has a mortgage on this debris!"

I thought she was a bit over the top by saying he didn't bother with me since he fixed and brought me my dinner each night and was still concerned about my health.

"So, you'd advise..." I asked, sensing her response before she spoke.

"That he raze the rest, of course. Including this forlorn little place.

Build some charming condos! Aspen Glen is realizing a great deal of interest. I have offers on units that only exist on paper!

"The view here is spectacular. I need waterfront, a lake, or even a creek. He could list it with me and put the entire place up for sale tomorrow. I have clients who'd sign a deed for the entire property, even in its existing state, if I had water. Confidentially, I already made him an offer, but he won't give it up."

I supposed if Brian stood to take a substantial financial hit from the storm, if he even cared about that, this would be a good time to consider her offer again.

"Are you, um, involved with him?" I asked timidly. I didn't know how to state the question, but I'd wondered about it and had watched them both for several weeks. So far, I hadn't perceived an exchange of tender feelings, but I'd been isolated in my pastel girly cell. "I mean, romantically," I added.

Cynthia laughed. "Not yet, but I'd like to be. I hope I'm not that obvious!"

I gave her a wry smile. Inside, I felt sick.

My reaction was perplexing. I barely knew Brian, and he and Cynthia had been friends for some time. Their relationship should mean nothing to me.

We were both silent while I attempted to sort out my ambivalent emotions, and Cynthia was probably dreaming of making this placid resort an annex of Aspen Glen.

She gathered our lunch things, interrupting my thoughts.

"I'll be happy to take care of your laundry," she offered. There she was, being nice so that I couldn't resent her feelings. "What else can I do for you? I'm heading back to Chicago in a couple of days."

"Maus Haus," I sputtered. "Could we take a drive over there? Would you mind? Ada must be anxious to know if her cottage has any storm damage."

Cynthia agreed that was an excellent idea. If I could convince Brian the time was right for me to move over there, she'd gain exclusive access to him. Win-win, right? At least for her?

"I called her again last evening," Cynthia admitted as we walked back to the bar. "Ada, I mean. She'd wanted me to keep her apprised on how you're getting along."

I knew, then, that Cynthia had told Ada about my injuries despite my asking her not to do so.

"And I said you were...that your Prius was..."

I also knew Cynthia was not a good liar.

Five

I found Ada's directions on the floor of my Prius, which would be towed away that afternoon. For a moment, I felt I should stick around to say goodbye, and I became choked up, patted a dented fender, and spread my arms to give it an awkward hug. Dash was happy to stay in Stumpy's care. We took off in Cynthia's sleek Porsche. She spun her tires in the gravel.

"What the fuck!" I exclaimed. "This is where I was headed the other night? In the storm?"

The Maus Haus turned out to be a shocking letdown.

"I don't think you'd have found it," Cynthia declared, "which would have been a blessing."

A discreet peninsula jutting out into Lake Sickle Moon provided a scenic site for the Vogel's cottage. Stumpy and Toad said they'd fished nearby and had seen the place from the water.

Ada's directions were correct, but we were frequently wrong and missed the turnoff where a gravel drive branched off the blacktopped county road, and a yellow "Dead End" sign should've been an easy clue. We also missed the path on the right, where a faded signpost on the ground had been engraved with a wood-burning pen to read Maus Haus. Cynthia made a U-turn in a circular area where cars could turn around: the dead end.

The building, nearly hidden by trees, faced the water. We approached it from the rear through a passageway of towering pines. The cottage had green clapboard siding with white shutters, a dark red asbestos roof, and a matching shed that leaned precariously at the end of the overgrown driveway where we left the car. A path around the left led to the front door, and a steep stairway of rocks went down to what remained of a pier.

Gus must have built a deck on the front before the advent of pressure-treated lumber, as the structure was missing more than a few boards. A metal front door opened off the treacherous platform and dangled from a rusty hinge.

Ada had given me a key, although we could easily have gained access without it. We kept the front door propped open while we stepped tentatively into the living room, where everything was damp. We decided the substantial hole in the roof had been there for a while as the black and red plaid shag carpeting was green and moldy in spots and oozed a rancid odor. The brick fireplace seemed intact and in okay condition. The leather sofa and chairs had served as a clannish habitat for dynasties of mice.

Maus Haus, indeed.

"Imagine if I'd arrived in the dark and had to spend the night!"

"This wouldn't have been a safe shelter from a tornado, Jenny. Seriously, I think we should be wearing gas masks right now."

Cynthia stood at an open bedroom door. "You know how they say it smells like something crawled in here and died? Come, have a look."

A cavity had been chewed through the outside wall. Heavy woolen blankets had been partially devoured. Feces from unknown animals were all over the place, and one corner held the rotten carcass of a raccoon. The striped tail gave it away; the skeleton could have been anything.

We escaped out to the deck to draw fresh air into our lungs.

"It's a toxic mess," Cynthia declared. "We can toss a coin to see who confirms that to Ada."

"You talked to her last," I suggested. We began to laugh. The situation was so ludicrous. "I wouldn't be here with my bruises and rattled brain if it hadn't been for this piece-of-shit cottage she so graciously gifted for my use. For free!"

"And you didn't want to look a gift horse in the Maus," Cynthia added.

We were nearly falling down, laughing, snorting, and wiping tears from our eyes.

"You'd have to be an acrobat to make your way down to the pier without breaking a leg."

Poor sweet Ada. She treasured her memories of this place, and it was a heartfelt gift of solitude. There was an ache in my throat.

"It's a teardown," Cynthia claimed. "No doubt about it. The location's okay, but what's left has got to go."

I didn't want to inform Ada, yet I knew the assignment fell to me.

"She still cherishes this place," I argued. "It'll break her heart to learn that it's become a putrid wreck. Besides that, she'll be mortified that she offered it to me for my use!"

"For free," Cynthia added, sending us off into yet another fit of hilarity.

The stench of the interior was drifting out onto the deck. We had been breathing so deeply that I'm surprised we didn't hyperventilate.

"You make the phone call, tell her we came over here to check on the place, then hand the phone to me," Cynthia suggested, wiping her eyes. Her mascara was smeared. "Greet her and let her know you're okay. Ada already knows I'm in real estate, so I'll give her my perspective. I'll be professional about it and explain her prerogatives: she can sell it as is; tear it down and sell it as waterfront property; have the place professionally gutted—torn back to the studs—and the lethal odor and germs and filth completely eradicated. New exterior and roof. Might as well start over! There's no way a realtor will handle this, even with rubber gloves and an oxygen mask."

"Building an entirely new building seems inappropriate when she cherished her memories of the original. She'll have to be convinced."

We left the storm door open because invading critters couldn't do much more damage. And we were somber as we headed back to the Porsche.

With more of an impatient swipe than anything, I opened the door to the leaning shed. It held a canoe, paddles, and a faded Volkswagen Beetle.

"Your new car!" Cynthia shouted.

"My new car," I echoed. "And it's even red!"

⁂

I bit the bullet when we returned to the resort, and I placed a call to Ada. She was relieved to hear from me and learn that I was okay. I'm certain, however, that she could sense my fatigue. I tried, but I couldn't entirely disguise how tired I was.

Then Cynthia took over to deliver the sad news. Ada took it fairly well and said she'd contact her insurance agent, who'd come by "lickety-split."

Damn, I missed Ada's effervescent spirit. Cynthia handed the phone back to me. Ada inquired about the resort where I was staying. Cynthia had told her I had a lovely room and was being cared for by a private nurse.

Only a minor hyperbole that I didn't bother to correct.

"Your Prius," Ada sighed. "By the way..." She went on to say that if we found a little Volkswagen Bug in the shed and it was in any shape to drive, the car was mine. She didn't want me to be without transportation.

"It's the least I can do for all you've been through, sweetie," she said. "I'm the reason you're way up there, and I hear you nearly lost your life! Are you getting inspired for the project we talked about?"

I fumbled to devise a rational response and told her I'd been distracted but would soon be formatting details. "It might go in several directions," I lied. Truthfully, I had given little thought to Lotta Morgan since I'd passed beyond the Tension Line. "I'll get back to you in a week or two. I might even be back in Madison by then."

Toad and Stumpy were wound up about the Bug. They towed it back to the resort the next day and began to fiddle with the motor in the remnants of Brian's garage, unable to mask their glee. Stumpy said he had a good idea of where to find parts. Toad claimed I'd inherited a total treasure. "It's a '67," he exulted. "A classic. This baby is vintage, one of the models collectors hanker after. If you go ahead and have it restored, it could bring big bucks."

I could read their disappointment when I said I just wanted to have something to drive and get me back to Madison when I was ready. Their shoulders slumped as they sighed and said they could have the car running well enough in a few weeks if that was all.

⁂

"Who was Bubba?" I asked Brian the morning after we'd had coffee and I'd shared the sad and silly narrative of our Maus Haus reveal. "So much for my plans to move over there to complete my rehabilitation and to begin my book" (the mention of which I added as an afterthought and a nod to Ada). That required some minor clarification as I wasn't sure I'd ever revealed my initial reason for coming north.

"Bubba?" I asked again. Before he asked for details of my "book," I wanted to change the subject. "There's a little headstone near the foundation of the bar with that name engraved."

He paused for a moment, checked his watch, then suggested, "Let's go for a ride. I hope your head's okay this morning because we won't be on the road."

I slid onto the seat of his beige utility terrain vehicle. I thought all these little machines were called ATVs and used for splashing through mud, like in the TV commercials during football games. This was more like a Jeep, and it was fairly quiet. Brian said he used it for hauling supplies to the cottages or reaching the far boundaries of the resort, which is where he took me—behind a dense grove of pines to a distant area I had not yet explored.

"It looks pretty good now because the grass has grown back," he explained. "This is where the previous owner kept his dogs. Try to imagine a dozen or more rusty overturned oil barrels scattered all over. Dogs, Plott hounds, chained to the barrels with rags, pieces of blankets, and old rugs to sleep on. When I was first shown this resort, no one had bothered to clean up their feces. And although it was claimed that they were being fed daily, it looked like the dogs were starving."

"Why would anyone want a Plott hound?" I was unfamiliar with the breed.

"For hunting bear. Bubba was a Plott hound and the lead dog for Bud Foster, who owned this resort before it was foreclosed. He was a hounder. Up here, that means using dogs to hunt bears. Plott hounds can be vicious; they're not like little Dash."

I obviously knew nothing about hunting bears with dogs.

Brian explained, as we drove back to the bar (and it was a bumpy ride), that Wisconsin sets time limits on when dogs can be trained for hunting bears, and it depends on the zone, but the training season in our zone began a few days ago.

"You might see their trucks around. They'll have six or more cages packed on the back of a truck, each cage with a dog. I've heard our parking lot used to be bumper-to-bumper with trucks like that because it was a popular gathering spot for hounders. They all revered Foster.

"Right off the bat, I let it be known that I am not a fan, and hunters who tree bear with hounds were not welcome here. I lost a lot of business during that first bear season, but it was worth it. Even had graffiti sprayed on the bar, and our 'Last Resort' sign was damaged, had to be replaced."

I asked if he knew what had happened to Bubba.

He said he did, but he'd save that for another day. It was a long story.

He parked the UTV, helped me down, and headed inside the bar, where Stumpy was chatting with a customer.

"Wait," I called. "Do you ever see bears around here?"

Stumpy and the guy he'd just served a beer laughed heartily at that.

"Jenny, we've got sixty-four thousand bears here in Wisconsin at last count, most of 'em up north," Stumpy said. "This year, hunters will take out four thousand five hundred, probably more."

"They're shy," Brian added. "If you see a bear, stay calm. Make sure you don't get between a sow and her cub. Otherwise, they'll most likely leave you alone."

"You're more likely to see a wolf or two," the customer commented. "They won't bother you neither, but keep your pup away from them. Nice little snack."

Stumpy explained, "They could see another canine as competition for their territory. Wolf-dog depredation isn't unusual, unfortunately."

The customer continued, "If you can prove your dog was killed by a wolf, the state will pay you two-and-a-half grand. Some hounders improve their pack that way." He snickered. "Take 'em out somewheres and let 'em have it."

With that to ponder, I went into the kitchen to fix a salad for myself. Cynthia was in Chicago, but I'd prepared a huge bowl of fresh greens with sliced tomatoes, green peppers, onions, and carrots and dished some into a smaller bowl for my lunch, which I then took down to Bluegill so I could eat on the porch. I missed my visits with Cynthia, especially now, when the future of Ada's cottage was uncertain.

There was one bedroom in the cottage, which I had yet to investigate. It had a window missing, but I found the screen on the floor and fit it back in place. The bed was littered with twigs and leaves. I shook the bedspread out on the floor, flipped it over, and lay down for a quick nap. Such a peaceful setting. I'd only intended to close my eyes and review what Brian had shown me. The Last Resort had secrets that I'd rather not have revealed. I wanted only the soft breeze, the yodeling loons, and the rhymical lapping waves I could hear at that moment.

I managed to catch Brian later that afternoon in the bar.

"Now that I know Ada Vogel's cottage is impossible for me to use, I was wondering if you'd let me rent Bluegill. I'll still be here on the grounds so you can monitor my recovery, and with my 'new' car, I can go back home as soon as I'm well enough."

"No," he said.

His curt reply was a surprise. I caught a glance from Stumpy, still in the bar, who merely shrugged and gave me a crooked smile. I was embarrassed. I apologized to Brian for asking but admitted I thought it was a reasonable idea.

He said he wanted to save Bluegill for a construction crew to use in case he decided to rebuild. The simplest thing would be for me to stay put. I might think I'd totally recovered, but I still needed rest.

"If you'll recall," he said firmly, "I assured my friend Singh that I'd be responsible for your well-being. You're due to check in with him at the hospital this Monday, two weeks since he last saw you." Blah blah blah...

⁂

That night I was already in bed by eight thirty, and the book I'd been reading had fallen to the floor. There was a tentative knock at my door. Dash, settled at my feet, barked in excitement.

"Sleeping," I mumbled and switched off my bedside lamp.

Brian stood over me while Dash bounced around, ready to play.

"I hate to pry you out of bed, but you have to come with me right now. If you don't, you'll regret it tomorrow. Trust me with this."

I grudgingly stuck my feet into a pair of oversized flip-flops.

"Wear your glasses and grab a robe."

I stumbled after him down to the T-shaped pier in front of Bluegill, where there was a wooden bench. Several lawn chairs had been placed there, and Stumpy and Toad were waiting. It was dusk.

"Don't want Jenny to miss the fireworks," Toad said in greeting. "We got everything set up for you."

Then I was very much awake! How had I not known it was the Fourth of July? I had admired many sunsets over water, but none since my arrival at The Last Resort. Now, Star Lake revealed a mounting profile of cumulous clouds in the west, warmed by the lowering sun's overripe blush. Across from us, the shore was a dark silhouette with the still water reflecting that image. As the sun set, the clouds developed a dusky pink hue that overspread the entire sky.

My lawn chair had a pillow on the seat (nice touch), and I pulled the terrycloth robe around my bare legs as the evening turned cooler when the sun disappeared.

"Keep your eyes over there," Toad said, pointing in a vague direction. He walked back up on land and was gone for several minutes. When he returned, the entire perimeter of Star Lake was encircled by red flares, including the edge of our shoreline—a necklace of glistening red jewels or glowing coals. I could imagine everyone on the lake feeling the same awe, and the impressive part for me was their mutual participation in the creation of that splendor.

When the flares burned down, fireworks began. Brian said Star Lake Lodge put on a little show every year. It only lasted a few minutes, but Dash, frightened by the first boom, scurried off the pier and hid beneath Bluegill's porch.

Brian went back to fetch him. Then he held Dash firmly on his lap and covered the dog's floppy ears with his hands.

It was not a flashy display, but I was delighted to celebrate this benchmark at the turn of the year with new friends. Mother used to close such an evening by saying, "Summer's half over now," and I'd respond with a bristly remark. Her rejoinder was always, "Swimsuits will be on sale."

"Rain tonight," Stumpy muttered as he gathered the folding chairs.

Toad replied, "Cooling off. Good sleeping weather."

The boys headed back toward the parking lot while Brian and I climbed the hill to the bar. Dash was lagging—a tired puppy. Every day was active for him; there was so much to explore. I nearly lost my balance a few times, slipping in the dew-wet grass. Brian caught my arm, and I left the flip-flops where I kicked them off.

Then I couldn't go back to sleep. The suggestion of a thunderstorm brewing in the distance was usually a summer lullaby. Later, when the rain began to sift through the curtains, I heard Brian come in to close the window.

A brilliant flash abruptly coincided with a terrifying explosion.

I honestly don't know what happened. I must have had a traumatic reaction to the thunder because the next thing I knew, Brian was comforting me. Dash had crammed himself beneath my pillow.

Brian sat on my bed and held me while I sobbed on his shoulder. Rain hit the roof in rolling waves.

"It's okay, Jenny. It's okay." His soothing whisper sounded in my ear. He embraced and rocked me as if I were a frightened child or a shell-shocked pup. Faint kisses on my forehead, gentle kisses on my cheeks. His beard was softer than I'd imagined. He smelled like soap.

"A touch of PTSD," he murmured. "Not unusual after all you've been through."

He continued to hold me and shared my bed for the rest of the night, although I was between the sheets and he lay on top of the quilt with Dash, who'd eventually emerged from his refuge. Silly boy. I was reminded of my first night at this resort when we'd slept in Brian's bed in a similar way.

My frayed brain invented passionate scenes with Brian that melted into a dream state, no matter how hard (or not that hard) I tried to push them aside.

Thunderstorms rumbled for hours. I didn't mind.

Six

Toad drove me to Cedar Springs the following Monday to see Dr. Singh. I'd hoped it would be my final exam, but after I flippantly quipped that I may have developed ADHD from my concussion because I was having trouble concentrating (partly my guilty conscience for lack of interest in Ada's project) and truthfully complained of recurrent headaches, he asked that I check back with him in two more weeks.

Note: It's not a good idea to joke with doctors.

On the way back, I asked Toad if he knew about Bubba. Yes, he did, and he knew about Bud Foster, too.

"I could go way back, but long story short, Bud messed up big time. He was a nice guy. Generous as heck. And there was this woman and her granddaughter staying at their cabin over on Sundog, so in a stupid, weak moment, Bud invited them to come along to see him and some others training their dogs. About this time of year, matter of fact. All the other guys knew Bud raised Bubba from a pup and how he loved that dog who was on his last legs, so to speak.

"Lo and behold, wouldn't you know that the girl and her grandma ended up watching a pack of dogs tree a bear. It was just a cub near a barrel of crap bait. Both women were scared to death that cub was going to get shot. Bud, he tried to rush them back to his truck before all hell broke loose, but before they got there, they heard a gunshot, and the girl turned around. The guys were already downing beers to celebrate, and the dogs were feasting on fresh bear meat. One guy told her it was so their hounds would get a taste."

Toad took a deep breath before he continued. I was sick at heart about the story he was telling.

"Later that day, the girl called the game warden. The guys lost their hunting privileges for three years and paid big fines. They were pissed as hell at Bud for bringing the women along. The next morning, Bubba was gone."

"Retaliation?" I asked. "Were the other hounders trying to get back at Bud?"

"You got it. After dark, the granddaughter snuck over and cut Bubba's chain, thinking he'd run away. But the poor old thing was blind and lame, somehow found his way to the door of the bar to wait for Bud, and fell asleep there. Bud's so-called buddies picked up Bubba, tied him up near a wolf rendezvous site, and all that was left of him the next morning was just his head and collar."

We were nearly back at the resort by the time Toad finished his story. I found it hard to speak.

"Does Brian know about that? Is that why Brian doesn't like hounders?"

"Hell, Jenny, a lot of folks don't like them. They bait the bears with sweets to get 'em used to coming to a spot, then set the bears up to shoot 'em when they do. Or the hounds get on the trail of a bear and chase him until he's exhausted. Or they can't tell what sex it is and kill a pregnant sow. Or shoot the sow and leave orphaned cubs. Either way, it's not a fair sport. Some states don't allow hounding. I could go on and on, but I figure that's enough."

I asked Toad if what happened had anything to do with the resort being for sale. He said Bud took off. Abandoned it all. To this day, nobody knows where he went. The dogs were left to starve, and eventually, the property went into foreclosure. After Brian toured the place and saw how their ribs were showing, he got somebody to finally give the dogs a new home.

"It was a goddamned pitiful sight, let me tell you. And guess who ended up having to clean up after all them dogs? Stumpy and me, that's who."

I could imagine Brian wanting to resurrect something that had been left so forlorn. It was his nature. And at that time in his life, he'd discovered a therapeutic project that would consume his energy and much of his time.

I also appreciated Brian's reluctance to share the rest of Bubba's sad story.

What happened to Bud Foster? What about the girl who'd called the game warden? Some mysteries there. I couldn't solve them all.

A note waited for me saying Ada had called: her insurance adjusters would inspect her cottage next week. To my profound relief, Cynthia had said she'd show them around.

※

The Last Resort had likely validated its awkward name many times. Old resorts like this surely had vast layers of anecdotes, and I briefly wondered about the hundreds of people who had arrived here over the years with a simple promise in mind—blissful solitude, quiet water, and no major concerns.

When I asked Brian what else he knew about the resort, he opened a drawer of his desk and said I was welcome to sift through the leftover collection of postcards there. Black and white scenes of the resort from the 1920s onward revealed its evolution. Some were comic scenes with enormous fish; others pictured the bar after various stages of transformation. Remarkably, photos of the cabins (at least Bluegill, the only one remaining for actual reference) revealed they had remained unchanged. I thought the cottages were sweet and closely resembled the one we rented at Birchwood Lodge when I was a child.

※

Sporadic vision problems caused reading to remain a challenge. Back home, I'd been addicted to my phone and laptop, checked email frequently, and kept close tabs on local and national news. At first, I'd suffered (in addition to everything else) an annoying withdrawal from lack of Wi-

Fi access and mild depression without the diversions of Facebook and Instagram. Eventually, Brian's Wi-Fi was up and running again, but I had adjusted to living without it by then.

I tried to Facetime my daughters. We had to settle for texting which, in retrospect, was probably a wise choice. My bruises were faded but evident; I was still avoiding mirrors. The girls were given modified accounts of the raging tornado and exaggerated descriptions of the glamorous bed of roses into which I'd fallen. Aware of my love of the Northwoods, neither questioned the length of my stay.

I was able to order new underwear online and a few clothes. I also ordered a larger collar for Dash, who had grown so much that his puppy collar no longer fit.

⁂

Around the lake, après-storm excitement was subsiding, with life returning to normal. On Monday nights, the bar was closed, and now that most of the larger debris had either been completely removed or shoved over to one side, a casual neighborhood ritual was reinstated. During the day, Toad and Stumpy gathered branches, boards, and anything combustible—not a problem at present—and piled them in a circular fire pit lined with stones in the center of the grounds. At twilight, neighbors came by with lawn chairs and snacks, bottles of wine or beer, and mingled with one another while the flames twisted and twirled. Eventually, Toad strummed his well-worn guitar with a clear, sweet sound. When he began to sing, everyone else joined in. The songs were old favorites like "Take Me Home, Country Roads" or "Sentimental Journey." Folks would harmonize, and the effect of campfire smoke in the long summer twilight amid tall pines beside the tranquil lake was familiar and soothing.

Following my initial bonfire, it seemed as if everyone present came over to shake my hand or give me a hug, expressing sympathy for my accident and wishing me well. I'd never experienced a community like that. Several commented on my stay at "Brian's Hospital," which they thought was hilarious. Maybe it was the wine.

※

Although he'd refused to let me rent Bluegill and move into the cottage, I inquired if it would be okay to at least borrow it during the day for my writing. I'd relocate as soon as his contractors arrived (if he was determined to rebuild).

To reach this point in my argument and gain his acquiescence, I offhandedly mentioned I could help in the bar after business picked up. Now that my balance was better, how hard could it be to wait on customers, hand them a beer, that kind of thing? In response, Brian asked, "How do you feel about serving pizzas?"

I wanted to say that his frozen pizzas sucked, but I gave him a bright smile and said, "Sure! That'd be great!"

Brian had no idea that I was a pizza snob. He'd been kindly providing me with his frozen pies for weeks, and I'd choked them down without complaint. Now he gave me instructions for the electric pizza oven that came with the frozen pizzas to advertise their brand. First thing: it was critically important to turn on the oven at the start of the evening so it would achieve optimum temperature and be able to pop out two fully cooked pizzas in around twenty minutes, give or take. When a customer chose from the handwritten menu on the wall of the bar (cheese, sausage and cheese, or the supreme—cheese, sausage, pepperoni, and mushroom), I had to dig deep into the kitchen freezer to find the selected item and tear off the plastic. Nothing else was added. The sauce tasted like SpaghettiOs, and the tough bits of sausage could've been rabbit turds. I'd have used a lot more cheese, but I'm a Wisconsin girl who likes mozzarella. When the bell dinged to say it was done, each pizza was served on a metal tin with small paper plates, napkins, and plastic utensils. Since we were currently without lodgers and because we were no competition for The Star Lake Saloon's hamburgers, our customers were mostly from the area and gathered for camaraderie, obviously not fine dining.

Tuesday, my first night as a pizza chef, had been quiet. Only a few regulars were there, including two old men who came every Tuesday evening to play cribbage. I privately called them Curly and Moe. After wiping off the table from the last customers, I was seated at the bar to finish a lukewarm slice when Brian inquired, "Tell me more about the subject you came up here to explore."

I couldn't admit that my enthusiasm for the project had expired. "Let's discuss your pizzas," I proposed instead.

That's when I came right out and confessed my pizza arrogance. It was a delicate subject since he'd been faithfully serving me these frozen slabs, and I didn't want to seem unappreciative. I hadn't lost any weight!

"The thing is, back home, I usually make pizzas from scratch. These are lacking in something. Maybe it's a human touch. I'm sorry."

I pushed my paper plate away with the edge of a leftover crust I planned to share with Dash, who sat at the foot of my barstool dangling a long thread of drool.

"Fair enough," Brian replied. "Show me what you can do. Make me one of your homemade pies. Give Stump a list of supplies you need, and tomorrow he can make a trip to the Antler IGA."

Dash caught the crust I tossed. What had I done?

If Brian liked my pizzas, and who wouldn't because they were fantastic, I feared my fate as a pizza chef might be sealed for a while. Would there be any time to handle a writing project in Bluegill? Not a worry—inspiration would have to strike before any real writing could commence.

My pizza process involved mixing my yeasted dough and letting it rise overnight in the refrigerator because that rendered the crust more flavor. Then I rolled it out thin and baked the crust on a hot charcoal grill so it got crisp and nicely charred. When it was flipped, I'd spread the toasty side with chopped garlic and crushed red peppers sauteed in olive oil, chopped tomatoes, onion, plenty of shredded mozzarella mixed with freshly ground Parmesan and sprinkled with torn basil leaves before I put the pizza back on the grill to melt the whole thing together. Red sauce was an option.

Without even closing my eyes, I could see myself gleefully flinging those frozen pies out of the make-believe kitchen like frigid Frisbees and

"Jenny's Last Pizzas" written in my hand on the menu on the tavern wall.

Did I want to work that hard? Then again, I could have perished in the wreckage of my car.

I owed Brian big time for taking care of me.

I'd managed again to avoid Ada's project, but I always found the act of kneading dough to be productive for managing anxiety and working things out.

⁂

When I'd joked with Dr. Singh about having ADHD, I wasn't entirely kidding. I'd never suffered from writer's block before. Ada's request had been straightforward: acquire information about an unsolved murder in Hurley over a century ago. That should have been a no-brainer. I could've lied and said I'd tried but found nothing there, yet I procrastinated like crazy and felt no urgent need to work it out.

Plenty of other up-north subjects had the potential to grab my attention. Yet, they didn't. How about a fictional multi-generational saga that followed a family of four who spent each summer at a Northwoods resort like this one? A kind of "same time next year," with the subtext disclosing a cautionary tale about the secrets we keep. With some effort, I could dig up the incentive for that, but it didn't fulfill Ada's request.

However, the topic touched upon a query that had emerged during my Bluegill daydreams: I was curious about the origin of the Northwoods' earliest resorts and what daily existence was like.

⁂

Cynthia liked the idea of the novel because she was a fan of historical fiction and said I could incorporate local visits from Chicago gangsters.

"Dillinger, Baby Face, Capone, they've been done to death," I argued. "Have you heard of the Southern Poverty Law Center? It's a nonprofit civil rights organization dedicated to fighting hate. If you check their website, they've compiled a comprehensive list of hate groups operating in Wisconsin, especially up north."

Cynthia wanted examples, so I listed the KKK. "And Proud Boys, Nation of Islam. Mostly neo-Nazis and white supremacists. I didn't dig deeply for details."

"But they're not around here," she countered. "I can't believe that."

With internet access restored, even as slow as it was, I promised to follow up and report back to her. She worried that racial disputes or extremist conflicts would be detrimental to selling Aspen Glen's condos.

I agreed it was a dark subject and assured her I was more intrigued with the historical aspects of resorts. "When you research a subject, you commit to living with it for a long time. Truthfully, I don't want to descend into an examination of evil."

⁂

Brian had told me he had no idea where "The Last Resort" name originated or who'd initially established the place. Toad insisted that I check with Ginger Kovalcik, the area's unofficial historian. He knew she'd been acquainted with a previous proprietor who'd owned the place long before Bud. I didn't have a longing to learn more about Bud Foster and his hounders, but Ginger didn't live far away, so talking with her would be painless. Toad said she had a cottage on Sundog, the lake adjacent to Star on the chain. The next afternoon, he took me by boat while Stumpy was shopping for groceries.

The white clapboard cottage had been christened *Lilypad*. Toad cut the motor and pulled up to Ginger's dock. Just then, Dash leaped overboard and began swimming off on his own. I stupidly stood up to grab him by the collar, lost my balance, and fell in.

I could hear Toad's laughter as Ginger, now down at the water's edge, grasped my hand and helped pull me onto dry land. "Don't be ashamed," she ordered, "happens to the best of us. Even Toady. I happen to know he's spent plenty of time in the drink."

"See you later, Jenny," he shouted, turning the boat and speeding away.

"Wait," I sputtered. But Dash was already onshore doing his happy Lab dance and nosing around trees and shrubs for satisfying scents.

"Aw, c'mon," Ginger admonished with a hug, "Let's get you into some dry duds. Then we can gab. Matter of fact, you might recall we already met..."

It turned out Ginger was the little woman with the cloud of orange hair who'd tried to keep me from leaving the Saloon when the storm was overhead. She was also the one who'd brought over the "Thank Your Lucky Stars" fleece jacket for me to snuggle in after my rescue.

We reached a large, screened porch cantilevered over a flagstone patio.

"I knew it was you who constipated our danged road with your cute little red Prius," Ginger confessed with a sigh. "Though that big white pine played a part. Nearly shoved me over on those slippery stairs, too, and look where it got you! Too uppity to take shelter with the rest of us, I guess."

Okay, I was ready to leave. Her accuracy was embarrassing, but then she flashed an apologetic grin. After I dried my hair, I sported a clean pair of old bib overalls and a large white shirt, the origins of which I didn't inquire. She indicated that I should unwind on the green pillowed seat of a woven cane loveseat.

Dash lay down to chew on a fresh ham bone. I helped myself to a chocolate chip cookie from a dark blue platter that Ginger offered.

"Nothing like chocolate to heal what ails you," she said, settling into a rocking chair. "But from the looks of the remains of those bruises, you're getting some better anyway. Good thing you couldn't see your face when I stopped over that night—you looked like you fell out of the Stupid Tree and hit every single branch on the way down."

She was petite and wrinkled, ageless, the color of a golden raisin but not quite that pale. Her orange hair radiated around her head like a carbonated aura, and she wore a chartreuse T-shirt with faded jeans rolled up at the cuffs to reveal a sturdy pair of athletic shoes.

I thanked her for the fleece jacket and for visiting me. "I *was* stupid," I confessed, "for not taking shelter. I was worn out from my long drive, and I wanted to get to a friend's cottage before the storm hit."

“Honey, it broke my heart to see you all beat up,” she replied. “You poor thing. Better have another cookie.”

She’d used dark chocolate chips, my favorite, and they were still melty from the oven. I took another and commented on her home. Ginger explained the cottage had been financed by her close friend, Lily Larkin, who’d only recently passed away. The women had been roommates for many years. “I miss my dear sweet Lily with all my heart,” Ginger said with obvious grief. “She was the kindest, most good-hearted, and most generous person I’ve ever known. One day she said to me, she said, ‘Ginger, when I pass, I’m leaving this and all my worldly goods to you.’ She paid for the whole place when it was built, you see. I lived here with her at her invitation. She wasn’t healthy from the get-go.

“Her last few years, sometimes Lily didn’t know up from down, but I took care of her the best I could. Horrible quiet here without her. I guess I need to get a cat or a pup like yours. I know some folks used to gossip we were lesbians or girlfriends, and I’ll admit I held and kissed her and comforted her, even slept with Lily in my arms. We weren’t lovers, but we were closer than sisters.”

One more cookie, and I’d quit.

Ginger continued, “So now, here I am, lonesome on my own, but with sweet memories, no worries, and not a single monetary need. A solid roof over my head, beautiful scenery like this grand vista to wake up to every morning, and friends galore. What more could an old woman want, huh?”

I shrugged and smiled. She seemed satisfied with herself. I nodded my thanks for a glass of lemonade.

“Two cents says you never thought you’d be accidentally laid up over at The Last Resort. I’d bet the table on that.”

She pointed to a smear of chocolate on my cheek and leaned over to wipe it with a piece of Kleenex enhanced with a dab of spit.

“I see you’re chumming around with Blondie.”

Of course, she must mean Cynthia. I said we’d driven around the lakes so I could get familiar with the neighborhood.

"She still set on sleeping with Brian? You been given any indications of that?"

I wasn't going to play that game.

"As far as I know, he's rejected her advances."

That was an accurate statement, and I hoped it would continue. The idea of Cynthia + Brian gnawed at me, although I knew it was ridiculous and most likely based on his being so kindhearted.

"That Brian's a sweetheart," Ginger said. "But he carries an air of sadness about him. Entangled emotions about his wife. A guilt trip, they all say."

That was another subject I wouldn't hypothesize about, even if Stumpy had reported that it was a common perception.

"I hope Brian doesn't fold like a cheap umbrella because Blondie's hot to take over. Everyone knows she wants to add his waterfront property to her condo project—easier now that it's all rubble. And if she's nice to you, take that nicety with a grain of salt."

"I don't have anything valuable to offer."

"In my experience," Ginger added, "oftentimes when a woman you think is doing something for you out of the goodness of her heart, the truth might be she's nothing but a nasty scheming bitch. Some of 'em are so crooked that they have to be screwed into the ground when they die."

I laughed at her preposterous comment, certain it had been utilized many times before. Her "colorful crotchety" persona seemed too rehearsed. Showing off? Could be a holdover from her days tending bar at The Star Lake Saloon. She said she'd been there for nearly forty years. Still, she made delicious cookies. I could be forgiving.

Dash was snoring, full of crumbs and treats. Occasionally he twitched his paws and wagged his tail as if chasing a squirrel. I had seen black squirrels up here, beautiful animals, sleek and shiny. Stumpy told me they were rare due to a genetic mutation, and this area was one of their few natural habitats. He also informed me of a superstition: squirrels can be one of the most trusting wild creatures, even learning to take food from your hand. "So when you see a *black* squirrel, it can mean that it has come to tell you to trust you're in the right place and doing the right thing," he said. "Trust the path you're on." But Stumpy might have made that up for me, knowing I needed reassurance.

"Why did you come up here in the first place, Jenny, if I might be so bold?"

Ginger slid around the question she was determined to have answered.

"I'm supposed to be researching a historical subject. Maybe or maybe not for a book."

"What about?"

I didn't want to admit my lack of focus, so I acknowledged, "Nonfiction, probably. Could be fiction. I've never written a book per se, mostly articles and the occasional poem."

"*Per se,*" she replied. "I've always wondered just what that meant, *per se.*"

"Sorry," I said. "There was a sense that if I spent some time here, I'd be inspired with breathtaking genius."

"That knock on the head call anything to mind. *Per se?*"

She laughed at the image she'd prompted, and I laughed, too.

Toad would not pick me up for another hour, so I asked, "One thing I'm curious about is the origin or history of The Last Resort."

"Good luck looking for genius there, kiddo. Not much dazzle, I don't believe. Of course, I knew Bud Foster; everybody did. And every summer, I went to his annual Roadkill Picnics just to be sociable. Always bring something for myself that I knew was safe to eat! None of his 'fricasseed fox' or 'sauteed snake succotash.' "

Then Ginger began to muse about her bartending days at Star Lake and bizarre interactions with patrons over the years. Finally, she reached a point where she mentioned that she'd been good friends with a long-ago owner of The Last Resort, Duncan Sunderlast, better known as Skipper because he enjoyed taking guests out in his pontoon boat to his favorite fishing holes. "Skip was one of our veteran resort owners and a colorful character, to boot. Wish he could tell you himself because he watched the business grow from the days of the canoe and rowboat to outboard and inboard motors. Didn't start with the dugouts or quite make it to those damned jet skis, praise the Lord!"

Back then, the place was known as Hideaway Bay, but Ginger told Skipper, "You should have your own moniker involved." So, they figured using *last* from his name would be effective, and that's how *The Last Resort* was born.

"Duncan Sunderlast," I repeated, making a note on the tablet on my lap.

"And it's a damn shame, too," Ginger continued, "what happened over there with the storm. I hope Brian tells Blondie to you-know-what and goes ahead and fixes his place up instead of surrendering to Mother Nature. Got any idea of what he's planning to do with it?"

"Not a clue," I admitted. "I'm sorry I didn't have an opportunity to see it before."

Ginger was getting more and more wound up. "I know there's plenty of folks came up north years ago and stayed at resorts like that when they were kids. Learned how to thread a hook and bobber from their dads or granddads, pulled in a sunfish or a walleye if they were lucky, went off to investigate trails in the woods, and were wide-eyed with surprise when they came upon a herd of deer or maybe a bear. Nowadays, all they want to do is fiddle with those electronic gizmos, and they might as well be vacationing on Mars."

"I was one of those long-ago kids with a bamboo pole," I confessed and launched into my sacred homage to loons, bears at the dump, canoes, and somnolent waves. But Ginger was way ahead of me.

"Jenny, I just now thought of something. There was a cardboard box that Skipper stored up in the attic over at the Saloon. He was packing to move up to Alaska to be closer to his kids, and he was about to pitch a hodge-podge of old clippings and papers he saved throughout the years. He had some last-minute hesitation about burning them, so I told him there was plenty of attic space next to the skis and ski poles and leftover fishing gear. It was years and years ago, mind you, but that box probably hasn't moved a jot nor tittle, and could be you might come across some bits of inspiration. Who knows? Skip came down here from Hurley, so I warn you there might be some spicy particulars." Ginger grinned at that and bounced in her chair as if she couldn't wait to investigate.

I agreed it wouldn't hurt to have a look. Now Ginger was impatient and unable to contain her enthusiasm.

"When Toad comes back to fetch you, I'll ask him to come by tomorrow with his truck, and we'll go over to the Saloon so he can help me hunt it down," she said. "I'll need to tag along to show him where it is. Meanwhile, why don't you take this one last lonesome cookie? Good for you. Let me get you another glass of lemonade to wash it down—should've done it sooner. I think you're spryer now than when you got here, am I right? You look better, anyway. At least you're finally dry. Go on and keep those soft old bibs. They're not sexy, but you're going to find them awful comfortable. I like to wear them, how do they say, *commando*?"

Seven

Cynthia found me in the kitchen the next morning, still sorting out the many bags of groceries Stumpy had delivered—ten pounds of flour, plenty of dry yeast, olive oil, Italian sausage, fresh mushrooms, pepperoni, green and red peppers, black olives including kalamata, fresh garlic, fresh basil, onions, and fresh tomatoes, lots of mozzarella and Parmesan cheese. Before I began baking, I wanted the ingredients to be convenient. But there was little storage space, and the refrigerator was small.

Ginger was right. The bibs were roomy, and I now wore them over one of Brian's T-shirts.

I didn't expect her to admire my fashion sense, but Cynthia showed a particular interest in my pizza: would I flip my crusts or roll them out, and if I rolled them out, how did I plan on doing it? I was not a flipper. Since I had little counter space, I said I'd probably use a beer can on the kitchen table. I was joking. I did have a plan but didn't want to share it with her. I'd ordered an oilcloth tablecloth from Amazon that I'd wrap tightly over the table and staple to the underside so it wouldn't shift. That should be sufficient with a lot of flour sprinkled on top. And instead of a rolling pin or even a beer can, I planned to use a bottle of wine.

Ginger called while I was talking to Cynthia, and I was on the phone with her when Brian walked through the kitchen. I tried to listen to Ginger and the two of them at the same time since I realized I'd never seen Brian interact with Cynthia, and I perked up when he called her Cindy. She asked if she could borrow his pickup and tossed him the keys to her Porsche as she was leaving. Meanwhile, Ginger was going on about Skipper's clippings which she and Toad had hauled to her cottage from the attic at Star Lake. She was chattering like a frenzied chipmunk.

"Just a minute." (I couldn't wait to tell her about "Cindy" offering Brian the Porsche.)

When I got back to Ginger, she hadn't noticed I'd been gone.

"...hotter than the hinges of Hell in that damned attic, and so close I thought I was going to puke. I forgot there's still oodles of Lily's things up there, too, from when she moved up here from her Florida condo, lamps and linens and all kinds of clutter. But after she passed, I didn't have the get-up-and-go to hold a sale or the heart to dump it without Chloe first looking it over. She's Lily's granddaughter and runs the Star Lake Inn. Have you met her yet? I told you about that, didn't I? Well, maybe not. You should meet Chloe. You'd like her, and she'd like you. But anyway..."

Stumpy had warned me that Ginger could talk the hind legs off a dog. I had no idea what he meant at the time, but I was getting an indication.

"Toad finally told me to shut up, have a drink of water and take a seat because I was a tad wobbly, and wouldn't you know it, I plopped my ass right down on top of Skipper's stuff. I had a flashlight along and couldn't wait to see what was inside. Jenny, you've got to get over here and see for yourself. We'll sift through everything. How soon can you come? This afternoon?"

I wanted to mix up a big batch of dough so I could make pizzas tomorrow. That could wait.

"Lunch?" Ginger was still talking. "C'mon over for lunch. I'll fix us some sandwiches. You like tuna? Have one of the boys show you how to start the motor."

Stumpy had gone fishing with the boat we used yesterday, and Toad hadn't yet returned from Ginger's, so I asked Brian if he could give me a hand.

On our way down to the water, Brian said he was glad to see me taking the initiative to use a boat by myself. I told him I'd rather be driving a Porsche, but that didn't draw any reaction, not even a smirk.

He tossed me an old Hills Brothers coffee can to scoop out standing water while he attached a motor to one of the last few dented rowboats that were still fit to use. Then he patiently demonstrated how to pull the cord to get it started. I apologized for how long it took me to catch on to the workings of the choke and the throttle and how to get the boat into reverse. After a dozen tugs and increasing perspiration, the old motor hesitated, then sputtered to life. I could hear Brian chuckling as I pulled away from the dock and into the lake. "Take it easy out there, Jenny," he warned. I had no intention of making waves and wanted to yell back, but he was already climbing the hill back to the bar.

Dash had naturally jumped in during my grueling efforts. We putted slowly across Star Lake, aimed for the center of the culvert that connected Star Lake to Sundog, happily emerged, and easily spotted Ginger out in front of Lilypad, where she furiously waved a white dishtowel to signal me ashore. I sideswiped the dock with the boat (Brian had shown me how to start the motor but not how to shut it off), so Ginger screamed, "Push the red button!" which did the job, but having overshot the dock by that time, I had to grab the oars to row back. Meanwhile, Dash joyfully leaped into the lake and began swimming away with Labrador glee.

"If I had to judge," Ginger said, "I'd say your brain might still be half a bubble off plumb. You might better be more careful next time."

Dash soon bounded up on shore and briskly shook himself before nuzzling Ginger's crotch and leaping to lick her cheek. His manners were terrible, but his sleek black fur gleamed in the summer sun, and he settled down when she pulled his ham bone out of her pocket. Then he stole off to a shaded spot near the porch to gnaw on his treasure.

"I understand Brian's got you making pizzas over there, now? Better watch out, Jenny. If you turn into an overnight sensation, you'll be signing yourself on to a long, drawn-out stay."

"I'll take that chance," I replied. I was due to see Dr. Singh again in two weeks, and I'd teach Brian and the boys how to make pizzas so they could handle the task themselves.

Dash carried his bone onto the porch with us, and we arranged ourselves as before. I sat on the white woven loveseat plumped with deep green pillows, and Ginger perched on a sturdy rocking chair on my left. Lunch was tuna fish salad on whole wheat bread, and Ginger shared my addiction to potato chips. We devoured almost an entire large bag of Ripples. A pitcher of real lemonade swimming with ice cubes and lemon slices slaked our thirst.

Even before we finished eating, she held up *The Pineries of Wisconsin and Upper Michigan*, a well-worn paperback thick with sticky notes.

"I came across this in one of my bookshelves and pasted in some reminders to help get you started. Like this. She squinted to read: *"One Northwoods tale tells of an 1890s fisherman who, when he heard piano music emanating from the main lodge of his favorite resort, turned to the guide docking his boat and said, 'Don't unload my bags. Where there's a piano, there's no fish.' "*

"So we know there were resorts up north in the 1890s," I said with a laugh.

"You bet," Ginger replied, turning to another page to report. "Even before that. Here it says that up at Lac Vieux Desert, a trading post from the 1860s was turned into a resort. That was around the time of the Civil War. It's the first resort around here anybody knows of. That's where the Wisconsin River begins."

It was a curious tidbit.

"And here," she added, "this is what I was looking for":

"Most of the early northern resorts were single lodges that had been converted from trading posts, postal and rest stations along tote roads, or abandoned logging camps or places that doubled as family homes. Paying clients were welcomed into the family circle, and the day's catch was shared equally at the dinner table."

"So, now you know. And the railroads built for logging brought the tourists up."

I began paging through a tattered guide to hotels and resorts in a magazine dated May 1929 that had been lying on top of a cardboard carton labeled *Blatz*. The box was heaped with a small mountain of yellowed newspapers, some torn into clippings and others folded into squares.

Dash had grown bored with his ham bone and got up to settle near Ginger, where he began to quietly tear apart the box of Kleenex.

"Would you prefer to rent a cottage at *Frying Pan Camp* or *Ye Olde Muskie Inn*?" I asked while scanning ads at the back of the guide. "Some of these were only thirty dollars a week."

"Holy smokes," Ginger said.

"I think I'd choose *Murmuring Waters* because it promises 'attractive wildwood surroundings.' "

"Hoo, boy," Ginger said. "You're talking *wild*? Girl, you ever been over to Hurley? That town's been wild since way before the first resort came about and still is. We'll have to drive there one day because you won't believe it until you see it. And you *should* see it, Jenny, to get a taste how things were up here back when because they still *are* like that in Hurley. I saw a piece about it in one of those magazines that tells about the Iron Range and how Hurley pulled in miners from all over for the iron ore and the copper, but curiosity always drew folks in to see what was happening. Still does. Lumberjacks used to play a big part, too. Way back when the town had those booming mines and lumber camps, Silver Street, that's the main street, was home to eighty saloons. Eighty! Eight Zero! It's a small town! And each saloon had three or four hookers working out of it and sometimes as many as a dozen. So, if you figure out the math, I'm guessing there might have been at least two hundred girls active and probably lots more because, you know, one girl can only do so much."

"*One girl can only do so much,*" I repeated with a hoot. Ginger put a hand over her mouth to smother her giggle.

"Used to be the girls posed in the windows to show off the merchandise. Then, in the 1940s," she continued with a satisfied smile, enjoying her story, "when the war was on, they painted the saloon windows black so nobody could get a free peek inside. Business didn't suffer any because the usual gambling and such went on, even so. It was a wide-open town, let me tell you. And it only cost a couple of dollars to bury the weasel."

Before I could help it, lemonade snorted from my nostrils. Ginger reached down and tossed me a Kleenex just in time.

"Oh, cripes, what do you think? I worked in a bar most of my adult life and served mostly men, so I bet I know a hundred terms for hanky panky—*horizontal refreshments, joint session of Congress.* A gentleman from England called it *rumpy-pumping*. I was rather partial to the way that sounded, especially with his hoity-toity accent."

Ginger took a long swig of her lemonade, then set the glass down softly and paused.

"Honey, you don't know what it's like to wake up in the morning and not have anything planned. I've been miserable all this summer until you showed up. It's Lily being gone, of course, and I've been laid up with a bum leg that's some better now. I've concluded that when you get old, the worst is not the aches and pains but a feeling that nobody needs you. You've outgrown your usefulness. That hurts the most."

I reached over to grasp her wrinkled hand and felt her fingers' fragile bones.

"So letting me help you with this stuff, it's a gift to me, Jenny; it really is. You got no idea."

I sensed that Ginger seldom cried, but now she was tearing up. Before I could lean over to hug her, she was reaching down to remove the remains of the Kleenex box from Dash.

"This isn't all going to be prizewinning stuff; I guarantee you that," she cleared her throat, and we dug into the box of clippings. "Skipper wasn't one of them hoarders like you see on TV, but he was known for saving all kinds of information doing with history. I figure if we sort it into piles, maybe we can begin to make some sense of it. Like over there on the chaise, I already started one pile just for lumber camps, and over there on the footstool, we can make one for mining. Those piles might get too big and have to be divvied up, but I bet you don't want to read about all the mines or lumber camps, anyways. You want to learn about resorts. The Iron County History Museum might want 'em, though. What do you figure?"

The woman barely stopped speaking long enough to take a breath. Dash put his head in her lap to receive some serious petting. His love could be bought with a ham bone and Kleenex to chew.

Out of curiosity, I asked Ginger if any Chicago gangsters happened to visit The Last Resort before or during Duncan Sunderlast's time. "I know about Dillinger and Little Bohemia, the shoot-out with the FBI."

"You been there, I take it," Ginger said. "Little Bohemia?"

"Years ago. I can't imagine it's changed much."

"Nope, about the same. The food's still good, and they still cash in with their museum, the bullet holes, and so on. Believe me, I can tell you plenty about Dillinger and Baby Face Nelson. More than you want to know. Buried treasure, lots of stuff. It was a whopper of a fracas. I got stories I could tell you that would take all night. A girlfriend of mine was a telephone operator, and she had the switchboard right in her house; they did that in those days. She said it lit up right off the bat with calls from all over the world, even Paris, France. Everybody wanted to know about Dillinger and if he got away or not."

"What about Al Capone? I heard his brother owned a bar up here."

"They say Al had trouble getting a handle on this area," Ginger said. "And you're right; his brother, Ralph Capone, had a bar up here. They called him 'Bottles.' He was a respected citizen, a generous guy. Everybody liked Ralph. And after Al got out of Alcatraz, oh, it must've been 1939, 1940, Al came up here to fish. He got a guide he liked and came back year after year, stayed at some ordinary place, just like anybody else, not sure where it was, maybe Lac Courte Oreilles, but Al never managed to get an operation going."

"Why did gangsters choose this area? Because it's easy to get to from Chicago?"

"Chicago's a good place to be from—as far away from it as you can get," Ginger joked.

As we began randomly sifting through the papers, Ginger dug a pair of bright pink reading glasses from her shirt pocket. Various headlines caught my eye. Fragments of clippings floated from my lap to the floor. Many were fragile, and some were from newspapers in the 1880s and 1890s, when reporters were paid for their stories by the inch. Skipper must have inherited someone else's cache. I was relieved that my vision had improved enough to read the tiny type if I squinted.

"*Monkey sets self on fire and burns down most of Ashland,*" I read. "In 1887. A monkey in Ashland?"

"Well, that's not far from Hurley, and why not a monkey? But wait a minute. I gotta get us some dessert." She stood up with a grunt, and I let Dash outside to pee. I took advantage of our break to use Ginger's bathroom.

When we returned, Ginger placed cookies on the table and said, "Okay, read me that bit about the monkey again. Print's too darned small for my cheaters. One of these days I gotta go back to the Walmart. Maybe you can take me."

She settled back into her rocker, tossed her glasses on the table, and closed her eyes.

Or maybe not, I thought. I wasn't a Walmart shopper.

"The headline says '*Some Monkey Work*,' " I read with gusto. "*A mischievous monkey burned the little city of Wakefield to the ground last night. He was given the freedom of the Vaudeville Theater by the proprietor, and at about midnight, the monkey had a circus with a kerosene lamp, the oil of which he put upon his hair and then set himself afire and scattered the flames as he ran about the room. His antics in the big windows of the building were watched by a crowd. A few minutes later the entire building was wrapped in flames...*"

"And it spread from there, I suppose," Ginger said, shaking her head, eyes still closed. "All over town. Am I right?"

I abridged the remainder of the lengthy piece. The buildings were made of wood. Looters took over. Hoodlums pillaged the stores as fast as doors could be opened. Revolvers were flourished by the drunken crowd, fed by liquor stolen from the saloons.

"I suppose somebody got shot? There was always a shooting."

"The man who owned the dance hall," I told her. "Here they refer to it as a '*dance hall dive.*' He was mad at the guy who ran the vaudeville house '*for allowing the monkey to run loose in his place. He damned him in vigorous language, accusing him of being the cause of the great calamity. O'Brien, of the theater became greatly enraged and shot Lewis of the dance hall twice, both balls passing through his hips. He will die. Both men are notorious characters in this section.*' "

"Well, there you go," Ginger said, clapping, eyes open now and bright with excitement. "Didn't I say it was wide open up there back then? Monkeys, dancing girls, prostitutes, hoodlums, bank robbers, murderers, you name it. Hurley was in Ashland County then.

"Now this bunch of old *Field & Stream* magazines, we can throw these away." Ginger, ready to get back to work, slung several magazines toward a corner of the porch.

I was about to sort through more clippings but saw that Skipper had circled something in red pencil on the same page as the monkey item.

"Have you heard of a woman named Maud Cassidy?" I asked. "Is she someone who deserves a category of her own?"

"Not familiar with the name," Ginger admitted. "But if the Skipper circled her, there must be a reason."

"She was a '*notorious abductor of young girls*' who was wanted in Chicago '*for inveigling girls to dens in the Hurley area.*' Wow."

"Yup, we better make a personal pile for Maudie," Ginger said. "Have to dig up more intelligence on somebody like that. *Inveigling*. Nobody uses that word anymore. It's a good one."

I found several more clippings about Maud Cassidy, a woman who, with her husband, kidnapped young girls in Chicago and brought them north by train, where they were kept in stockades to service customers. The Cassidys were paid twenty-five dollars for each girl they handed over, and the girls were not allowed to escape. Sex trafficking was apparently alive and well in Wisconsin's early days. That topic grabbed my attention.

"Here's a story about a woman named Irish Annie who was murdered at a Hurley saloon. Did you know about her?"

Ginger replied that Skipper mentioned a murdered prostitute once upon a time. "But the name Irish Annie doesn't ring a bell. What else does it say about her?"

"She was shot in a tavern in 1897. According to *The Ironwood Times: 'The murdered woman was one of the old timers among Hurley's tough element and had been in town ever since it started.'* "

"Poor thing," Ginger shook her head. "Annie didn't have the luck of the Irish, did she."

I stuffed a grocery bag with the pieces that I felt bore more scrutiny and began packing my things to leave when Ginger came across a manila envelope stuffed with news of another Hurley homicide: Lotta Morgan.

"Okay, here we go," she said excitedly. "Sit yourself down and wait just one more minute!"

Lotta Morgan. The cold-case murder that Ada wanted me to explore.

I sat down again and rested the brown paper bag on my lap. Skipper must have been the one who regaled Ada's husband, Gus, with Lotta's story. I could feel my heart beating faster.

"This here is an important murder, Jenny. To this day, it's a cold case, never been solved. And Skipper played a hand in it. And it was big.

"When he was a young man living in Hurley," Ginger explained, "Skipper was first on the scene to discover Lotta Morgan's mutilated body in an alley. He got other bystanders to help carry her into a nearby rooming house. Apparently, her head had been bashed in with an axe the night before. Skip relished relating the story over and over, sometimes elaborating and throwing in more gruesome details.

"Lotta still had all her diamonds and cash on her," he'd say, and "Hurley made a great big fuss. Said she was a popular 'woman about town,' and her funeral was the biggest event they'd ever seen."

Ginger handed the envelope over to me. Skipper's brush with fame. And my key to Ada's questions. "Read all about it for yourself," she said. "The $500 reward has never been claimed!"

⁂

Back at the resort, mid-afternoon, I found a surprise! Cynthia had asked her carpenter to install a marble top for the kitchen table. He'd even nailed supports to the legs to support the frame. It was wonderful! Brian said she'd told him they had surplus marble from one of the condos. I wanted to roll my eyes but decided not to make a Cynthia joke because, really, her gesture would make rolling out my pizzas much easier.

"She's a very thoughtful person," I said instead. And she was. I liked her. I just didn't want Brian to sleep with her. Or sell his resort to her so it could blossom with fancy condos.

There were a few additional items among the groceries that Stumpy had claimed he liked on his pizzas (jalapeno peppers, Canadian bacon, artichoke hearts). I told him I'd include them in my first pizzas and asked if he'd bring the bag of newspapers from the boat and upstairs to the lounge. "Can you add extra cheese when you make 'em tomorrow?" Stumpy asked. I assured him I could. Then I washed my hands so I could begin stirring up some dough.

Lotta Morgan. Wow. I was eager to return to Ginger's treasure.

I had the ingredients, but my utensils were minimal. Ideally, I'd be using a heavy-duty KitchenAid mixer like the one I used to have, to stir up several batches of dough. At least now I had a flashy tabletop to spread out my tools. I found a large dishpan beneath a cabinet, scoured it well, rolled up my sleeves, and got to work. The kitchen was warm, so it didn't take long before I'd kneaded the flour, water, and yeast, and an enormous batch of dough was rising. I'd planned to refrigerate all of it to add more flavor, but the temptation was too great. I tore off enough for a sample pizza, made balls for three more, and was about to set them aside when I realized one pizza would never be enough. I rolled out dough for four of them, got the gas grill going out in the back, and carefully slid the crusts on, one at a time, so they would get crisp and bubbly on both sides. After everything was oiled and toasty, I liberally smothered all with shredded mozzarella and a variety of toppings and slid the pies back on the grill to quickly melt. I could only bake a couple at a time.

Brian, Toad, Stumpy, and I ate our pizzas on the screened porch with a couple of customers who begged to sample at least one slice, sometimes two. My pizzas were, as I'd expected, perfectly exquisite. I was especially proud of my bubbly crisp thin crust, nicely browned and sporadically charred.

No words were uttered. No one said, "Holy cow, this is great!" or "Jenny, you're the best." Instead, there were just the sounds of chewing and moaning, almost sensual pleasure.

"You're hired," Brian said at last with a grin. "Can you make these every night?"

I told him I could show him how, that I could fill the freezer with enough dough to hold him for several weeks, and Stumpy already had the necessary list of ingredients.

"It's not hard to do," I assured him. "It just takes a little effort."

"Hot damn," Toad exclaimed. "We're going to be swamped with customers. *Jenny's Last Pizzas*. Might have to add more tables and chairs."

"Word'll get around," Stumpy agreed. "These here are your gourmet pizzas. And no tomato sauce, either! I'll be damned. And I'll help myself to another slice, thank you very much."

When Brian closed the bar that evening and came up to his apartment, I was sorting through more of Skipper's fragile clippings in the lounge to see if I could find more about Lotta. He sat on the ragged loveseat next to me.

"Congratulations," he told me again. "We'll donate the rest of our old frozen pizzas to the Antler Food Pantry."

I asked if he was familiar with the name *Duncan Sunderlast*. "He owned this resort years ago, and Ginger says he's responsible for the name. This grocery bag is only a small part of his legacy left behind when he moved to Alaska."

"Never heard of the man, but I guess the name makes sense," he said as he made a move to get up. "Sunderlast, *Last*. Clever."

"It was Ginger's idea. She also said she'd felt discouraged before I arrived because she didn't feel needed, but my questions about Northwoods history have revitalized her. And today, we discovered some material that revitalized *my* ideas for what I might write about. Which arrived at a convenient time, actually."

Brian sat down again. "Because..."

I responded with a deep sigh.

"I had an email tonight from Sue, my building manager. Turns out my plants are okay, but my mail's piling up, and my condo maintenance fee is past due."

I was unintentionally hugging the grocery bag as if its brittle contents would buoy me. Ada had promised to underwrite my expenses for a year. The agreement, however, was dependent on my research and writing. Now that Lotta had made her appearance, my feeble excuses were dissipating. One expense I needed to cover was my vacant Madison condo.

I felt Brian's arm circle my back, and he cuddled me. "It'll all work out, Jenny. Have your mail forwarded to this address; that shouldn't be a problem. The book idea will develop if you don't work so hard to find it. You said there was some potential in Sunderlast's collection, right?"

"Like here," Brian reached into the grocery bag and pulled out a vintage magazine at random. "Inspiration at your fingertips. Listen to this:

Fancies stray at the close of day
—those dancing ghosts!
Only the stars, only the moon,
Only the wind and its rhythmic tune
Causing the trees to slumber

"*Fancies stray at the close of day.* Tell me you're inspired! *Dancing ghosts!* That sounds like a haunting idea for a book."

I let my head drop on his shoulder and pretended to snore.

Part Two

Life is either a daring adventure or nothing.

—Helen Keller, *The Open Door*

Eight

Dash's new collar arrived in the mail, and I was ready for some exercise. We headed out for a walk on Friday before the day got too warm. I didn't want to go far, just a mile or so from the resort but not toward The Star Lake Saloon, where I'd have to pass the roots of that demon pine that still skulked on the shoulder. In my pocket, I had another item I'd ordered, a can of pepper spray. In case we encountered a bear, I'd be prepared.

It was a glorious early morning, still wet with heavy dew and smelling earthy and fresh. I heard birdsongs I could not identify, probably northern species we didn't have in the southern part of the state. Maybe Ginger could help me with that, too. After about twenty minutes, I was ready to turn back, but when I tugged the dog's leash and yelled, "Heel," a black squirrel emerged from a pile of brush along the wayside. Dash easily slipped from the collar I'd so recently buckled (not tight enough), sprinting after the squirrel and disappearing down the road.

Of course, he did not respond to my demands to return. What dog would, with a frisky squirrel spurring you to chase. With leash in hand, I angrily marched forward, reproaching myself. Why hadn't I utilized some of my long, lazy days up here by training my dog? *Stupid, stupid, stupid.*

Soon, on my right, I heard hammering. There were pickup trucks in the driveway, and a crew was working on a cottage with dark log siding like the bar at The Last Resort. The roof had been damaged, and glass was missing from several windows. One of the carpenters was down on his knee, petting Dash, who slavered with joy as the guy, heavyset, wearing a plaid flannel shirt and pair of patched jeans, made a fuss over him.

"Sorry," I said. "He got away from me."

The guy reached for the collar, slid it back over Dash's head, and notched it more tightly this time. He spoke sweetly to Dash and called him a beautiful pup. I agreed; he *was* beautiful: shiny, sleek, and mesmerized by squirrels. "Show me a dog that isn't," the man replied, getting up off the ground with a mild complaint.

"Took a hit in the tornado, huh?" I said, not being easily conversant with carpenters. Considering the debris piled off to one side, it was a dumb remark. Then I tried to make up for it by saying I had a cottage that needed work and attempted—not very successfully—to explain what remained of the Maus Haus. "Any chance you could check it out and give me a bid?"

Cynthia was in charge of that, but she was now in Chicago, and I had only briefly spoken with her since we'd learned that Ada was determined to rebuild. We presumed her damages were not entirely covered by insurance because Ada added she would "sweeten the deal" from her savings. And as long as I was comfortable, could I help Cynthia by sticking around to keep an eye on things?

Oh, Ada. What could I say? Now, at least, I had Skipper's material to work with if I felt like compiling more data in response to her initial request. And the least I could do was help Cynthia acquire an offer from a local firm to recreate Ada's beloved retreat.

"You'll have to check with the boss." The carpenter pointed to a burly man retrieving tools from one of the trucks. "He's the one."

Larry was tall, broad-shouldered, with a messy mane of brown hair that stuck out from under his backward baseball cap. Why do guys do that? It always looks like a dunce cap or a sign that says, "I am so stupid I don't know how to wear a cap." They might as well wear beanies. He also had strands of barbed wire tattooed around his neck and looked menacing until he smiled.

"What can I do you for, young lady?" he asked, pulling his arms out of the sleeves of his jacket to expose an image of a fierce mythical beast on a black T-shirt. Brawny arms were swathed in tattoos, as were the knuckles of the hand he held out for me to shake. I couldn't see his eyes; they were hidden behind mirrored glasses.

"Larry Boone," he said. "Storm loss. Whereabouts?"

I gave him my name and explained the location of Vogel's Maus Haus on Sickle Moon. He said he knew where it was and agreed to meet me there late that afternoon. "I'll take a quick look around, and then in a day or so, I can give you a guesstimate," he said. "Can't guarantee that we'll get at it right away 'cause there was a helluva lot of damage around here, but we could add you to the list. Might be late summer. Just so's you know."

If Cynthia could find someone to handle it sooner, hooray for her. We were both eager for that project to get moving! My spirits were lifted as Dash and I trekked back to the resort.

My good mood lasted until I proudly told Toad and Stumpy that I'd asked Larry Boone for an estimate on Mrs. Vogel's cottage and that he'd look the place over later today.

"Where in the heck did you run into that sleazeball?" Toad asked.

"Aw, c'mon. He's reasonably harmless," Stumpy added. "Used to come in every weekend to pick up one of our pizzas. Wait 'til he gets a taste of Jenny's!"

"He did serve time," Toad said.

"Well, that happens when you write bad checks."

"And hired a fellow to take out his wife..."

"With said bad check. So, the bozo only smacked her with a baseball bat, for Pete's sake. I hear now she's married again and living in South Dakota. His daughter's still here, though. Lives with him. From all accounts, she's a good kid. Smart. I see her name in the paper every once in a while, on the honor roll."

I continued to sip my morning coffee, ignoring their baiting chitchat.

"Careful you don't get romantically involved, Jenny," Toad nodded toward me. "Unless all them tattoos turn you on!" Then he added with a snort, "He did tell you he's the Grand Dragon of the Ku Klux Klan in these parts, didn't he?"

The boys had a good guffaw. I choked on my coffee and coughed until tears streamed from my eyes. I may have noticed a Confederate flag on the bumper of the massive black pickup, but I was too concerned about catching Dash to make a serious note of it.

"You're kidding," I accused Toad.

"The hell I am."

Crap. The guy had my name and number. And Ada Vogel was Jewish. My high spirits plunged, and I attempted to mop up my spill, but I'd have to change my shirt because the coffee had soaked through.

I tried to blame my precipitous actions on Dash, but that excuse bombed. I'd already emailed Cynthia with the guy's contact information and my gleeful news that I'd requested a bid from a local crew. She would be driving back up here this weekend.

Brian had overheard our conversation and joined us on the porch. He assured me I didn't need to carry pepper spray or a baseball bat. Just meet the guy at Maus Haus and be me. Larry Boone and his men did respectable work and could be trusted to finish the job.

"But it's unethical," I argued. "It's against all my moral values to support someone so vile. It's not right."

"Boone blows a lot of hot air," Stumpy promised. "He likes the attention. And all those guys are on the Antler Fire Department and EMS besides. They've got families, love their kids, pay taxes."

"His crew is probably in the Klan, too, and they insist that because they have light skin, they're genetically superior to Blacks. Christians are better than Jews. Protestants are better than Catholics."

My voice grew louder and louder, and I would have kept going, but Brian calmly interrupted.

"Jenny, when Cynthia arrives, tell her about Boone. Let her take it from there," he advised. "She'll be looking for more bids and can always cross him off her list."

It took me several deep breaths to recover from my tirade. Brian's advice made sense. I'd hand everything over to Cynthia with sincere apologies and explain that my affection for Ada Vogel would take precedence over a low bid by the Klan. Meanwhile, that afternoon I had an appointment with a Grand Dragon.

⁂

My zippy "new" Volkswagen Bug had a full tank of gas and was ready to roll. The boys had treated it as the precious relic it was, tapping out dents and giving it a good vacuum, wash, and polish, inside and out. They could do nothing about the mouse-nibbled upholstery or the aroma of rodent urine. Sadly, I was warned that if I put down the rotten convertible top, it might not come up again. There was also a maximum probability that it leaked.

Rumbling misgivings about meeting with Boone had not subsided, but I was eager to take the Bug for a drive. Toad opened the driver-side door for me, slapped the hood of the faded red survivor, and shouted, "Give 'er hell, girl," as I climbed in. Dash squeezed into the back seat, although I hadn't planned to take him along. I would be delighted if the scent of dog would replace *Eau de mouse.*

I shoved in the clutch, pressed down the accelerator, turned the key, and the motor started up right away. Stumpy and Toad beamed like proud new fathers. I suspected driving a stick again wouldn't take a second thought, and I was right. We were off.

As I left the parking lot, I heard Stumpy holler, "Hitler loved the Beetle," which, I guess, was supposed to reinforce my confidence in the upcoming encounter.

⁂

Dash had already met Larry Boone, and if I didn't overthink the situation, he did seem like a normal guy, albeit covered head to toe (as much as I cared to discover) with a massive amount of ink. I tried to mask my apprehension and realized I was talking too much, so I told him to go ahead and tour the interior while I remained on the deck. A few minutes later, I called through the door that I'd be waiting down by the water, where Dash had already ventured.

Rocks had been rammed into the ground to simulate steps, and the grade was precariously steep. A railing would have helped, but I grabbed nearby saplings and whatever else I could to keep from sliding. Sections of earth and stones had eroded the soil. What remained of the dock was barely enough to support a lop-sided bench.

Even without the conundrum of Larry Boone, I had deeply mixed feelings about this project—whether it was Ada's desire for renewal or restoration. I recognized that my hesitancy had less to do with Maus Haus than my restlessness. The reality of my day-to-day existence had become so disordered. In addition to my previous lack of motivation, I lacked control, and it was freaking me out.

Waiting for Boone, I stared at the lake and wondered, as I always do, at its ability to mesmerize. I could see Star Lake from my bedroom window. One morning the lake would be slick as a mirror; the next, it would have little ripples skittering on the surface like they were now. It was like my horoscope—if the water was smooth, that meant the day would be perfect. This morning I hadn't checked it out.

My contemplation halted when I heard Larry swearing as he skidded downhill, rocks tumbling ahead of him in a noisy cascade. "Goddamn steps," he said when he reached the dock. "Could kill a guy."

I hoped he wasn't getting any malevolent ideas. I stood up from the wooden bench on the pier, made room for him, and then sat down again.

"It's a disaster, isn't it?" I was talking about the cottage, but the bench, dock, and stairs were also lumped in there. "What do you think? Is this worth restoring, or is it a total loss?"

He sat down next to me and removed a worn, spiral notebook from his shirt pocket. A pencil stub was tied to it with a string. He licked at the whittled point of the pencil and made some notes. I scooted over a few more inches so his leg wasn't touching mine.

"Smell's enough to choke a horse," he said. "I nearly spewed. But once the crap carpet and other junk's pulled out of there, it might not be such a big frigging deal to bring it back. Have to go through my notes before I can give you any numbers. First of the week be all right?"

I again explained that I was partnering with someone else and we'd be seeking more bids.

"You go right ahead," he said. "Everybody I know's full up at the moment." He placed the pad back in his pocket, shook a cigarette from a crumpled pack, and lit it after offering one to me. "But you might as well give it a try anyways."

I refused the smoke and attempted to enjoy the quiet motion of the waves.

"Beautiful spot." After exhaling a lung full of smoke, Larry said, "And you're not bad lookin' yourself," he gave me a friendly grin. "How come I never seen you around here before?"

If I moved any farther away from him, I'd slide off the end of the bench. I quickly explained that I was from out of town (didn't want to be too specific) and visiting friends at The Last Resort.

"They said you like their pizzas. Give me a week or two, and they'll be even better."

Were we done? Could I go now? I wondered how far I could swim if I had to jump in to get away.

The only time I'd been in the water this summer was when I fell out of the boat at Ginger's. I loved swimming but didn't like tangling my legs in the slimy weeds along the lakeshore. And now it was Dog Days. Was that recognized up north? Dog Days—the hottest time in summer—when duck parasites in the lakes would guarantee swimmer's itch.

"You have any children?" he asked.

"Dog Days," I said. "The Dog Days of Summer."

The look Larry Boone gave me clearly revealed he thought I was nuts.

"Sorry, this time of year," I apologized. "After the Fourth of July, I mean. Like now. It's the hottest time of the summer, but when I was a kid, we couldn't go swimming because of Dog Days, which meant we'd get a rash.

"Speaking of dogs, I got my eye on yours," he replied. "Determined little guy."

Dash was attempting to round up a pair of loons that were successfully eluding him.

"Dog Days doesn't really have anything to do with dogs. I know that."

For some idiotic reason, I felt I should clarify my comment. "Except for the Dog Star, Sirius, the brightest star in the sky."

Oh my god, I was rambling. I had to get out of there.

"I was asking if you had any kids. I got a daughter," he said. "Teenager."

"Ah, I remember those days," I said. No risk sharing a trace of nostalgia. "I have two girls, both married now and living far away. As rough as those years were, I'd give anything to have my moody teenagers back again. They grew up too fast. I have a grandson, too."

"You don't look like a grandma," Larry said. There was that super-friendly smile again.

"Thanks," I said, and despite my unease with his attempted geniality, I could feel myself choking up. It had been over a year since I'd spent much time with Charlotte or Emily. We Facetimed frequently, but Charlotte's little Henry was almost three, and Emily was expecting her firstborn in a few months. What was wrong with me? Why couldn't I play grandma like any normal, loving mother? Why hadn't that occurred to me instead of heading north? Was I really that dense, so self-absorbed? Sure, they lived miles away, but I wasn't afraid of flying. My condo was too small to accommodate families, so I couldn't invite them back home. I should have kept the house. The next time I spoke with Emily, I'd pledge to be with her when the baby arrived.

I cleared my throat and swallowed. "What's her name? Your daughter's."

"Rebel Rose," he said. "She hates the 'Rebel' part and just wants to be called Rosie. I know what you mean; they grow up too fast. I'd do anything for that kid."

He took another long drag from his cigarette.

I didn't know how to conclude the conversation. I called Dash, who swam over to the pier, climbed out, and shook himself all over us. I'd informed Cynthia of the hate groups in the Northwoods, and here I was, sitting next to a fucking Grand Dragon.

"I hear you're involved with the KKK."

Without Toad's warning, would this man still possess the power to frighten me?

"You heard wrong."

He tossed the stub of his cigarette into the water beyond the dock, where it landed with a sizzle.

Dash, alert, turned to see what made the strange noise.

"Got to get moving," Larry slapped his knees, rose to his feet, and began to climb back up the hill.

"Who told you I was in the Klan?" he asked over his shoulder.

"Oh, someone in the bar," I threw back, which was not a lie. We kept climbing; it was slow going. I was glad to have him ahead and not behind because I could trace his footing. It's always intimidating to be wagging your butt in somebody else's face, and if that somebody was a Grand Dragon, well, you get my drift.

When he emerged, Larry reached back to give me a hand. I was short of breath from exertion. His hand was thickly callused, but his grip was firm.

"That shit's got to be replaced," he nodded. "Nice wood steps of treated lumber with a railing off to one side. Be a shame not to add decent stairs to reach the lake. Go a hell of a long way in selling this place. And the view from here would open up, too, if this brush was cleared away. The downed trees, too."

I agreed.

"I got to confess," he said, looking me straight in my eyes as I pried myself from his grasp. "I told you wrong down there. I am in the Klan. 'The National Knights of the Ku Klux Klan.' But people around here pretty much go about their own business, and nobody gives a damn. My work crew's in it too. If it upsets you too much, I won't bother making a bid."

I nearly wiped my hand on my jeans but inserted it in the front pocket instead. "Let's see what kinds of numbers you come up with, okay?" I pulled out one of Cynthia's cards and gave it to him. "Here's the name and number of my partner, Cynthia Curtis. I've already told her I'd be talking with you. She's experienced in real estate, and if you send her your bid, she's the one who'll be getting back in touch."

My last contact with this bloke, I told myself. Cynthia could handle further discussions, but I'd warn her ahead of time that I didn't want to be involved. He seemed nice enough, but hate groups and what he represented made me ill at ease.

Dash was already waiting for me by the Bug.

⁂

After dinner, I drove to Lilypad to return Skipper's clippings and show Ginger my "new" car. She wanted a chance to sort through Skip's entire collection again by herself.

"Larry Boone," she mused after I mentioned him. "Name sounds familiar, but I've never had the pleasure of meeting the bloke. Might've seen him around. Wouldn't recognize him, except now I'll watch for that cavalcade of tatts and that Confederate bumper sticker. That's some nerve."

She handed me a mug and a teabag while she put the kettle on to boil.

"He's a head of the Ku Klux Klan, a Grand Dragon."

Ginger was speechless. "Up here?" she managed to squawk.

"Before I met with him at Ada's this afternoon, I Googled *Boone.* In one interview, he mentioned it's been a lot easier to recruit for the KKK since 9/11."

"Oh, for the love—"

"I also Googled *Wisconsin hate groups* again, and besides the Klan, there's at least a dozen more. We've got the White Devil Social Club, that's anti-Jew; the White Boy Society, a 'biker brotherhood' that aims to protect the heritage of white people; New Order, which says they hate Jews and love Hitler; ACT for America—an anti-Muslim hate group that promotes conspiracy theories. The list goes on and on. Wausau has the White Nationalist Women for Aryan Unity, and their website describes their primary goal as '*Kirche, Kuche, Kinder, or church, kitchen, and children.*' They even have a kids' coloring book called *Children's White*

Heritage."

"Boy, that stinks up to high heaven," Ginger said, rolling her eyes.

"Most of these aren't involved with actual violence; they just get their kicks from the rhetoric. But it's upsetting."

Ginger put her head in her hands as if she had a migraine.

"All that hate and rage up here," she said. "I hate to see it. People who think they're better because they've got white skin or they pray to Jesus. Makes me sick. I had no idea."

"And neither do most of our tourists," I replied. "Welcome to the *Northwoods nobody knows.*"

"Sounds like a dandy title for a book," she said with a sarcastic smile. Then she gave me an apprehensive glance. "Are you thinking you might want to write about stuff like that?"

I shook my head and said I was simply gathering information. "You know, the saying '*knowledge is power*'? I think that was originally Sir Francis Bacon long ago. And Thomas Jefferson after that." Then I added, "I did notice that the Klan is having a rally in Upper Michigan this weekend. Tomorrow, in fact."

"Oh, Jenny," she said, her eyes suddenly taking on a playful sparkle. "Oh, Jenny. We're driving to Hurley tomorrow, right? Upper Michigan is just across the railroad tracks up there; other side of the Montreal River."

I raised my eyebrows and pretended I had no idea what she was talking about.

"I got a bunch of old sheets I can stitch up and make us some robes," she offered. "No one will know who we are. You game?"

"No! Absolutely not. What in the world?"

There were so many adventures I still wanted to fulfill. I wanted to spend at least a year or more in the Outer Hebrides, where I could learn Gaelic. Another dream I still vaguely held on to was to become a trapeze artist. There was a circus camp near Madison where I could enroll, although they might have a cut-off age for a woman over fifty. Skydiving was on my list. Learning to play the mandolin. Sharing hugs and reading to grandchildren was swiftly scooting up to number one. But secreting myself inside a Klan costume (for what are they but creepy "costumes") had never been, was not, and would never be a goal of mine.

"Ginger," I finally had to sigh. "You're too much. I agree that would be an interesting gambit. But it's too dangerous, really. Even more important, *pretending* to be part of the Klan seems ethically wrong. Unforgivable. Their beliefs are too evil to treat with mockery. And what if there was a riot? What if we were found out? What if we got hurt? What if we got arrested and were labeled as members of the Klan? What then?"

Ginger's enthusiasm ebbed, but she proffered a deal.

"Okay, how about this: If we just *happened* to drive past where they're holding their rally tomorrow, we could park the Bug and sneak up and have a little look-see."

I assured her I would make no promises. "It's not like my little red car wouldn't stand out on a city street," I proclaimed. "And if Larry Boone saw me spying on him and his men, recognized me..."

"So what?" Ginger argued. "Maybe they got women in the Klan, too. It's not as if you don't know who he is; he told you so himself. I'd kind of like to see what happens at one of their rallies. What they espouse."

"*Espouse?*" I practically spat the word back at her. "What's with you? *Espouse?*"

Chagrined, Ginger admitted, "I've been reading a lot of old newspapers. You might find me *espousing* lots of opinions from now on." She handed me a book. "And here's a novel by a famous author, Edna Ferber, who wrote a book you better read."

The book, *Come and Get It,* was a hardcover still wrapped with its faded green jacket and quite worn.

"They made a movie from it," Ginger added. "This here's Skipper's autographed copy. Ferber wrote famous books like *Cimarron* and *Show Boat.* If you ask me, this one's cut out of a lot of whole cloth, but she came up to Hurley herself for the research."

Inside the cover was a page torn from an August 1936 issue of a monthly journal of some sort, *Monthly Bulletin,* with a glamorous photo of the author in a dramatic pose: "*Edna Ferber was born in Kalamazoo,*

Michigan, but she spent her childhood in Appleton, Wisconsin. The inside flap of the book jacket declared *Come and Get It "was rich with the exciting quality of life itself."*

"Come to think of it," Ginger said, "I recall Edna Ferber was a Jew."

I began to protest, but Ginger put up her hand to stop me. "Nothing wrong with that; I'm not like your buddy Larry Boone."

I closed my eyes and sighed.

"Just kidding," she said. "You know I'd never say anything bad against a Jewish man or woman. I'm not in the least bit racist. I've got my share of Indian friends—excuse me, Native American—and I've also had plenty of friends who were Jews. But what I *am* saying is that Miss Ferber probably didn't find a lot of other Jewish folks up around Hurley. Matter of fact, I'm recalling now that she ran into some narrow-minded people up there who did not appreciate having a Jew in town, and Skipper relayed that she had to get out of the fancy hotel where she'd ensconced herself to the house of a wealthy Jewish family on a nearby lake where she was more at ease."

"*Ensconced* and *espouse*. Ginger, you're beginning to sound like a sage."

"Read the book," she said flatly. "I'm not asking you to memorize the gol-danged thing."

I opened the cover as soon as I got back to my room.

⁂

Ginger *espoused* a personal opinion the next morning when she complained, "I don't remember these Beetle Bugs being so tiny. Or so frigging hot."

Saturday was warm. We weren't debuting Jenny's Last Pizzas until the following weekend, so I was free. Meanwhile, I'd made a fantastic discovery. While fiddling around online to find a collar for Dash, I found a propane-fired pizza oven that could reach a temperature of nine hundred and fifty degrees in fifteen minutes and cook a pizza in only sixty seconds. With that, I could turn out a lot of pizzas in a very short time, so I ordered one. My gift to The Last Resort for taking me in. I'd have Stumpy place it near the kitchen door on a couple of sawhorses and a slab of a Formica countertop that I'd spotted in the dumpster. My usual technique would have to be modified a little, but the pizzas could potentially be even more delicious and ready to serve in minutes. Brian might grumble about my expenditure, but he'd have to admit we'd be able to serve a crowd in a hurry.

I hadn't told him exactly where Ginger and I were going today except to say we were taking a test drive, and it might be late when we returned. I knew Cynthia might be looking for me, but there'd be time to check in with her tomorrow to give her a heads-up about the results of my meeting with the Dragon himself.

My little car motored along beautifully. We were approaching a hill, so I shifted down to second and gave it more gas. The muffler's potato-potato burble sounded sort of like a Harley. Meanwhile, Ginger fussed with the window vent and rolled her window down and up, down and up, because she didn't like the wind blowing her frothy hair. "Can't get any flow over here," she complained. "Tell me again why we can't put down the gosh-darned top?"

The far northern landscape was generous with assorted shades of green, dense with wetlands, pine savannas, thick tamarack bogs, and plenty of lakes. If you looked at a map of this part of Wisconsin, it resembled a natural sponge. We met flatbed trucks piled high with logs, heading south. Once, I had to shift down and wait for a mother bear and her cub to pad across the blacktop. I loved that loud muffler, even though I could conceivably be arrested for the noise.

I completed a speed-reading of the Ferber book the night before. It was not a literary gem, and only the beginning mentioned much about Hurley. Ferber analyzed Lotta Morgan, but there was no mention of her gruesome murder. Instead, the author created a new life and love for Lotta, providing her with a stunning daughter whose awesome beauty resembled her own. Many pages were devoted to Lotta's sordid background, and I told Ginger about the posters Ferber invented for the Alcazar Theater that supposedly portrayed the actress as a loose woman who'd become a star after she escaped from a crude stockade like the ones where Maud Cassidy delivered her kidnapped girls.

"She made Lotta blonde and Swedish when Skipper's clippings quoted Lotta as saying her mother was a Spaniard. I know the book is fiction, but I don't think it's appropriate to reinvent rudimentary details and ignore her brutal death!"

"Maybe the historical society in Hurley will have some real pictures of Lotta," Ginger offered. "And share information."

"But get this: Ferber also gave Lotta a tattoo! At that time in history, during the reign of Queen Victoria, it would've been unusual for a woman to have a clandestine tattoo."

"A tattoo of what?" Ginger asked.

"Well, that's so odd. It was a crucifix. Between her breasts."

"Jesus," Ginger said.

"Exactly. Jesus on the cross. And Ferber cruelly described the other actors, Lotta's friends, as "*half-witted children*." In the end, she didn't treat Hurley very favorably, but I suppose they were flattered to have a fabled author in their midst."

"Some of them weren't as impressed as you think," Ginger replied. "Remember, I told you she had to check out of that posh hotel and ensconce herself out of town."

Nine

"I'm getting so hungry, my stomach's going to think my throat's been slit," Ginger complained.

I'd heard that quip before, and I hadn't even known her that long.

"Let's find us a place to grab a bite before we amble off to see the sights."

As we drove into town, I caught a glimpse of the Iron County Historical Museum—a large dark red building with Romanesque features. It had been the county courthouse in a previous life. I assured Ginger we'd get lunch and make a brief stop on our way home.

"Don't forget that KKK rally," she added faintly. I pretended not to hear.

Hurley's Silver Street could have been the Main Street of any Wisconsin small town, with the usual two-story buildings built of brick or lumber, some storefronts altered with awnings or shutters or a false façade. But it didn't take a closer look to note all the taverns. Some had neon signs in their windows proclaiming "Girls" (or "Girls Girls Girls") still dark in the late morning.

"Here's one that's open," Ginger pointed to the Nip 'n' Nudge. She claimed a tavern would have more local color and better hamburgers than a run-of-the-mill café.

As I'd expected, it was dim inside and had that familiar tavern smell. Ginger slid onto a barstool with practiced ease and began perusing a menu wedged next to the sugar dispenser. A woman behind the bar slapped paper coasters down in front of us and asked with a cheerful smile, "What can I get for you gals today?"

"Give me a burger with the works, medium rare, and a Miller Lite. She'll have the same."

Ginger gloried in taking charge.

"Diet Coke," I amended. "And make it medium; add a bag of chips."

"Tell me, Fawn," Ginger pointed to the woman's name tag, "Does this little metropolis still live up to its shady reputation? What I mean is, you still got strippers up here, right?"

I excused myself to use the restroom, and when I returned, she was conducting an interview.

"Okay, so we see a lot of these taverns up here advertise *Girls* and *Dancing*. Elucidate for Jenny here, just what that stands for."

Fawn, washing glasses behind the bar, nodded. "I understand you want to learn about our tittie bars?"

I was a little taken aback but said, "Sure, if that's what you call them," and threw Ginger a quizzical look.

"You've never been to a strip club? Never saw a pole dance?"

Our burgers were set in front of us. They smelled greasy and good.

Fawn began with a grin, "You gals are sitting in a so-called 'tittie bar' right now. Only at the Nip, the tits don't start swinging until after dark."

Ginger's mouth was now full of hamburger, so she added a sip of beer and then explained.

"The reason I ask is because Jenny here is interested in the olden days up north. I'm helping her investigate." Ginger took a moment to swallow and then continued, "One of the things we found out that you might enjoy, Fawn, is an article in an old paper that I read. It said back then, 'working girls,' meaning prostitutes, worked out of the saloons. And the owner of the saloon took the girl in and let her stay at his home like a friend of the family or a hired girl on a farm. She ate her meals right at their kitchen table, and his wife was okay with that arrangement."

Proud of her research, Ginger gave me an elbow in the ribs. "How 'bout that? I'm *elucidating*."

Fawn admitted surprise, as did I, mostly because I wasn't aware of my friend's independent homework.

"I dance at the clubs sometimes, just for fun," Fawn admitted shyly. Her long black hair was too dark to be natural, and she wore a tight red ruffled top that exposed a toned midriff above the waistband of her jeans. "A bunch of us locals dance to pick up extra cash or during deer season or when the snowmobilers come up here without their wives. But we're not prostitutes, for God's sake! We're not sex workers."

She pulled her hair back, secured it with a scrunchie, and then got busy rinsing glasses. "You might hear that one of the girls gave a blowie in the parking lot, but that's her business. She's not tied to a john. The Nip 'n' Nudge is pretty tame. It's not like our bigger bars. We get girls more like the girl next door. What they do after hours is up to them, and some make enough income dancing. They might be saving up for college or a new car; you never know. It depends a lot on their situation. Have a kid at home or maybe staying with their mom. Might even have a hubby who doesn't mind her dancing as long as she doesn't turn any tricks on the side and stays clean."

The hamburger was large and juicy with nice crispy edges that stuck out of the bun, but I could only manage to eat half, so I pushed it aside to concentrate on potato chips and a dill pickle. Ginger's mouth was still full of ground beef. Out of curiosity, I asked Fawn which club featured the best dancers. To be honest, the subject was beginning to intrigue me. I think it was the mention of "the girl next door."

Fawn sighed and wiped her hands on a bar rag. "If you're talking local, Psycho Suzy's usually pretty good. But there's a rotation, a regular circuit of professionals who come into town on Thursday afternoons. They'll dance through Sunday night and then leave for someplace else. Each club is different, and each weekend is different, too."

Ginger finished her burger, swallowed the rest of her beer, wiped her mouth, issued a mild burp, and asked, "So what does it feel like? Taking your clothes off in front of strangers and standing there buck naked? Is the first time the worst, or is it scary every time?"

Embarrassed for our waitress, I quickly stated I might have a few questions later and asked if that would be okay.

Fawn nodded and recommended the local historical museum to get a take on Hurley's history. "But I can certainly fill you in on what it's like in Hurley right now. We're pretty much like any other small town. We've got a fire department, chamber of commerce, grocery stores, hardware, library, schools. But the big difference is, with a population of only fifteen hundred, we've got at least twenty-five bars and seven strip clubs. If you want, I can introduce you to some of my girlfriends who might have more to add. Here's my email." She took a pen from behind her ear and scribbled on the edge of a colorful brochure listing the Hurley and Ironwood attractions like the "World's Tallest and Largest Indian," located in Ironwood, Michigan, which was just across town.

"And here's my cell. Give me a call anytime."

I pulled the brochure toward me while she added, "I got to warn you, though. There's no way to visualize our girlie shows if you haven't seen one in person. We're not big on glam, not like Vegas or Reno! And most places don't bother with a website; they operate by word of mouth. Some clubs have an 'amateur night' when any girl who wants to can get up on stage and swing her tush." She squinted at me and grinned. "You might even want to give it a try. Shake those girls, honey!"

I blushed, although I privately thought my body wasn't bad for a woman in her fifties. Or at least it looked good to me when I stepped out of the shower. And the mirror was veiled with steam.

"Now I've got to get back to work or get fired," she said.

Ginger had opened her purse and was reapplying lipstick. That meant it was time to go.

I paid for lunch and took the rest of my burger for Dash in a doggie bag.

"Before we go, can you show me your stage?"

The Nip 'n' Nudge featured a raised platform in the back of the building where a rope of colored lights encircled an area about as big as a king-size bed with two chrome poles jutting up from the middle. Three high-top tables sat off to the side, or you could find a seat within a messy assortment of folding chairs. There would, of course, be a view from the far end of the bar.

"It's more impressive when the flashing lights are moving and stuff. It gets pretty crowded," Fawn suggested. "So if you show up at any of our local taverns for purposes of entertainment, be sure to get there early, or you might not find a seat!"

"Can I give the pole a try?"

I just wanted an idea of the degree of difficulty these girls faced.

"Help yourself. If you're interested, some bars rent out their poles by the hour so the girls can practice their act."

I was the schoolyard champion on the monkey bars in eighth grade but soon found that skill wouldn't be of any help with the slick silvery rods.

My partner was getting impatient; she wanted to survey the town.

⁂

Ginger insisted on walking up and down the entire length of Silver Street, which, to be truthful, wasn't that long. She had to gawk inside each tavern to observe their stage setup, which varied significantly, but none were as remarkable or imaginative as I'd supposed. Many of the doors were locked, and the bars wouldn't open until late afternoon. Still, we were able to enter a few. One carved a stage out of the side of a wall, a sort of indentation that extended back maybe six feet and provided twelve feet of exposure across the front—a tight fit. Another boasted two stages, and we were assured they both would have simultaneous action. A different tavern had poles extending from the top of the bar.

The historical museum closed at six, so I encouraged Ginger to shorten the tavern tour. I was already considering another visit to Hurley when I could explore on my own.

⁂

The ornamented Richardson Romanesque building was made of pressed red brick. I'd never observed that architectural feature before. It was constructed in 1893, originally as the Town Hall. It had an enormous clock tower plus three floors of historical artifacts, mostly devoted to the development of the local mining and lumbering industries responsible for Hurley's early establishment. The museum director, Jeffrey Draper, welcomed us and reminded us of the closing time, so we had a couple of hours to peruse their collections. I looked around while Ginger regaled him with descriptions of Skipper's newspapers. She was pleased to learn the museum would accept them for their archives.

"A lot of famous people stayed at the Burton House," Mr. Draper began. "You may have seen it advertised in those old newspapers of yours. Sarah Bernhardt stayed there; she made three appearances in town. Benjamin Harrison, during his 1888 presidential campaign. Grover Cleveland signed the guest book in 1889. The Burton House was the model of the hotel in the novel Edna Ferber wrote about our town. In fact, Miss Ferber spent several days browsing through the old structure and its records to gather material. She referred to it as the 'Ridge House.' "

Ferber's book. I asked Draper about the location of the hostelry, and he pointed in the general direction but said it sustained significant damage during a fire in 1894 and burned to the ground in 1948. "The hotel was financed by a mining speculator for $100,000. As you might guess, that was a fortune in 1886."

Photographs revealed the architectural grandeur. It showcased four stories and one hundred rooms, all elaborately decorated with ornate wallpaper and decorative woodwork of oak, walnut, and ash. In addition to the dining room and café, there were double parlors, meeting rooms, a ballroom, and an expansive veranda.

I was unable to feign further interest in the hotel and foolishly asked if the museum had their card catalog on computer—a ridiculous question. But when I specified my area of curiosity, Lotta Morgan, Draper referred me to a substantial file of period newspapers with details of her murder. He also furnished more narratives about stockades where young girls had been imprisoned.

"Reminds me of those articles we saw about Maud what's-her-name and the girls she brought up from Chicago on the train," Ginger remarked.

"Cassidy."

"That's the one. Maud Cassidy." She informed Draper, "We want to know more about Maud Cassidy and how she went about operating her lousy rotten game. I'd also be interested in what happened to the tough old bird after she was captured."

Director Draper promised to check their files and said he might have more information if we could schedule another visit in a day or two. He could even locate a couple of portraits of Lotta Morgan.

Meanwhile, Ginger was growing nervous, pacing the floor and checking her watch.

"What's your problem?" I took her aside to ask. "Do you need to use the restroom?"

"The rally," she replied. "It begins in two hours. I'm going to need a sandwich or something before then. I can feel my sugar running down."

I assured Mr. Draper that I'd return, and to placate Ginger, I stopped to pick up a couple of Subway subs which we took to a park bench near the giant Hiawatha statue in Ironwood. We were now only a few blocks away from Hurley and on the other side of the river.

Ginger consulted the brochure. "Says here, this statue is fifty-two feet tall, and we're right on top of an old iron mine. He's looking north toward Gitche Gumee or Lake Superior."

I silently wondered how much longer it would take before Longfellow's epic poem and this humongous fiberglass depiction would be called racist, referring to the Ojibwa as "noble savages" plus the additional cultural appropriations and make-believe legends conflated by a bearded old white guy who made vast financial gains with his book.

Ginger began reciting

By the shores of Gitchee Gumme,

By the shining Big-Sea-Water,

Stood the wigwam of Nokomis,

Daughter of the Moon, Nokomis.

Dark behind it rose the forest,

Rose the black and gloomy pine trees.

Rose the firs with cones upon them;

Bright before it beat the water,

Beat the clear and sunny water,

Beat the shining Big-Sea-Water—

I cut her off before she got any further. "Do you want to see the giant Stormy Kromer cap, too?" I asked. "They're made here in Ironwood. I'll take your selfie there if you want."

Ginger said she didn't need a "selfie," whatever that was, and she already had two Stormy Kromer caps, one in navy and another in red plaid. "Bet you thought you could kid me about those wool caps. They're damned good, keep you warm in winter with the ear flaps, and don't blow off in the wind. You stay here through January, and I'll see you wearing one and be overjoyed you got it!"

I was more than ready to head back to Star Lake, but Ginger was adamant about the KKK rally. "Do you suppose they'll burn a cross?"

"Ginger, it's probably just a handful of men who get together over beers, wrap themselves in sheets, talk up a storm, and want to make a few headlines."

I had to consider that she'd been kind enough to accompany me on my initial visit to Hurley, so I tried to be as patient as possible and waited until twilight, then sought the rally's location in Ironwood. Nothing to see. We stopped at a service station only to learn the rally was at the Gogebic County Courthouse in Bessemer, the county seat, about seven miles east on U.S. 2. Maybe we'd be too late. If only. I knew squat about Michigan's Upper Peninsula. The broad slab of land was once part of Wisconsin, and its inhabitants were called Yoopers. That was the extent of my knowledge.

We arrived after the rally was supposed to have begun, which was okay with me. When I turned off my headlights, my little Bug was not that conspicuous after all. I pulled up to the curb opposite a large red brick courthouse with a tall tower on the front. We were partially concealed by a couple of trees.

Nothing was happening, and there wasn't much of a crowd.

"Should we get out?" Ginger wanted to know.

We agreed to leave the car but stay within a short distance.

Only seven or eight members of the Klan remained on the lawn, but it didn't take many hooded bodies in long white robes to appear intimidating. They stood in a clump with a couple of law enforcement officers off to one side. I doubted anything serious was going to break out. It was weirdly quiet.

Finally, I steeled my courage and approached one of the officers to ask about the rally.

"Canceled at the last minute. Almost everybody's gone, and those guys are leaving now. Maybe you can ask one of 'em what happened. And if you find out, let us know, okay?"

A placard leaning up against a black van read: *KKK hate every rase but for wight.*

Another sign said, *White Jeans are Best.*

And yet another, *Ragheads Go Home.*

The spellings were problematic, but the message was clear. These were also Larry Boone's sentiments, which gave me a chill.

"Excuse me," I asked a nearby fellow still dressed in his white attire and beginning to disrobe. It was frustrating not to be able to see his eyes.

"What's going on?"

"A-K-A-Y?" he asked. I knew that was code for "A Klansman Are You?" If I were, I would reply "A-K-I-A," meaning "A Klansman I Am."

"No," I replied, "but I'm a friend of Larry Boone. Where's your Grand Dragon?"

"You tell me," he replied. "Called a half hour ago and said to cancel the whole f-ing rally. And he says now our klavern's disbanding, too. Sounds like he's having an f-ing nervous breakdown or something. Traipsed all the way up here to f-ing learn that."

"Ragheads," I said. "Does that refer to Sikhs?"

"Them guys with the brown skin and the turbans," he said. "Sometimes we call 'em Towelheads."

"And you hate them...why?" I asked, playing stupid.

"Because they ain't white! Cripes, that's what we're about, White Power. Jeez."

"The rally's canceled," I told Ginger after I informed the police. "They feel threatened by people like Dr. Singh, Brian's friend at Cedar Springs, who's been treating me for my concussion. Brian told me two more Sikhs were working out of the hospital in Ironwood."

It was as if Ginger were reading my mind. "You know, if Cynthia goes ahead and accepts Larry Boone's bid on that Mouse House cottage, it'll be her responsibility and not yours," she said. "It's not like she's entering into cahoots with the Klan."

"Ginger, I'm the one who foolishly invited him to give us a bid."

"He'd have heard about it one way or another and finagled his way. Do you think there are that many construction jobs around up here in this economy? Even after the storm? Guess again, sweetheart."

When I dropped her off, Ginger said she'd stop by the resort to try one of my pizzas next week. "I bet you're going to make another trip up there, aren't you?"

"Just overnight. Maybe two nights. But not right away."

"Tell Brian he ought to install one of those stripper poles. That might bring in even more patrons than your pizzas."

Ginger patted my thigh as she opened the door to the car.

"The pole would be easy," I replied. "Finding a stripper might be more of a challenge."

"I saw Fawn looking you over," Ginger shut the car door, then chuckled, sticking her head through the open window. "Dim the lights, Jenny, and you might be able to carry it off!"

Ten

There was sexual depravity all over the country back then," I told Brian, "but the national newspapers liked to focus on Northern Wisconsin."

"Because?"

"Because there was such an abundance of sordid behavior up here in the late 1800s. Colorful characters! Debauchery! Corruption!"

I was struggling with a five-pound bag of flour, water, and yeast that I was trying to mix with a wooden spoon. I should have used only half a bag and stirred up two batches. A white cloud flew over the edge of the bowl, then hovered and settled on the table and my shoes.

"Why don't we change places," I suggested. "You can stir the dough and entertain *me*."

Brian shrugged, rolled up his sleeves, washed his hands in the sink, and grabbed the wooden handle. I removed the apron I'd been wearing and flipped the strap over his head.

"Then, if you enjoy this, you can knead the dough when it's ready."

My hands ached.

Sunday morning. The bar was closed.

"I had a super KitchenAid mixer once," I told him. "It was the most expensive model, the kind with a head that tilts back so flour and other ingredients could be added without spilling everything. And it had a nice, large bowl. Six quarts."

"What happened to it?"

Brian was beginning to see how stiff the dough was before it became more flexible.

"It was a gift from my mother-in-law. Second marriage, but I don't count that one because it was so short. She kept a list of every present she ever gave me, including the KitchenAid. During our divorce, she insisted I return it all—the sterling silver I received every Christmas, elaborate spoons, knives, and forks—to fill out the setting chosen by her son's first wife. Same with the fancy gold-rimmed china I hadn't chosen, either. Then there were necklaces, a wristwatch, a toaster, and other odds and ends she and my father-in-law—a truly nice man—purchased during their many trips abroad."

The pizza dough was beginning to come together.

"I never missed the watch, had no use for the sterling or china, surely didn't miss her son, but I always regretted losing that mixer."

He threw me a rueful smile.

"Okay, back to illicit sex."

Brian paused to wipe the sweat from his forehead with a towel.

"This area, between Northern Wisconsin and the Upper Michigan border, was a hot spot for prostitution and gambling. And *boodling*. How's that for the word of the day?"

"Boodling," he repeated. "Sounds like a video game."

I explained it was in all the headlines then, and the practice never died out. "Political corruption involving money. They ought to bring back the term; it's fun to pronounce."

I dusted more flour on the new marble top of the little pine table and told him to dump the dough out on it. Then I demonstrated how to knead: press down on the mound of dough, fold it over, stretch it, and turn it again.

"How long does this take?" Brian asked, up to his elbows in the very sticky mixture. I dabbed his forehead since he could not.

"It's mostly by feel," I said. "When it gets shiny and reaches a point where you can poke your finger in it, and it springs back, or if you pull the dough and it doesn't tear, you know it's ready to set aside to rise. We'll cover it with a clean dishtowel, and after it's grown to twice the original size, we can make a bunch of smaller balls that we can freeze like that or roll out as pizza crusts to use right away."

Toad and Stumpy wandered into the kitchen just then and had a good chuckle when they saw Brian wearing an apron.

"I didn't see you guys laughing when you were knocking back the last of Jenny's pizzas the other night," Brian said. "Besides, she's about to entertain me with tales of sex in the Northwoods."

The boys each pulled up a chair and said they sure didn't want to miss that, so I told them about Razorback while Brian fought with the dough. "She must've been a beauty," I said. "Up in the UP, she chewed Peerless tobacco, a brand still manufactured in Milwaukee. No idea where her nickname came from, but she liked to dance with the men who visited her brothel—danced them conveniently toward the door where they were seized by her john and robbed of all their cash. Many of the prostitutes took advantage of men who'd already removed their pants and went through their pockets."

"Still happens today," Toad said soberly.

"Like you'd know." Stumpy elbowed him in the ribs.

"Well, I got ears! I know what's going on! Say, Jenny, you ever hear about Lumberjack Ida?"

Stumpy asked if that was Lumberjack Ida from Antler.

"Yup. She worked with Tootsie, Ruby, and Big Florence."

"Personal friends of his," Brian added with a smirk.

"Oh, go on and hurry up with that there dough," Toad advised. "You know yourself that was way before my time, back when the Milwaukee, Lake Shore and Western still came through town. As I heard tell, the girls had a house of ill repute next to the railroad tracks and served the lumberjacks who came into town on payday with fat rolls of cash. There was this bouncer, see, who, from time to time, would relieve an unconscious body of his money roll and arrange him just so on the tracks in time to be run over by the next train. The undertaker was paid to swear it was an accidental death."

"Finally came to an end," Stumpy added," only because one day the train had engine trouble and was running late. The conductor had time to spy the body and got the brakes on just in time. The undertaker took one look and had to admit the target had a bullet in his ear."

"Ida hung herself in jail with her stockings," Toad said, shaking his head.

We were silent for a moment, as if in respect to the deceased madam. Or because we had nothing to add that could top that tale.

Brian was tired of kneading. "You think this is ready yet?"

I checked the dough and told him to keep going. There was a lot of dough, and it took another twenty minutes before we could dump it into the bowl and wait for the magic of the yeast to do its thing.

⁂

I drove up to Cedar Springs alone to see Dr. Singh the next day, Monday. After his genial welcome, I casually mentioned that I'd heard about a Klan rally in the UP over the weekend that protested the presence of Sikh doctors.

"I've sewn up at least a half dozen of those men, including Larry Boone," he sighed. "Treated them for broken bones and cuts. They never seemed bothered by the color of my skin when they were bleeding."

We considered that paradox with good humor, and after my exam, he concluded that I had fully recovered. "You could not have been rescued by a better man than my old colleague Brian Cullen," he said. "How long has it been since your accident, just over a month?"

I agreed.

"Good luck to you, Jenny," he said as he shook my hand. "I hope to see you again, under different circumstances. Someone said you make an excellent pizza!" Then he added, "Your impromptu visit to The Last Resort has been of immense benefit to my friend. Having you to look after seems to have vastly improved Brian's mental health. I'm sorry a tree fell on your head, but I'm happy for the outcome."

A tree fell on my head. I'd use that in the future to describe my bizarre introduction to this Northwoods "holiday."

⁂

In the beginning, I'd been eager to escape from The Last Resort as soon as I could. A month after the tornado, I was still there, and it seemed everyone who wanted to view the damage to the landscape had already done so.

Now we were packed with customers every night. *Jenny's Last Pizzas* were a huge hit, and with the new pizza oven, I could rapidly turn them out. I had a new routine:

Before going down to Bluegill to write, I spent at least an hour in the kitchen of the bar, where, depending on the day of the week, I mixed and rolled out at least a dozen crusts or more from yesterday's refrigerated dough. The ones that weren't baked that night would be stored in the freezer. It was a big task and usually took longer than I wanted. I often put off mixing tomorrow's dough until the afternoon.

After that, I reported to my "office" with my charged laptop and a folder of clippings and assorted notes to be transcribed. The wobbly kitchen table in the cabin had become my desk. Dash had become proficient at opening the screened door with his nose and came and went as he wished.

Of course, Bluegill had no power or Wi-Fi, but the placid location seemed to motivate my imagination. Occasionally, however, my wonderings led me to less-than-useful thoughts.

Cynthia had made arrangements with Ada to take full responsibility for rebuilding the cottage with Boone's Construction, and they were able to begin work sooner than expected. I delayed a trip over there to celebrate the subsequent demolition, blaming my absence on innumerable newspaper accounts of Lotta Morgan's life and death that I wanted to make note of and compare.

⁂

When the late summer weather finally enticed me to get outside, I collected Ginger by boat, and we made our way over to the Maus Haus via water. She'd been informed of the crude stairway from the dock to the cottage and said she was content to rest her eyes while Dash and I did a quick survey.

The once-unspeakable structure was in the midst of a remarkable renovation. Two dumpsters held putrid evidence that had been pulled out of the place. Boone wasn't there (a relief since I didn't want to encounter him after the bust of the Bessemer rally), but a teenage girl sat on the edge of the deck, head in hands. Dash quickly made friends.

I introduced myself, and she said she was Larry's daughter, Rosie. She didn't look at all like I'd imagined she would—she was pale without makeup, no tattoos, no piercings, no absurd color in her long dark blonde braid.

"What's up," I asked as I took a seat next to her. "Helping your dad?"

She said she was supposed to be, but she hated it.

Without another word, Rosie stood and made her careful way down to the pier with Dash at her heels. I knew she'd run into Ginger and a catalog of questions, but I didn't stop her.

Dash had smuggled a tennis ball along and was playing fetch with Rosie when I got there. I informed Ginger about the cleanup progress. Rosie complained that Cynthia had given her instructions to pull up the moldy linoleum from the bathroom floor today. "I'm not in the mood."

"Don't blame you, kiddo," Ginger replied. "That sounds like a revolting job. What else could you be doing this summer if you weren't working out here for your dad and Blondie?"

"I'm only fifteen, so I'm not old enough for some jobs," Rosie replied. "I tried to find housekeeping work at local resorts, but the ones I tried hired the same girls they had last year."

"Do you like pizza?" Ginger asked.

"I could use some kitchen help," I explained, "at The Last Resort."

Rosie showed up the next day, and I began tutoring her. She learned fast and soon had perfected all the necessary techniques. She was suitably impressed with our slick pizza oven. Cynthia was okay with my rescue of Rosie and said she'd only taken her on at Larry's insistence; he wanted to keep his eye on his daughter. I was pleased since I could report to Bluegill earlier each morning.

※

There were a few unusually humid days in early August until thunderstorms brought a cool breeze from the north. Each night I pulled the soft, faded pink comforter up to my chin and gave thanks for my return to health, my cozy retreat, the luxury of my freedom, no real deadlines or work to realize, except for the pizzas and my immersion in Lotta's story. I pledged to enjoy the now, no matter what it brought forth. In my other life, as I thought of it, I'd been a crazy news junkie. Up here, I had been ignoring the national news. No one much cared what happened in Washington, DC, Madison, or Milwaukee. I didn't have to set an alarm clock. If the fish were biting and the sun was shining, everything was right with the world. I was living one day at a time.

"Things will sort themselves out," Ginger assured me, and if they didn't, she had a spare bedroom that she'd be happy to share. Dash and I were welcome to move in with her any time.

※

That turned out to be the week that Cynthia revealed her scheme to beguile Brian. It was also when I began to seriously consider leaving Madison and making my home up north.

But first, I heard back from Jeff Draper in Hurley. He'd been in touch with a friend who ran a local B&B with a cancellation. Without asking, he'd made a weekend reservation for me.

"You can ignore it if the timing doesn't work out," he promised. "But Myrna's usually full every weekend in summer, and in winter, she and her husband relocate to Florida. Snowbirds, you know. The thing is, here they have a special 'Lotta Morgan room.' Myrna collected items from Lotta's day, like oil lamps and lace curtains, a canopied bed, and other vintage pieces, and she made copies of Lotta's photographs. The room's always in demand for anyone who's into history, especially those who like mysteries like Lotta's murder or who are inspired to track down ghosts."

I was confused by the last reference and asked if the room was haunted.

"It's Lotta's ghost. I did mention that to you when you were here, didn't I? There have been reports now and then that she's made appearances downtown since her death."

I told Jeff I'd see what I could do about the weekend and get back to him later in the day. The excursion sounded interesting. I had zero interest in ghosts, but I could complete my investigation, get together with Fawn—the waitress at the Nip 'n' Nudge—and learn about Hurley's lurid nightlife. I was excited.

Well, I was excited until Cynthia told me she'd made weekend plans with Brian.

At my request, she was giving me a tour of Aspen Glen. I had perused the packet of information she'd given me shortly after we'd met, and despite initial hesitations, my interest had been piqued. Natural woodlands sheltered the fairly large cottages. The forty-acre development was only a few miles from The Last Resort. I had no idea the landlocked locale was that close. Thus, her avid wish to obtain Brian's lake access. Now it made sense.

To be honest, I'd weighed many possibilities and memorized the blueprints for each Aspen Glen cottage. If I sold my condo in Madison—a prospect that gradually became an actuality in my mind—I could almost afford one of hers and move to the Northwoods full-time. It was appealing. My daughters would enjoy visiting me here, and my grandchildren would, too, with a chance to fish and swim, watch loons dive, maybe see a bear—all the things I'd loved about up north as a kid.

Any fears that the community would be too luxe for me were easily quelled when Cynthia showed me a two-bedroom, two-and-a-half-bath home. There were two decks and a beautiful wood-burning fireplace. Dash and another pet (maybe a cat?) would be welcome there.

"I'm sure you can appreciate the modern cottage ambiance," Cynthia said (whatever that was). I didn't need much persuasion; I liked the air conditioning and beautiful fieldstone fireplace. I was smitten.

The eventual clubhouse would feature indoor *and* outdoor pools, tennis and pickleball courts, exercise rooms, a spa, and "every convenience necessary for modern-day life in the woods," according to a glossy brochure. I must be getting old, I decided, because "rustic" had lost much of its charm. Streets were plotted and would be cleared as the project evolved. Three finished condos were available, including the one Cynthia occupied—a model she'd staged for prospective buyers. Eventually, they'd have over fifty homes altogether. She had already sold ten.

"The only thing we lack for this "modern-day life in the woods," Cynthia mourned, "is access to a lake. We'll have groomed walking paths throughout, and with minor acquisitions of adjacent vacant land and some alterations, we'd be able to highlight a forested drive to the scenic shores currently occupied by The Last Resort. I'm still working on that."

In my head, I was already in Madison, listing my condo and packing my furnishings. In actuality, we were seated on the edge of the covered front porch of her Aspen Glen cottage, where I was picturing a couple of rocking chairs and a place for Dash to nap.

"So, a couple of months ago, I made a reservation because they have to be made that far in advance," Cynthia was saying, "and Saturday night, I'm treating Brian to dinner."

Cynthia frequently mentioned how much she cared for Brian, but I tried to remain noncommittal and neither encouraged nor discouraged her. I did, however, closely observe their interactions whenever I could.

"I'm sorry," I blinked. "I wasn't listening. Where?"

"*Bonfire.*" She laughed. "You're already moving in, aren't you?"

"I have to talk with my banker and make some arrangements in Madison," I admitted. "But I'm sensing a strong possibility."

"Fantastic!" Cynthia exclaimed. "We'll be neighbors! I'm going to stay on as the resident caretaker!"

Her hug was spontaneous and warm. I knew this was more than just a sale; we'd become close friends.

"Just let me know when you're ready to discuss the details, and we can make it happen."

I was still preoccupied as she continued, "I was saying Brian will be joining me for dinner at Bonfire on Saturday night. It's a restaurant deep in the woods near Manitowish Waters. Last month *Gourmet* praised it for its *exquisite cuisine in a casually elegant setting*, and *Travel and Leisure* had a feature story on it last year. Since the tornado wiped out his property—conveniently for me, although I hesitate to admit it—I think Brian may feel more motivated to hand it over."

I agreed that Brian was still undecided. "Your scheme involves reaching Brian through his stomach?" I tried not to laugh at her simple strategy. With unusual control, my response became affable but muted.

"Oh, Jenny, you know I'm not that naive," she grinned. "I've had a lot of time to design this plot. My dazzling effort will involve feminine cunning, carnal lust, and single-malt scotch. Wish me luck!"

⁂

If I drove up to Hurley on Saturday morning, I reasoned, that left me Friday night to subtly influence Brian before Cynthia and her Bonfire strategy. Precipitously, perhaps, I texted my daughters on Thursday to tell them of my thoughts and sent them a link to Aspen Glen. Their joyous replies underscored the certainty of my resolve. By Friday, I'd texted my condo manager to say I'd be selling within the next month or so. She said she had a waiting list of interested buyers.

I was especially interested in one of the Aspen Glen homes under construction but nearly complete. I preferred the secluded location, and it had a floor plan like the one I'd toured, but the fireplace would have a rough-hewn mantle, and the second-floor master suite had an attached study and sitting room. I could envision myself there with only a slight hesitation: what if Cynthia and Brian became a duo? I didn't know how I could adjust to that. I had become extremely fond of each for separate reasons. And in the future, I'd be much happier if I could keep the two apart.

I wondered if there was some way I could design a plot of my own—find a means to thwart their relationship. Although it might be rude, I decided to hazard that risk.

Brian had left to run errands in town, so Stumpy and Toad joined me for lunch. I fixed egg salad sandwiches which Toad, who was missing several teeth, always enjoyed because he could chew them. Dash sat next to Stumpy, supremely content but alert to the possibility of a dropped potato chip or snaring one that was surreptitiously shared.

Since I had the opportunity, I asked them if they knew what kind of settlement Brian's insurance company had offered him.

"You know the place wasn't in prime condition before the wind came," Toad said.

"No idea," Stumpy confessed. "Brian keeps a lot of stuff close to his vest. If I had had to guess, though, I'd bet he surrenders the place. Too much work to get it running again. Don't believe he has the incentive or the energy anymore. A couple years ago, it was a different matter."

⁂

Delicate forget-me-nots with bright yellow throats still hemmed the shoreline in front of Bluegill. There was no way I could concentrate on my work. I slipped off my sandals and sat on the pier to dangle my feet in the water while I watched a bald eagle ride the thermals. Dash lay beside me, his black coat wet and gleaming. I wanted to embrace the entire tableau in my heart, but I couldn't entirely. I didn't want the "resort" enchantment to fade away.

I was convinced this peace and ease could be cherished by tourists in the future as they had for so long. If Brian got the resort back and running, it could thrive with a few changes. Ginger had come across another box of Skipper's, a shoebox hidden under her bed. Assorted photos and snapshots documented the resort's early days, including some saved by previous owners. Grinning fishermen spread their arms wide to display prize muskies, and hunters swollen with pride embraced their rifles and knelt in the grass next to bucks with large racks.

We delighted in photos of kids gripping inner tubes or standing on the dock goofing off with skinny arms around each other's shoulders. These children were now grandparents or, more likely, gone.

Ginger knew I was a hopeless romantic, but she agreed that the pictures captured the essence of Northwoods escapes before electronic adventures took over. Simple pleasures were treasured then, and an annual vacation at The Last Resort was the favorite focus of a family's summer.

⁂

Brian accepted my invitation to the Friday night fish fry.

Rosie was on hand to take care of pizza orders. Toad and Stumpy were glad to handle the bar. My plot, much simpler than Cynthia's, had been easily arranged.

I had reserved a table at The Star Lake Saloon, and the enthusiastic welcome Brian received there was, I could see, an embarrassment to him. Our dinners epitomized the iconic Wisconsin fish fry: three flawlessly battered, deep-fried perch; golden-crisp French fries that sparkled with salt; a generous glob of creamy coleslaw, and a slab of dark rye with a cold slab of butter. It was every bit as delicious as Ada had described.

Later, we watched the reflection of a pink and orange sunset settle upon Star Lake as we shared the last drops of a bottle of wine.

"Tell me again what you expect to find in Hurley," he asked.

"First, I want to sort out the hyperbole about the Wisconsin Pineries. One rather stupid account said loggers and miners came north to avoid serving in the Civil War. But the war was in the 1860s, and the mines and logging camps did not enjoy their heyday until the 1880s. The UP had a hundred and fifty lumber mills by 1889. That's when they employed thirteen thousand men."

"Who made good money with no place to spend it."

"Right. Hurley had the most to offer. Nearly every building on Silver Street was a saloon—many, many more than they have today! As I mentioned before, newspapers loved bawdy tales, and reporters complied by embellishing every dubious anecdote. Their accounts were reprinted word-for-word in St. Louis papers, St. Paul, Detroit, Nebraska, Kansas, and dozens of other cities. Like the story about *Piano Annie.*"

"She was a musician?"

"For twenty-five cents, she'd turn a trick behind an upright piano in the corner of a little bar in Eagle River."

Brian mused that perhaps The Last Resort should replace the jukebox with a piano.

I had yet to explain Duncan Sunderlast's involvement in the Lotta Morgan murder, so I previewed what I knew of Lotta's story and added that I hoped to learn more about that, too.

"Was Lotta an actress or a prostitute," Brian asked, "or was she both?"

"In those days, merely appearing on stage was enough for a woman to merit a shady reputation. Who knows for sure if she slept with men for money. Let's say it was assumed. I've read tales of so-called theatrical agents who lured young women north with promises of leading roles on the stage. Then when the girls stepped off the train in Hurley, they were billed for their travel and clothing, which they had to repay by wearing scanty attire and 'performing' at disreputable dance halls. Some of these girls were only in their early teens."

I wanted to describe the stockades and Maud Cassidy's evildoings, but he asked if Lotta Morgan had been duped into coming to Hurley. I had to admit I didn't know for sure, but it was another of the mysteries that I hoped to solve.

"The historical museum has limited hours, but the Lotta Morgan murder remains a significant part of the city's history, and the director has taken a special interest in my research. He's allowing me to come in on Sunday so I can have the archives all to myself. He's already set a few articles aside.

"Then, late tomorrow night, I may visit a tittie bar."

Because I had described their shabby stage, Brian had a good laugh when he suggested I don some scanty attire and dance at the Nip 'n' Nudge.

"Hey, that's not so funny," I teased. "I've already been encouraged to audition!"

Eleven

We returned to The Last Resort after sunset, but there seemed to be a mutual desire to not end our evening that early. "The only nightcap I can offer you is lukewarm tea from a thermos that I left down at Bluegill," I offered. Brian said he wanted to check with the boys in the bar and grab a flashlight; he'd meet me there.

Twilight lasted longer in this part of the state, so it wasn't yet completely dark. Fireflies mingled with stars' reflections in the water. Loons, always melancholy, yodeled along the chain: Star Lake to Sundog and then Lake Sickle Moon. On the porch of Bluegill, I already occupied the beat-up rocking chair where I liked to relax and read. "My office is in there," I pointed to the darkening kitchen.

Brian pulled the other wicker rocking chair closer to mine. "I'm going to miss this special place," I said with more regret than I'd meant to reveal. My voice cracked. I cleared my throat.

"This is where you're supposed to say, 'You're only going to Hurley for a few nights. We'll still be here when you get back,'" I reminded him.

He took my hand and held it in his.

"Not sure how much longer old Bluegill will be here," Brian replied, lifting my fingers to his lips. "My insurance company gave me the go-ahead, even though rebuilding costs would be substantial. Reconstruct the demolished cabins, for example, and tear down or gut and fix the problems with this one. Do something major about the septic system while everything's in chaos because a total update's overdue. Quite honestly, it's a lot to think about. I'd rather not get more loans to sink into this place.

"Cynthia made me a generous offer before the storm, shabby as it was, and she's assured me that her previous proposal still stands. I want to hear her out. I owe her that. I wouldn't mind getting out from under so much debt."

"She's been your friend for a long time," I offered.

"Ellen's, too," he replied. "She's a good person. Cynthia has a good heart."

I agreed with him about that, but I left a lengthy silence before remarking that the property was pretty much unoccupied now, so there wouldn't be a lot to raze. "What about the bar?"

"Well, yes, the bar. But it's not in great shape, and it's been here for a very long time. Duncan Sunderlast wasn't the first owner. Not much of a loss as a building, except for the regulars who like to stop by and would miss us just out of habit."

"And the pizza connoisseurs, of course," I joked.

I removed my hand from his grasp, trying hard to keep it light and refrain from mentioning what was really on my mind: that I'd hoped he would feel a responsibility to maintain a family resort.

"I heard some statistics the other day."

"I thought you said you weren't keeping up with the news," Brian teased.

"I do listen to the radio occasionally, and this was on NPR. I figure that's acceptable."

"Oh, c'mon," Brian said, laughing. But I recapped the story told by a man who'd written a book about changes in the way families now spend their vacation time. He mentioned how the old family resorts had been split up, with their cottages sold off as condos.

"That's hardly news."

I was silent for a moment, wondering how to phrase my comment so it would seem more appealing.

"You're right; it isn't news. But you probably weren't aware that one morning this week, I came down here to write and found a strange woman sitting in my chair."

"*Your* chair?"

"Yes, my chair," I said. "This chair. In the morning, after I fuss with the pizza dough—which Rosie is helping with—I like to come down here and read. Or meditate. It's *my* chair. The wicker seat and the pillow have gradually been formed to fit my butt. I sit like this, with my feet up on the little edge that runs around the porch where the screens are fastened, and then I'll lean back with my book on my lap. It's very peaceful. Eventually, I'll work on my writing."

"Jenny," Brian interrupted. "The woman. Your chair. What are you getting at?"

"Okay, this is the cottage where she first stayed with her parents in 1974. It was a hot day in June, and by the time they got here, the dog had thrown up in the car. Her mother began crying and wanted to go home. Her father convinced her that the kids *should* at least have a chance to swim, and he wanted to fish. So they stayed. They came up here every year after that until her parents died and her brother moved away. Then she and her husband rented this same cottage every summer and brought their children. Her husband passed away last spring, and after the tornado, she thought she'd never see this cottage again or have a chance to sit on this porch and review all her memories."

"Spare me the sob story." Brian's voice had a sharp edge.

"It is sad, I know," I replied. "How do you think I felt when the woman started to cry? She said this resort represented everything good about family. They laughed and played games, they swam, they went out in the boat, and the kids learned to fish. Every year they'd take a family photo next to the same tree and later compare the pictures to see how the family grew. Eventually, they rented additional cottages to handle the grandchildren. She said this resort was a magical place for them, and it became the one week a year when they didn't have to think about anything else."

"I've heard similar anecdotes," he admitted. "Every once in a while, somebody will show up to reminisce. They'll have a couple of beers, and the sentimental narratives begin to drip. But I'm sorry, I don't think this place ever made a living for anyone, including your Skipper or Bud Foster and his hunting hounds. It costs a hell of a lot to keep a small resort like this up and running, and you can see for yourself how futile that can be. Winter is a huge challenge, too, if we don't get much snow."

"Unless you've got a good snowmobile crowd. And you do have that, right?"

"If there's a spectacular winter."

Okay, I'd said my piece. I didn't want to press my luck.

"I know what you're getting at, Jenny. Your argument isn't exactly understated. But this simply isn't a reliable way to make a living. I was barely earning enough to get by before the storm hit."

"But what if...what if you fixed it up? You could raise your prices!"

I was diving off the deep end with that proposition. I'd given it a lot of thought, and it was now or never, so I spoke fast.

"I mean, okay, build all new cottages with the insurance money. Raze this one, too. I'm thinking *modern* cottages that look old, kind of *retro*; use new logs and new shingles but furnish them with reproductions of furnishings that were used in the 1930s and 1940s. Duplicate activities that an escape to the Northwoods used to mean back then for families, parents, and kids. Put in a sandy swimming beach and a raft; that wouldn't cost much. Kids could learn how to make s'mores and how to thread a worm on a hook, how to sit on the dock and watch a red and white bobber. It would be radical. You could be at the forefront of a new wave of resort living in Wisconsin. When I was a kid, my family used to come up north every summer."

"As you've frequently reminded me."

I exhaled a very deep sigh. I wasn't getting anywhere.

"You've never owned a business!" Brian said flatly. "And neither had I until I bought this place on a whim."

I apologized. "I know I'm a dreamer. Always have been."

"And you want to reach back and drag out strumming ukuleles and Parcheesi and sing *"Kumbaya"* in four-part harmony, ignoring the bankruptcies, the suicides, the sheriff's sales."

That was all true. Except for "Kumbaya." And I hadn't considered ukuleles.

"Wait a minute," I interrupted. "You seem to forget that I'm reaching back to investigate this area's sordid history. That wasn't a carefree time for anyone, including the lives those loggers and miners and miserable women were challenged to lead. I resent your accusation that I'm relentlessly starry-eyed."

"Jenny, just drop it, okay?"

But something in me couldn't stop nagging. Maybe it was the wine. Maybe it was because I knew my time was limited. Tomorrow night he'd be subjected to Cynthia's maneuvers and allure.

I readjusted my rocking chair, but my stubbornness remained.

"Forget about the resort. If you go out of business, Brian, or sell this property to Cynthia, what will happen to you? Will you go back to nursing? Get a job at a hospital? What will your life become?"

"What difference is that going make to you? Jenny, what the hell."

"I'm almost certain that I'm going to move to Aspen Glen. The condo I intend to purchase isn't finished yet, but Cynthia says it'll be ready by Thanksgiving. I've already invited my daughters and my grandchildren for Thanksgiving dinner. I want to show them around The Last Resort, have them meet the man who saved my life."

Early in my recovery, I somehow managed to suppress the rush of desire I'd felt for this man. Yes, I was dizzy then, too concussed to realize its depths, but hadn't I been recalling his loving touch ever since with profound longing?

"Thank you for taking such good care of me," I said, more softly now. "Dr. Singh claims I was lucky. I don't know what would have happened to me—and Dash—without your help. I'd probably be dead."

Brian was rocking, silent. Perhaps he'd be glad to have me out of there. Oh, dammit—maybe by saying, "I'd be dead," I reminded him of Ellen.

I'd gone overboard. Big Mouth Jenny. I attempted to explain:

"I was on my way *from the fish fry at* the Saloon when I was 'hit on the head by a tree,' as Dr. Singh defines it, and tonight, now that he says I'm finally healed, I returned there *to the fish fry* with you to bookend my stay. It's been a considerable amount of time, and I want to compensate you for that—for the rescue, for the room, for my care, for my meals."

I took a folded check from my pocket and tried to place it in his hand. It was written to cover what I'd figured the monthly charge for a cottage would have been, but that didn't include the ice packs, the food, the therapy, and companionship.

I couldn't read his expression in the dark, but Brian brushed me away and left the porch. The screen door slammed with a crack that shattered the calm.

"We were having a nice evening," he said over his shoulder. "For god's sake, did you think I did what I did for you because I'd be paid?"

It was still a lovely night. Far off, I could hear the lonely howls of a pack of wolves. Rippling circles on the lake intersected where fish surfaced to snap bugs.

I had soured the atmosphere.

"I've been here for six weeks," I hurried to follow him up the hill.

"And writing a check, that's supposed to...what?"

"Bring some closure. I'd feel better if you knew how grateful I am."

Brian turned and roughly grabbed my arms, nearly knocking me down.

"Grateful," he said, his voice suddenly hoarse. "You're grateful. I get it. Maybe I'm grateful, too. Maybe I enjoyed—although enjoyed isn't the right word. You suffered a concussion and bad cuts and abrasions, Jenny, and having you under my care was something I've been trained to do."

He pulled me close, held me tight, brushed my hair from my forehead, and whispered, "And maybe I liked having you here, near me. What about that?"

I felt I must resist the force of his grasp. But wasn't this what I dreamed of all those nights when I tried to generate some crazy ESP to draw him into my room and have him join me in bed? Those half-conscious fantasies I'd invented about the loving ways he would touch me, his warm hands on my breasts, tenderly parting my thighs.

Brian brusquely pushed away. I landed on the dew-wet grass; not because of Brian but because I was such a fool.

"So, this is it," I said to Dash, who ran down to me, freed from the bar by Brian. I got to my feet and went back to retrieve my sandals from Bluegill's porch. I sat on the steps. Mosquitoes swarmed and buzzed while I hugged my dog and hid my tears in his ebony fur.

"I blew it, Dash," I told him. "It's over." And, finally, "Let's just go to bed."

Twelve

Even with an extra sleeping pill, I laid there, eyes wide open, and when I finally dozed off, it was a fitful night. Yes, I'd hoped to meddle with Cynthia's forthcoming gracious offer, but my desire to provide financial compensation for my stay was a stupid last-minute impulse. Dr. Singh claimed that my body had been healed. I was not that certain about my addled brain.

I could hear Rosie in the kitchen assembling ingredients for mixing dough, so I joined her, and we worked together for several hours. Leaving her to handle the kitchen by herself on our busiest day of the week caused some apprehension, but Stumpy had offered to serve the tables if Rosie kept the pizzas rolling out, and she was fine with that.

No one knew where Brian had gone. I grabbed a quick lunch, said goodbye at noon, and left for Hurley, relieved to have missed him. Remorse and misgivings. Why was I so often driven to act on impulse when it invariably caused second thoughts?

⁂

Jeff Draper welcomed my arrival and guided me toward a desk he'd prepared for my use. On the top were three formal portraits of Lotta Morgan that he had already scanned for my files. One was a full-length studio portrait, and the other two concentrated on her face and shoulders. She appeared exceptionally stylish and wore dresses of dark silk or satin fabric (burgundy or black?) that were heavily adorned with elaborate capes of beads and jewels. Each dress buttoned to her throat, where a bar pin with three gold discs was fastened. Further diamond ornaments were attached to Lotta's bodice and nestled in her thick, dark hair. Large diamond pendants swung from her earlobes. A floss of curls on her forehead had been an *au courant* fashion back then. We remarked upon the serene gaze of her eyes, her discreet smile. One portrait bore her signature: "Yours truly, Lotta Morgan."

I spent a couple of hours squinting through spinning microfilm, a slow and patient task for me due to the inevitable motion sickness it triggered. I much preferred yellowed newsprint. Draper was able to provide that as well. At my request, he copied articles that mentioned Lotta and featured acts at local theaters during her time. A related piece in the *Ironwood Times* bore this headline: "Lottie Morgan was 'Tame' Compared to Irish Annie," whose own murder occurred seven years later, and stated: "Hurley is keeping up its reputation as the toughest town in the Northwest, and has this week added another murder to her list of disreputable occurrences." Annie was shot "in one of the Dago saloons on the main street." Moreover, Annie was "one of the worst characters that the [Iron] range ever saw. The police of Hurley have at this writing been unable to find any trace whatever of the murderer, and it is probable [sic] destined to remain an unsolved mystery and an unpunished crime, as is the murder of Lottie Morgan, which occurred there a few years ago."

I expressed my gratitude to Draper for his generosity and packed a tote bag with documents to keep me occupied until the next day.

⁂

Before checking into Myrna's B&B, a pink clapboard home in a modest neighborhood, I stopped to pick up a few snacks. Plumply stuffed into jeans with an oversize red sweatshirt and gray hair pulled back in a ponytail, Myrna greeted me at the door with a squashy hug and appreciation for my stay. I was given a tour of the Lotta Morgan Room to the right of the entryway. A four-poster bed filled the compact space nearly wall to wall, but a small, windowed bay facing the street had space for a potted fern and a vintage glider. Photos of Lotta I'd recently studied were displayed in fancy gilt frames.

"I'm open to any suggestions for personalizing the room even more," Myrna stated. "The only true item I have of hers is this silver hand mirror."

She handed it over. The heavy item, including the handle, was about ten inches long, with an ornate Victorian design. The mirror portion had oxidized, and one area toward the top of the frame displayed a cloudy shadow. The mere thought that Lotta's face had been reflected beneath my gaze was decidedly creepy. I turned it over and set it aside.

There was an attached bathroom, pocket-sized but efficient, most likely created from a closet. I hoped I could fold my body into the minuscule tub.

"Breakfast is from eight to ten," Myrna paused before leaving, "But if you prefer a different time, Jenny, I can arrange that for you. We have four other guests this weekend, but I want you to be comfortable."

Myrna beamed.

Just then, my only preference was a lengthy nap.

I slept until six, and when I woke, I immediately imagined Brian meeting Cynthia for dinner. Or getting ready to meet her. Would he stop for her at Aspen Glen in his pickup, or would she come for him in her Porsche? How did a woman dress for an exclusive Northwoods supper club? I'd never seen Cynthia in a skirt.

I felt restless and edgy, so I dined on a cheese stick, Ritz crackers, and a glass of rosé while I forced myself to page through the additional photocopies Draper had provided—anything to keep my mind off Cynthia and Brian. I could picture them arriving at Bonfire and being shown to a table in a shadowy corner.

An early *Ironwood News Record* referred to Lotta as "a habitue of Hurley's very earliest variety theater and saloons." The *Gogebic Iron Tribune,* published in Hurley, identified Lotta as "a sporting woman." But a book of Northwoods history boasted, "Of all the girls of Silver Street in the old days, the most celebrated was beauteous Lotta Morgan...strictly a high-class girl. Like most of her sisters, she worked out of a saloon."

Eventually, I gave Fawn a call. My invitation to dinner was tempting, but she and a couple of her girlfriends were dancing at the Silverpalooza that night. It was not far from the Nip 'n' Nudge. And if I still wanted to see what their dancing was like, I should be there around nine to see them work. I thanked her for the info, made no promises, but hadn't I told Brian I'd visit a tittie club?

According to Ginger, a first-person report on these strip clubs would be revealing in a hypothetical manuscript for *The Northwoods Nobody Knows* except for those who intentionally sought out that sort of thing. There'd be no comparison between the Silverpalooza and the original saloons, the Alcazar Theater or Variety Theater, or the Hurley Opera House where Lotta and her other friends executed their acts. Still, Fawn had been so patient with Ginger's interrogation that I could not simply ignore her invitation. Plus, ambiance, milieu, spectators, curiosities, details, descriptions, etc. Research.

In truth, my concentration was not at its best. In the back of my mind, I was imagining current events at Bonfire while at the same time remembering what happened last evening. Our dinner conversation, the argument on the shore, and then the outburst of emotion that followed. Hadn't Brian said he enjoyed having me near him? *Only three nights*, I told myself. Three nights in Hurley, then back to Star Lake, where I could decide where to go next. Madison would make sense. I could sort out my condo and arrange for its sale. Before heading off, I should take some "after" photos of the progress at Ada's Maus Haus. She would be thrilled by the dramatic improvements. I hoped Cynthia had made a photographic record of what it was like "before." Knowing her, she would likely keep a calendar to track the evolution.

⁂

To blend in with the Silverpalooza crowd, I wore jeans and a long-sleeved black cotton T-shirt. Women over fifty were invisible to men, right? Fine with me. I was only gathering local color.

Fawn had warned there'd be a crowd. Silver Street swarmed with pickups and SUVs. Neon lights flashed from strip clubs like sheet lightning, and the clash of loud music fleeing bars was an assault to my ears. I must have lingered a moment too long in front of the Silverpalooza, a square cement block building painted gray with one frosted window in the front, because I reaped lewd glances from a cluster of young men crouched, smoking weed near the heavy door. Their remarks were garbled in the din. I guess I wasn't exactly invisible, but it was promising.

The odor hit me the moment I went inside—the usual rancid tavern whiff plus sour vomit, stale cigarette smoke, heavy perfume, and sweat. I'm not very tall, so my nose was at armpit level, and with the dense throng inside, I had to shove aside damp bodies to squeeze up to the bar.

I got a beer and wedged farther back to an area where I was directed toward the stage. My comfort zone was miles away at this point, and it was difficult to breathe in such captivity where I was jostled and shoved and probably felt up—it was hard to tell. I began to feel lightheaded. A young woman skidded off a barstool, and I rudely grabbed it away from her; this was not a time or place to be genteel. There I could rise above the rowdy multitude for a better look and took a few slow, deep breaths, redolent as they were.

Women of all sizes wore shrunken tank tops that revealed their bra straps. What is it with this popular fashion faux pas that only I seem to mind? Men didn't bother to remove their caps indoors (many worn backward), and nearly everyone flaunted at least two or more tattoos.

In the middle of a bright red enameled floor that projected into the room like a massive glossy tongue (a crude reminder of The Rolling Stones' logo) a tall chrome pole gleamed like a phallic sentinel. Strings of colored Christmas lights blinked around the edge of the stage. The crowd became more raucous when Ruby appeared in flimsy white lingerie over a red sequined bra and matching thong. The crowd chanted her name as lights dimmed and a cacophony of blue, white, and red spotlights spun in rotation. Was this meant to be patriotic? I had to squint to keep from feeling carsick, but Ruby worked that pole like they were having sex: she licked it, rubbed her butt up and down, and squeezed it between her thighs. She climbed the pole and spun around in circles. I guess there may have been music in the background, but the shouts and whistles of the crowd drowned it out.

Lotta Morgan? She and her sisters would have been anachronists, kicking a cancan in their flouncy skirts.

I briefly caught Fawn's beckoning gesture from a back corner of the room, but it was only luck that I spotted her since Ruby was the focus of everyone's gaze. Now strobe lights made it seem as if she moved in slow motion. Some people get seizures from strobes, but I get migraines, so I closed my eyes.

Still, I heard the whistles, the jeers, and the crude and disgusting comments. Someone shouted in my ear, "For fuck's sake, take it off!"

Ruby was into the second number in a dim red haze. She had discarded the lingerie top, was clad in her sequined bra, and seductively removed her brief thong to reveal a sequined G-string. The old-fashioned term "bump and grind" aptly described Ruby as she rolled around on the floor, jutted her butt in the air repeatedly, and swung her breasts from side to side with her bra straps undone. When she stood and discarded the bra, only sixty seconds were left. She circled the edge of the stage and held out the elastic of her G-string for men to tuck folded bills inside.

I fumbled through the crowd and found Fawn wrapped in a floral polyester kimono. She was nervously sucking on one of those vape things. She said professional dancers that were hired for the weekend by other bars, got rough with local girls when they competed with them for tips. But the Palooza preferred the locals, and she couldn't take too much time to chat because she had to be on stage in a couple of minutes. After her dance, she'd be working the crowd.

"Can you hang around?" she wanted to know. I told her I would, but that was a lie. I'd already seen more than enough, so I wished her luck and blended back into the swarm where I could discreetly disappear.

Back at Myrna's, I folded myself into the tiny tub. My knees touched my chin. I scrubbed until I'd used up the little bar of Ivory soap and washed off Silverpalooza sleaze. I was so far out of my element in that place! Hurley's girlie bars had nothing to do with the dancers of Lotta's day and even less with any study of Northwoods lore. Good grief.

⁂

Was Brian waking up in Cynthia's bed? That was my first thought the next morning. I'd slept better than I'd expected and harshly reminded myself that I should be more concerned about the fate of The Last Resort instead of whether they'd slept together. Dammit, all to hell.

I left a note for Myrna, saying I would not be having breakfast after all, as I had my own plans that morning. I was meeting Fawn and Ruby for brunch at Timber Ridge. Lumberjack breakfasts seemed to be a thing up north, and the huge restaurant on the highway featured an oversized menu to correspond with its logging theme. Thick chains, crosscut saws, and other lumber camp trappings were displayed on the walls, with photographs of teams of oxen hitched to sleds piled with gargantuan logs. In some of the photos, lumberjacks posed triumphantly on the pinnacle of the colossal pile.

"So, what'd you think?" Fawn immediately wanted to know as I slid into the scarlet vinyl booth. Her friend Ruby managed a tired smile. "About last night?" I asked as I rolled my eyes and exhaled loudly, not wanting the girls to suspect my exit from the Silverpalooza had been premature. I ordered orange juice, coffee, and eggs over easy, with hash browns, three slices of bacon, and a cream cheese Danish. This breakfast was going to last me all day.

"I don't know how you do it," I confessed truthfully as I handed my menu back to the waitress. "Not only are you lithe and athletic, but you girls are fucking fearless!"

"There is an art to it," Ruby insisted. "It's not just tearing off your clothes in front of a bunch of rowdy men. It's something you need to learn."

"And women," Fawn added. "I know you must've seen some gals in the audience last night, too, right? But Ruby's dead-on; what we do is an art form. You get to know what moves work and what moves don't, and how to do what and when. There's a lot of timing involved. And you've got to be strong and flexible, too. Ruby and I, we exercise in a gym. We work out with weights. We do lots of yoga."

At first, Ruby was more subdued than the night before and shrugged. "It's a tough life, but at least I'm not unemployed. I'm just doing it until I get on my feet. When that's going to be, I don't have any idea. But right now, this is as good as anything."

When she mentioned "get on my feet," I recalled her crouched on the stage, rhythmically jutting her spangled ass in the air, and tried not to smile.

In daylight without makeup, Ruby could be anyone's daughter. She said she had dropped out of technical college after two years and now had to begin paying her student loan. She had short brown hair and looked nothing like she had when working the pole on that giant tongue.

"I'm a little embarrassed because I've always considered myself a very modest person, even though I may be liberal-minded and free, you know? When I'm working, it's like my body's my instrument. Like a piano player's hands. It's what I use for my work, and it's even sort of like my body doesn't belong to me sometimes."

I asked if they felt exploited because that seemed to be a common feminist perception about strippers.

"Hell, it's a job, isn't it?" Fawn replied. "It's just a fucking job. It's show business. It's entertainment. You got to have strength and character. Your audience depends on you to perform for them, and when they come into the bar and pay for a dance, it's all up to you. Just you, up there on stage! Forty or more horny guys in the crowd could tear you limb from limb if they felt like it, and all you've got are your wits and your talent."

"Your wits and your tits," Ruby added, laughing. "And your talent. So what you do is you look down at them like the animals they are. I'm sorry, but that's what I do."

Both women claimed they were making good money, the work was easy, and they didn't feel harassed. Instead, they felt empowered. "We're completely in charge of what we're doing," Fawn said. "I have the upper hand when I strip. I'm in total control, and if a man tries to give me a hard time, I can always just walk off. Screw 'em. Like that."

I was making notes, and Ruby leaned over to share her secret. "The best advice I ever got is this: When you go on the stage, you tell yourself, I'm the best goddamn stripper there is; nobody's better. I admit I like all the attention, everybody looking at me in the spotlight. It's a great feeling. But the men can't see it for what it is. Like, it's 'I've got you eating out of my fucking hand.' That's what it's like."

Our breakfasts were served, so our conversation momentarily eased before Ruby took up the subject once more.

"I know how to dance. That's all. Like I said, I didn't finish college. I can't do secretarial stuff. I couldn't be a teacher, and I'm not emotionally cut out to be a nurse and deal with all that blood. The only thing I can do right now is dance or be a waitress, and I don't want to waitress for the rest of my life. You know, like that girl just did, say, 'Here's your food,' boom, and pass the time until she gets your tip. I had a waitress job when I was in college, and all the guys could think about was grabbing my ass or looking up my skirt."

We each accepted refills of our coffee before our server took our plates away.

"Sometimes, at the Palooza," Fawn began, "I don't know if you sensed this when you were there, but it does get rowdy. And there are some strippers who strike me as being absolute pigs. There were a couple of pigs there late last night; maybe you were gone by then. A woman's body is beautiful, but not the way they pushed it. They weren't from around here. I think they were washed-up professionals trying to pick up an extra buck. You can strip very elegantly, very beautifully, but that's not what those old girls did. I'll be goddamned if I'm gonna push it right in somebody's face like that."

"So, Jenny, why do you want to know about all this?" Ruby asked. "Fawn says you're writing a book? Are we going to be in it?"

I was struggling to finish my lumberjack breakfast and still had the cream cheese Danish to go, but I showed them Lotta's portraits and told them I was intrigued by this woman who was an important part of Hurley's history, a featured performer who sang and acted on stage and was admired for her beauty. "In 1890, she was murdered in an alley not far from here. The whole town turned out for her funeral. The newspapers, in her obituaries, claimed she was a high-class prostitute.

"I'm not sure about the last part," I admitted, "even though it was written that she was a 'courtesan to lumber barons, mining speculators, and wealthy businessmen,' and 'a lady of the evening.' But if you don't like blood, Ruby, you'd have been out of luck if you came across her body. She was murdered and struck in the head with an axe. And when she was found in the alley the next morning, she still wore her diamond earrings, her diamond bracelets, and rings. No jewelry was taken, and the money she'd carried was still in her purse."

"Oh my God," Fawn remarked. "I can't believe I never heard of her. What's her name again? That's terrible! I mean, I suppose it's a great story for a book and everything, but a terrible, horrible murder. Lots of blood, I'll bet. Did they get the guy who did it? I mean, I presume it was a guy, right?"

We talked a little more about Lotta's death and how untamed Hurley was back then.

"Too bad they didn't know about DNA," Fawn said. "I suppose it's too late."

"Well, I'm not an actress, and I'm not a hooker," Ruby exclaimed brusquely. "I just dance. That's all. I swear."

"There's a bunch of us," Fawn interrupted. "Five dancers. We're definitely not sex workers, but we're all friends, and we hire out freelance to dance for parties."

"Four," Ruby interrupted. "Angel got knocked up."

"Okay, four dancers, and we hire out freelance for parties and stuff. But there's no sex, not like some guys expect from us. We dance and strip and collect our pay and go home. Alone."

"Except for Angel," Ruby interjected.

"Well, yes, Angel stayed after. I guess she was no angel, huh?"

I let the waitress remove my plate before I brought Edna Ferber's book out of my bag and read the part that described Lotta's appearance and "the blood-curdling poster of a girl standing poised for a death-defying leap from the top of a high wall."

The girls had never heard of the stockades or the young girls brought up north and imprisoned there, so I shared what Ginger and I had learned about stockades and the insinuation that Lotta had escaped from one. "She was pursued by howling buh-lud hounds. She leaped a forty-foot wall. Lotta Morgan, the bravest little girl in the north country...

Then I described how Lotta sang on stage at the Opera House and the poster of her doing the cancan. They'd never heard of that, either. I explained that the cancan, a French dance, was considered scandalous because, in the nineteenth century, women's pantalettes had an open crotch. This meant that when the dancers did a high kick, men in the audience could get a revealing look beneath their flouncy skirts.

Fawn said, "This Lotta was probably more of an exotic dancer. Like us."

Ruby said, "I can't see this beautiful woman as a waitress today. And these days, she wouldn't have to escape from bloodthirsty dogs or a stockade. I feel sorry for her."

Meanwhile, Fawn was digging in her vast faux leather handbag and brought out a folded poster of her own.

"Okay, I picked this up for you, Jenny. Here's something you should think about for your book."

She unfolded the poster and smoothed it on the table with her hand.

"There's this brand new gentleman's club just outside town that opened only a few weeks ago. It's a very classy place, and they're trying to build up a following. Ruby and I can't compete because of our local reputations, but you could give it a try and see what being an exotic dancer today is like."

I glanced at the poster, covered it with both hands, and pushed it back toward Fawn with a hearty laugh. The poster advertised an upcoming Amateur Night.

"Thanks, but I have my research pretty much wrapped up."

"Their next Amateur Night's on Tuesday, and it's only Sunday morning now," Fawn argued. "You could stick around until then, right? Why don't you pretend you're in one of those 'variety theaters' and get a feel for it. The Dancing Bare is modern and clean, and on amateur night, maybe three or four girls show up. Usually there's only a small crowd, maybe ten or a dozen men."

"We can dress you in a wig and high heels and other stuff. Nobody would know who you are. Let's think of a new name for you!"

Ruby was becoming quite animated by the notion.

"And Jenny, you wouldn't have to take *everything* off, just enough for a tease. It's all about the tease," Fawn added. "Let us teach you a few moves. Never know when they might come in handy. By the way, in case you're wondering, they don't allow any cameras."

Ruby said anyone who tried to bring a cell phone inside had it confiscated by security.

"They have a phone check like some restaurants have a coat check. You hand in your phone when you enter the building and get it back when you leave. It's for the protection of the employees and the patrons."

"That includes the girls who dance on Amateur Night," Fawn added with a wink.

Ruby licked her lips seductively and grinned.

Oh, God.

Thirteen

I left Fawn and Ruby with their coffee at Timber Ridge and headed to the majestic building where Jeff Draper had granted me exclusive access. He'd set aside an article on my desk that mentioned Maud Cassidy. In 1887, Chicago's *Daily Inter Ocean* ran a story entitled "Experience in a Pinery Dive," an account of Julia Howden, a Chicago woman who claimed she had been "forced into depravity" and brought to her downfall by the evil Maud. Wisconsin's Governor Jeremiah Rusk was notified of the statement and others like it relating to the growing shame of our state's northern dens of infamy and rumors of sordid stockades. The governor demanded the authorities "*take immediate steps looking to the removal of the great evil which has so disgraced our commonwealth.*"

Howden's story was told with the lurid enthusiasm fancied by newspapers of the day. It began by describing a fight on a Chicago street in which a younger woman "*about twenty-five years of age, with a handsome face showing traces of recent dissipation*" stamped her foot on the pavement and stole the hat of "*another woman some ten years her senior,*" then ran off with said hat to a police station crying, "*Lock her up!*" as she pointed back toward Maud Cassidy, the woman in hot pursuit.

Reporters of the day were paid by the inch, so the story naturally continued. Cassidy had hitherto been aware that Howden's marriage was unhappy and had convinced her to go north with her to work in "*a pleasant place in the country.*" They took the train from the city and, upon reaching Northern Wisconsin, were met by a carriage that took the woman to "*what seemed to be a quiet kind of saloon and hotel.*" Howden was fatigued (or drugged) and fell asleep until she was "*awakened by the sound of music and laughter, while loud jests and profane language were plainly heard through her open window. She arose and found that her clothes were gone, and in their place were short skirts of bright-colored silks and hosiery of fancy patterns. Then for the first time, she knew where she was and soon discovered that she was expected to join a crowd of girls in the parlor and, clad in the short skirts, was to sell liquor to the men who came in.*"

The incredulous woman claimed she tried to escape several times, but ferocious dogs tracked her down, and she was "*brought back to slavery,*" along with a ladylike little creature named Blanche, only fourteen years old, "*who begged daily to be released but was eventually sent to Hurley.*" National newspapers picked up Howden's tale of woe and Blanche's, too, freely augmenting the stories and shouting headlines such as "*Foul Blots on the 'Scutcheon of One of Fairest Lake States.*" More sensational stories appeared, confessions of young girls who'd been "*entrapped into one of the dancehouses and of life while an inmate there.*"

In the end, Governor Rusk, known for helping to suppress Milwaukee riots the year before and stating, "I seen my duty and I done it," was reluctant to make a dutiful move this time. He concluded there was "*more smoke than fire...I am convinced that no such deplorable and infamous condition of affairs exists and that there is no call for interference on the part of the State.*"

Sadly, Hurley's historical files held little more about Lotta Morgan than the accounts that Ginger and I had already explored. Draper left a note for me, however, saying that Lotta had been deeply affected by the 1887 fire at the Alcazar Theater, where she had frequently performed. The blaze destroyed five downtown blocks, including seventy buildings. All the actors lost their lives, and their charred remains filled only two coffins. In her grief, according to Draper, Lotta was especially impressed with the hymn sung at the funeral, "Ashamed of Jesus," and asked that it be sung at her own. Ironically, that would take place only three years hence:

Amazing tho't! Lord can it be
I sometimes am ashamed of Thee?
Sometimes forget that Thou did'st die
For willful sinners such as I?
Ashamed of Jesus, that dear friend
On whom my hopes of Heaven depend?
No, when I blush be this my shame...
That I no more revere His name.

※

Due to my substantial lumberjack repast, I could easily forego lunch, and although my bottle of wine was running low, my dinner duplicated my snack of the night before. When Fawn called to ask if I'd like to take a break on Monday, I was ready. "I hope you've given up trying to sell me on Amateur Night," I warned. We shared a hearty laugh.

Thus far, I had not noticed even the slightest presence of Lotta in my room at Myrna's, nor had I touched the silver mirror that remained face down on the table near the window.

The historical museum was closed on Monday. Fawn, Ruby, and I headed north into the UP to Little Girls Point on Lake Superior, where I was introduced to the sport of hunting for agates on a beach densely packed with wave-smoothed stones that had been pleasantly warmed by the sun. I couldn't resist the temptation to lie on my back and soak in the heat absorbed by the slick oval stones, aware of the lulling sound of the waves washing ashore.

Next, we went to a small café where we had cudighi, sweet and spicy Italian sausage formed into a patty, served on a hard roll, and overlaid with mozzarella and tomato sauce. The UP is one of the only places in the country where this classic can be found. It was introduced long ago by

Italians from the northern regions of Italy who came to work in the iron mines.

As we headed back toward Hurley, the girls insisted on making one last stop. My suspicions proved correct; The Dancing Bare was just off Highway 2 north of town and resembled an immense log chalet. Ruby was friends with a maintenance guy named Billy. So even though The Dancing Bare didn't open until five o'clock, he let us in, and I was given a tour.

"Just for fun, Jenny," Ruby said when I demurred. "This way, you'll see what else we have to offer besides our itty bitty tittie bars."

In my wildest imaginings, I could not have envisioned an establishment like The Dancing Bare. The open interior of blond wood felt like a vast mountain lodge with vaulted ceilings and peeled tree trunks extended up from the floor as though they'd grown there naturally. In the central expanse, a generous elliptical span provided space for several dancers to work a dozen or more chrome poles. A bar bordered the stage where captivated onlookers could enjoy their drinks and savor the view from swivel armchairs.

Several smaller areas were set aside along the outside walls for more intimate shows. There were separate booths for lap dances. Downstairs, Fawn said, they had shower rooms. I figured, foolishly, that they were for girls who worked up a sweat while they were dancing. Fawn and Ruby gleefully informed me that's where men reclined on sofas to watch strippers take showers. The girls would wash each other with loofahs, get all sudsed up and press their boobs and bottoms against the plexiglass.

I was hopelessly naive.

In the heart, near the stage, we saw Ruby's pal Billy high overhead on a ladder where he was fussing with a cluster of spotlights. Billy called down to say it was okay if I wanted to have a look around the stage. I welcomed yet another opportunity to further my knowledge of this mysterious subculture. It was a much more professional platform than the Silverpalooza's red tongue.

The pole I chose to play with was cold and slippery, thicker than the one at the Nip 'n' Nudge. I was wearing linen shorts, so I tried hooking one leg around a pole and leaning back as Ruby had done.

"Some girls climb to the top of the pole to lean like that," Fawn said. "But you have to have bare legs and strong thighs that you can squeeze together. Anyway, dancing here isn't about doing fancy pole tricks; it's all about the tease. Like we said before."

"If your Lotta was alive now," Ruby said, this might be the kind of place where she'd kick up her heels."

"None of our Silver Street saloons for her," Fawn added. "From what you said, Lotta was too high class for those."

I gripped the pole more tightly, one hand, one leg, spun around, and grimaced at the squeaking sound I made. I hoped I still carried a small bottle of Purell in my purse.

Billy yelled down that the manager rented out poles for practice.

I hollered back, "Thanks. I've had enough!"

The Lotta I'd envisioned would have seen pole dancing as coarse and vulgar. I wanted her to be more regal and imposing. Edna Ferber was the one who dressed her in black stockings and put her on stage with thigh-high boots. And a limp. No doubt Ferber invented the limp because Lotta jumped over the stockade fence to escape the blood-thirsty hounds the author had invented as well.

Witnessing this dodgy "show business" in connection with Lotta's history seemed disloyal. But sleazy as it was, The Dancing Bare itself was fascinating. I should've majored in cultural anthropology instead of journalism because I've often found human beings and their behavior profoundly perplexing.

The dressing rooms revealed a less-than-alluring side to The Dancing Bare. This congested setting was where the make-believe was crafted.

"Usually, there's a retired older dancer who's like a big momma back here, and she keeps everything moving along," Ruby said. "She makes sure the girls aren't drunk or drugged, and they get up on stage on schedule. There might be fifteen girls in here at a time, maybe twenty on hunting weekends. Things can get rowdy."

"I thought you said it's only been open a couple of weeks."

"Maybe it's been a couple of months," Fawn hedged. "Weeks, months. Doesn't matter, does it? Could be it's been a year. Anyway, it's brand new compared to all the old clubs in town. You can see for yourself!"

A desk in the center of the dressing room held a large plastic bowl with tampons, dental floss, Midol, breath mints, gum, and travel-size bottles of mouthwash. Another bowl, smaller, was cryptically labeled "meds." Beside the desk was a rack hung with a wild array of garter belts, thongs, and G-strings.

Lighted mirrors ran above dressing tables down two sides of the room. They were littered with overflowing ashtrays and lighters, curling irons, combs, brushes, wig stands with a vibrant variety of wigs, cans of hair spray, "freshening" vaginal spray, and other cosmetic accouterments. The space was highly perfumed with sweet, cheap fragrances and personal odors. As we headed toward the exit, both girls called my attention to the large poster that announced:

Tuesday Amateur Night

Tell Your Friends — $250 prize

No Previous Experience Welcome

⁂

I might as well confess right here and now that the balance of my time in Hurley had nothing (almost) to do with Lotta and everything (almost) because of my desire to be more of a free spirit. Like Ada. Which, in retrospect, closely resembled my proclivity for impulsive behavior and ended with an unfortunate debacle.

I've done some truly stupid things in my life. Many were experimental. Going back to when I was a toddler, I tried to flush myself down my grandma's toilet. She found me standing in the bowl, flushing and flushing, in tears because I didn't disappear like my doody did. Then when I was twelve, I walked downtown and back home blindfolded, using a cane I'd painted white. I wanted to see what it was like to be blind. And one autumn, I massaged a poison ivy leaf on my wrist to see if the red leaves were still potent. I'd never had poison ivy before, so I rubbed the leaf until a rash of pimples appeared. The dermatologist said it was the worst case of poison ivy she'd ever seen, and now I'm highly allergic to the plant.

I went ahead with this admittedly reckless initiative, even though I'd recently had serious cause to reflect on how a seemingly small decision can change one's entire trajectory, such as not heeding a warning that a tornado is heading your way. Or trying to repay Brian by writing a check for his kind and thoughtful care.

Even in contrast with those examples, this adventure (Ginger would say) took the whole freaking cake.

⁂

On Tuesday, I picked up the remainder of my material at the historical society and said farewell to Jeff. I expressed my gratitude for his invaluable assistance, assured him I'd keep him apprised of my progress, and most certainly let him review my chapter on Lotta Morgan.

Then I became an amateur stripper named Misty Dawn.

Fawn glued long fake fingernails painted blood red on my fingers. Ruby deftly used a handful of colored Sharpies to create rather beautiful and intricate tattoos on one of my arms and the opposite thigh. I wondered how long the permanent markers would take to eventually wash off. How long was "permanent"?

Ruby loaned me her stripper shoes, seven-inch platform heels made of clear Lucite. She said she got them at Sears for forty-two dollars, which was a surprise in itself. Sears? The girls insisted that I practice walking because they make you so tall that your stability is challenged, and you don't need much of a wobble to fall flat on your face. You must take tiny, mincing steps and move your hips and shoulders and head in tandem to keep your poise. It was hard to do.

"They raise your butt," Ruby said. "They help you look slimmer."

I was all for slimmer, although Ruby's feet were a whole size larger than mine. And I had only recently regained my balance (such as it was) from my concussion, so the trial was even more daunting.

From somewhere, the girls produced a long blonde wig and said I should take off my glasses even though I'm annoyingly nearsighted without them.

They watched me strut and made suggestions for my costume. "You don't want to go into Amateur Night looking like a stripper," Ruby warned. "You've got to pretend you're their neighbor's wife, their kid's teacher. The waitress at the local café. Wear what you would wear to PTA."

PTA was far in my past, I nearly told them, like being a den mother for a Brownie troop and hawking Thin Mints. I was a grandmother, much too old for this, and if my daughters knew about it, they would die of embarrassment.

But I had never signed on to be a conventional mother. Or grandmother, either. So, I sighed. In for a penny, in for a pound. Wasn't that the expression?

Ada would be vastly entertained.

I decided to wear an extra-large men's button-down shirt over Ruby's old Miracle Bra; the invention was popular years ago due to ample cushions in the bottom of each cup that sent one's boobs bulging over the top. Then I'd wear a pair of Fawn's tiny cut-off jeans because my chosen role was "the wife next door," which, I was guaranteed, many men found remarkably sexy. I wanted to wear an apron over everything as it would give me one more item to shed, but the girls insisted that was too "French Maid" and claimed "nobody wears aprons anymore," although I do when I'm making pizzas.

When making pizzas...

I gave Rosie a momentary thought and hoped she and Stumpy had been able to keep pace with orders. I came very close to calling her to see that everything was okay.

Where I was now was so remotely detached from where I'd been over the past few months and especially The Dancing Bare, where I was scheduled to appear in a very short time! Fawn and Ruby proudly presented me with my very own garter of shiny red satin, with a blue badge and ribbon that read: "Sexy Gramma." The garter stretched enough to go around my left thigh on top of the tattoo and would be, I was assured, where men in my audience would delightedly wedge their cash.

Later that afternoon, I practiced my moves in my room at Myrna's. I could have used a full-length mirror to view the wig combination and those crazy shoes. My routine would involve gradually unbuttoning the men's shirt and stripping only to my bra. I'd keep the shorts on.

"You're probably not going to win without showing your tits," Ruby had warned. But the $250 prize was not what I was playing for. This was a personal dare, a rare opportunity to pretend to be someone else for a very short time. Fawn and Ruby were the only ones who'd know what I'd done; nobody else would ever have a clue. And if I didn't do this now, when would I have another chance?

I felt one nipple accidentally pop out of my bra. I wondered what Brian would think of this raunchy burlesque. Would he think it was sexy? Or would he find it hilarious? I collapsed on the bed in laughter because the whole idea was so recklessly insane.

Maybe he'd find it disgusting.

Suddenly, there were tears.

I had to use Lotta's silver hand mirror to repair my mascara and re-glue my eyelashes by the time Fawn and Ruby came for me. If Lotta disapproved, she did not reflect a warning.

Myrna had gone to Wausau to shop at Walmart and said she'd be stopping at a Minocqua restaurant before coming home. I escaped the B&B without her observation.

When we arrived at The Dancing Bare, I signed in, chatted with the DJ who'd play the song I wanted, and gave him my stage name, *Misty Dawn*.

"Mitzi," he said.

"*Misty*," I replied.

Billy walked past and greeted us with a mumble. His extension ladder seemed to be perpetually attached.

The girls helped me with extraneous details and showed me backstage, where the other girls waited. It was surreal.

I practiced a relaxing breathing technique and peered through the burgundy velvet curtains in time to watch Cherry Delite, a freckled preteen with auburn hair and breasts only budding, as she looped a leg around a silver pole. She leaned so far back that her long hair grazed the floor. My reaction skirted amazement, then revulsion, which quickly became a mothering sort of anguish. This little girl shouldn't be on stage like that! What kind of parent would allow her daughter to be so exposed?

Beefy hands stretched toward her and snapped folded bills into her G-string while she teetered around the perimeter in treacherous red plastic heels.

"Hey there, no touching," the announcer warned an impulsive patron who charged toward Cherry and briefly grabbed her wrist.

Granted, I couldn't see that well. My vision was impaired by nonprescription dark glasses purchased at a filling station and the rank dishwater blonde wig that kept falling over and into my eyes.

I'd expected to be gutted with fear, but Fawn had crept up behind me and advised, "Keep a big smile on your face! Get ready to doff those duds and work that beautiful ass. Interact with everybody you can. Ruby and I are going out there right now to shout your name and get the guys jazzed up!"

I reminded myself this was supposed to be fun. If nothing else, it would make an entertaining first-person story (by "anonymous") for my book. With the platform stilettos on my already sweat-slippery feet, I'd try to perform like the free spirit Ada claimed was exhilarating.

Even before Cherry's final moves, the lights were getting weird. Not like the strobe lights at the Silverpalooza, but the clustered spotlights near the ceiling would swell brightly for a few seconds and then fade away for a few more. There were snapping sounds, and once I thought I saw a few sparks.

Her music faded, and I parted the heavy curtain so Cherry could retreat backstage. Her mascara was smeared from sobs, and black rivulets trickled down over her freckles. Naturally, I reached for her as she stumbled against me. I held her arm for balance while she removed those awful shoes. Yes, she was just a child. She was trembling, and I was troubled by her presence in this louche locale, even as the DJ was now calling for *Mitzi Dawn.*

With my aid, Cherry limped over to collapse on a metal folding chair, and I was shoved aside by a tall, black-haired woman who jerked the girl back to her feet. She wrapped a large hooded sweatshirt around Cherry and pulled her away.

Men chanted, *"Mitzi! Mitzi! We want to see your titzi!"*

"Mitzi Dawn, Gentlemen," the DJ repeated. "Let's have a big Northwoods welcome for our next contestant, Mitzi Dawn, everybody. Mitzi? Mitzi, are you missing, Mitzi?"

My music had started, and so had a massive hot flash. I was glowing with perspiration emanating from every pore. I muttered an expletive, laughed at myself, shook my head, and fluffed the fusty wig with both hands. Then I tugged at the too-tight bra and adjusted the crotch of my shorts. I was ready.

I glimpsed Cherry's phone left behind on the folding chair. I swept it into my bag and carefully shuffled out on stage.

This version of "Misty" was barely recognizable. The underlying bass thumped behind the pumping melody while an unknown vocalist tried to imitate Johnny Mathis.

"Mitzi! Mitzi!" the crowd hollered in rhythm.

"It's Misty," I shouted back, but I shouldn't have bothered. My sunglasses were sliding down my nose, and I brushed a forefinger across the moisture on my upper lip to snap it dry. A deep breath challenged the hooks on my Miracle Bra.

Above, flashing swirls from a mirrored ball revolved in the flickering spotlights and caused a woozy rush of motion sickness.

Fawn had sworn there'd only be a dozen or so men in the audience. It sounded like there were several dozen, two or three deep around the edge.

A hard swallow barely staved off the good chance that I would vomit. I dithered across the massive stage from one chrome pole to another with a halting version of the seductive moves I'd rehearsed.

I am a feminist, I told myself. This is an anthropological study. An exploration of human behavior. This is science. Research!

Smile!

You are completely in control. You're in charge.

"Take it off!" one guy shouted. I'd forgotten about the shirt, so I slowly unbuttoned the top two buttons. Not fast enough, according to the boos. Hastily, I ripped the shirt off, and buttons bounced onto the floor. That brought cheers.

I swung the shirt beside me in a wide circle and let it drop.

I heard Fawn shout, "Bolder, Misty!" So I did a clumsy dance move which was not a good idea, as both breasts popped up and out of the Miracle Bra. I tried, unsuccessfully, to tuck them back in.

"Grab a pole," Ruby hollered, so I minced baby steps toward the pole nearest me. I tried to mimic the moves that Cherry had made, hooked one leg around the pole, and bent over backward as far as I could, which, it turned out, wasn't very far because sweat had gathered behind my knee. In what felt like slow motion, I slid to the floor in a graceless heap.

Maybe this would be a good time for a downward dog, I thought. But in that yoga position, my sunglasses slipped away. It was also not an effective posture in platform shoes, so I just knelt and waved my butt at the audience as Ruby had done in town. Fawn's too-small cut-off jeans were rubbing me raw. I had to hold onto the pole to climb back to my feet like the old lady I had to admit I was.

My wig was askew, and getting back up took way more effort than expected. I was wilting, nearly breathless, and thankful the music was winding down. A nearby drunk held out a twenty-dollar bill, so I slid over to let him tuck it into my garter.

"I'll double that, honey, if you meet me in the parking lot," he slurred.

"Fat chance, fuckface," I yelled at him, backing off. I'd had enough.

The men around him enjoyed my remark, but he angrily reached out to grab back his donation. I nearly lost my balance as I hastily spun away. He threw his empty beer glass at me, and it bounced off my hip. At that very second, the cluster of spotlights above me blazed brighter than ever. It was blinding.

The spotlights exploded.

Shards of glass fell upon me like razor-sharp confetti. I could feel the jagged edges stabbing my skin.

Everything went dark.

The stage became feebly illuminated by cigarette lighters. No one had cellphones, but a few carried flashlights.

Someone hollered, "Get off the stage, you fat old cow! Time for you to limp back to the barn."

I could feel the crunch of broken bulbs beneath the soles of my shoes. I began to skid, lost my balance, and fell. My right hand came down on the beer glass, which broke beneath my weight. The floor turned slick with blood, making it even harder for me to stand, which was challenging enough wearing those stupid heels. When I did manage it, my left ankle throbbed with pain.

Everything around me was becoming disorderly and boisterous. The impatient crowd booed. Litter was hurled on stage. The drunk who'd given me a twenty stood on his chair and flung his body on stage to try and catch me, but he was pulled off and then threw a punch at the fellows who'd grabbed him. Fistfights broke out. Everything was happening so fast, but I could see shuffling bodies in the meager fluorescence.

For an instant, it seemed as if new lights above began to flutter and then grow more intense. I looked up and watched in awe as flames swiftly unfurled along the length of the varnished beam.

"Fire!" someone shouted. "Call 911!"

"Call the sheriff," a woman shrieked. "Somebody find a goddamn phone!"

"Get out!" men began to yell. "Head for the exit!"

I staggered toward the curtains, where arms reached out and pulled.

"Get me out of here!" I cried to Ruby and Fawn.

We could already hear sirens in the distance.

Fourteen

I told the emergency room staff at the Ironwood Hospital that I was a writer from Madison and in town to research a book—a true albeit feeble explanation that didn't remotely clarify why I was dressed like I was, why I looked like I did, and why I had been brought, bleeding and bruised, to the hospital from The Dancing Bare. I silently blessed the doctor and nurses for their sense of humor. The bit about "the book" brought knowing smiles. They may have figured it was a ruse, but I didn't care at that point.

My right hand was given a numbing injection while shards of broken glass were carefully removed (of course, I'm right-handed). After cleansing, irrigation, and much exploration of my palm, my hand was sewn up and then bandaged. They said there may have been damage to a tendon, but that would require an inspection by a hand specialist.

Little bits of glass were tweezed from my face, shoulders, and back—a result of the exploding spotlights. None had caused any real damage, but the spots were cleansed with alcohol and dabbed with antibiotic ointment. I was also given a tetanus shot because I couldn't recall when I'd last had one.

My left ankle was x-rayed, braced, and bound. It turned out to be a second-degree sprain which meant I'd torn some ligaments. Rest, they said. I should keep weight off that foot for two or three weeks. I was given a clunky foam boot and a crutch.

I called Myrna to say I'd been in an accident, and before she could become unduly alarmed, I told her doctors had examined me and I was fine, but I needed to leave. My friends would stop by to pick up my things and hand over my credit card.

Ruby, who could drive a standard transmission, drove me in my Bug back to Ginger's door, where I'd promised she would take me in. Fawn followed in her car because they needed a way to return home.

There was no answer when they knocked at Lilypad. Granted, it was nearly two in the morning, but surely Ginger and even folks across the lake would have heard the racket those women made.

After a long, awkward silence, I said they might as well drop me off at that little place we'd passed—the one with a bar.

"The 'Last' something?" Fawn inquired. She stubbed out her cigarette in Ginger's gravel with her sandal. I knew Ginger would immediately spot the butt and be suspicious.

"Resort," I said. "The Last Resort," I mumbled. "Fucking hell."

One car was still in the parking lot, but I knew Brian must be ready to close. I slumped in the passenger seat while the girls went inside the bar.

After a few minutes, Brian came out and opened the car door. I cowered in the feeble dome light. *Mortified* does not come close to describing the way I felt.

"Well, who do we have here?" he asked with a make-believe frown. "Is this Misty Dawn? Or is it *Mitzi*?"

He helped me climb out, an awkward shuffle with the clumsy boot, pain, lack of space, and my bandaged hand. Then he carried me upstairs. I would have attempted an explanation, but Brian said my girlfriends had filled him in on the details, which was exactly what I'd feared.

Dash did his happy Lab dance, so glad to see his mom. No doubt, I exuded an inscrutable essence. I was desperate for a shower and shampoo. With the bandage on my hand and the splint on my foot, it would be difficult, but Brian got some plastic bags and rubber bands to seal off my wounded body parts. Instead of a shower, Brian ran hot water in the tub. He said it would be good for me to soak in warm water for a while, as he was concerned about chafing from the skintight shorts, which he had to cut off with scissors. I asked him to cut off the constricting bra as well. When it fell to the floor, he reached around to cup my breasts in his warm hands and nuzzled my neck. My shoulders shook as I tried to stifle my tears.

"All in the name of research, I presume."

I'd held everything in for as long as I could and finally fell apart in his arms. I cried, big hiccupping sobs, soaking the shoulder of his shirt as he held me and patted my back.

"I'm so stupid," I sniffled.

His dinner with Cynthia, The Dancing Bare debacle, my bloody body—I let it all out until almost nothing was left.

Brian helped me into the tub, added more hot water, and arranged my sprained ankle over the edge as well as my wounded hand. Seeing me naked was not a big deal at that point, although I must have been less than alluring with my massive parade of tattoos and multiple bruises.

"Lean back," he directed before he tenderly washed my face. He scrubbed my body with a sudsy washcloth and washed my hair. His fingers deftly massaged my scalp and released any tension I'd been holding back. The tub had one of those sprayers on a flexible hose to rinse me with. While I soaked, he gave me a pill to help me relax. Soon I could feel my anguish melting away. Eventually, he helped me out and toweled me dry. I was guided toward my bed, where the quilt and sheets were already folded down.

Dash placed his glossy head on the pillow next to mine. I reached for Brian with my good hand and whispered, "I'm so ashamed."

He leaned over to give me a soft kiss. Then he placed his hand on my cheek, gave Dash a gentle stroke, said goodnight, turned off the light, and closed the door.

⁂

I slept late the next morning. I ached all over. I also didn't look that good. It was a warm day, but I wore a long-sleeved hoodie and sweatpants to hide what I could. Shortly after noon, Brian helped me down to the porch and brought out my breakfast. I knew Fawn and Ruby had filled him in on my fiasco, but I was determined to explain my version of the weekend down to the last revolting plunge. I anticipated an expression of surprise or scorn from him after I finished, but there was nothing.

"You made the paper," he said finally, displaying the *Ironwood Daily Globe* to share the headline with an enigmatic smile:

"Blaze Destroys Gentlemen's Club During Melee."

There had been a malfunction in the electrical system. Everyone inside the building had been accounted for except the girl who'd been on stage when the fire broke out. Anyone with knowledge of the whereabouts of Mitzi Dawn was asked to call the Hurley police.

"I already talked to them," Brian said, "so you can relax. They didn't ask for your real name or age; they just wanted to know if they should bother sifting through the ashes for your teeth."

I recalled Billy fussing with the sputtering spotlights. I may have incited the scuffle but didn't cause the fire.

Stumpy and Toad came in just then. "What in the hell happened to Jenny?"

Brian quickly said, "She wasn't the driver this time," which satisfied them because an even bigger concern was the pizza disaster that had occurred while I was gone. For some reason—nobody knew why, and she hadn't called to warn them—Rosie hadn't shown up to work in the kitchen on Sunday night. Brian had removed twelve balls of dough from the freezer, but after they'd thawed, there was no one to roll out the crusts and assemble the pies except for Toad and Stumpy, who were required to do the same on Tuesday.

"They tasted okay, I guess," Toad said. "We copied your routine. But they didn't look that good. Sort of cockeyed."

"No complaints how they tasted," Stumpy added, "except for the ones that burned. Anyway, we sold all the good ones and a couple that were kind of black. But jeez, we sure got gripes about the long, drawn-out service. If Rosie was here, it'd been okay because she knows her way around the kitchen and makes those pizzas almost as good as you."

"You better find out what happened to her," Toad said. "I promise nobody's going to see me in a goddamned apron again!"

I agreed to have a word with Larry Boone if I could get a ride over to the Maus Haus later in the day. Boone could assume, too, that I'd been in a collision. That wasn't even too far from the truth.

⁂

Boone and his men were loading tools into their truck by the time we arrived, and I leaned out the window of the pickup to hail him with my good hand. Of course, I was anxious to see the work they'd completed, but tomorrow would be okay. They had wrapped up and were in a hurry to leave.

"Hey, what's the deal with Rosie?" I asked as I waved him over. "I was out of town for the weekend and heard she didn't show up for work."

"Damn right," he said gruffly. "My daughter's done working for you."

I reached across my body with my left hand to grab the passenger door handle, but Stumpy placed a firm grip on my shoulder to discourage me. Boone continued, "You probably wouldn't know, but they got a good hardware store up in Hurley. Ain't that right, Stump? One of my boys was up there a week or so ago. Said he seen you and that old hen from the Saloon parading up and down Silver Street, trying all the doors to the strip joints. Even seen you go inside. Figured maybe you was looking to take on a side job besides the pizza kitchen, and I don't want my little girl associating with somebody that leaves her working at that tavern all by herself while you're up at Hurley shucking your clothes."

"Excuse me," I sputtered as my face tingled with heat. "Don't you think I'm a bit old for that? I'm a grandmother, for God's sake! I can't believe you'd even think I would do such a thing!"

Stumpy coughed and coughed again.

"Anyways, you hear about the fire up at The Bare? We got called to dispatch our company in the middle of last night and got there just in time to see the whole fucking place come down. I was hung up there 'til noon. Probably smolder for a month or more, all that timber."

"I'm glad nobody was hurt," I told Larry, trying to keep from glancing down at my boot. I slipped my bandaged hand underneath my sweatshirt.

"Larry, I'm a writer. I'm researching a book about the Northwoods, and because of its colorful history, Hurley has to have a chapter. I can't write truthfully about that town without mentioning the girlie clubs. That's why Ginger and I were there—to gather details on what they're like."

He harrumphed at that and said, "Only way to do that is to catch some of their stripper shows, but that raunchy shit would shock the bejesus out of you. And what about the Klan rally at Bessemer? One of my boys said you was there, too."

"But the rally didn't happen, did it?" I replied. "Maybe you can fill me in on why it was canceled at the last minute and what it would've been like."

Boone looked away and then slowly shook his head. Silence.

"Again, I was merely observing activities in the Northwoods. You can't have a problem with that. You said you were in the Klan, and I wanted to get an idea of what an actual rally was like. I've never been to one of those, either."

His expression changed. Boone was clearly tired and now deep in thought. He approached the truck, put a hand on the door, and leaned through the open window. His voice was low.

"This is confidential, got it? So don't you go spreading it around, neither of you. The truth is, I had to quit the Klan," he whispered. "Dispersed my Klavern, too. The reason's not for you guys to know, but I'm not going to be in it anymore."

Stumpy took his hand from my shoulder to cover another coughing spell.

Boone said he'd talk with Rosie, but I could probably count on her help tomorrow night.

⨯

The next morning, Thursday, Brian drove me up to Cedar Springs, where I saw Dr. Singh once again. My smile revealed more than a little chagrin. My ankle was x-rayed, and so was my hand. He deemed that the foam boot could be tossed after I'd worn it for a week, and then I could rely on Brian's bandaging and the crutch. My ankle wouldn't be strong enough to shove in the clutch, so I couldn't drive my car. My hand was another matter: it had sustained significant damage from the broken glass, and X-rays revealed a couple of hairline fractures. The stitches I'd been given at Ironwood were acceptable, but Dr. Singh felt I should also be using a splint, which he applied.

Back in Brian's truck, I checked my texts. Fawn had written with added details of the fire and questions about my well-being. "We thought the night was going to be a joke, just like you did. Turns out it wasn't very funny after all, was it? Ha Ha. Hope you get well soon."

"This ride to Cedar Springs seems uncomfortably familiar," I told Brian. "I suppose you want to know why I did it? Amateur Night?"

"Well, I don't think you counted on winning," Brian gave me a kind smile.

"Let me tell you a true story," I began. "Once upon a time, there was a monkey. This was in the late 1880s. And this monkey was part of a vaudeville act. He got out of control and rubbed his fur with kerosene, and then he set himself on fire. That must've scared him because he went crazy and ran all over, and soon there were flames everywhere. The dance hall next door caught fire, too; the whole town suffered damage. Lots of drinking and looting resulted, and, in the end, someone got killed."

"And this is relevant...how?" Brian asked.

"I'm the monkey," I replied. "I played with fire."

We drove on for a few miles, Brian deep in thought and me feeling sorry for myself. Finally, he said, "Jenny, I think you're making too big a deal about it."

"About this?" I held up my bandaged hand and pointed to my foot. "And here on my face, these spots aren't chicken pox!"

"Nobody was killed," he said. "You played a role. It was theater. You wore a costume. You were pretending. At least I hope you were."

"You didn't see it!"

"No, but I wish I had. Never saw a woman next door wearing a bra like that."

He didn't comprehend how much I was suffering.

"Were you responsible for the electrical malfunction?" he asked.

"No, of course not."

I told him about Billy and his extension ladder and explained the spotlights were already acting up before that night. "But I sort of incited the mob."

"And how did you do that?"

"I called a man a name."

"That's not the same as lighting a match. Did he deserve it?"

"I thought he did. He tried to touch me. He tried to grab—"

"He what?"

"He tried to grab his twenty-dollar bill from my garter."

"Your what?" Brian seemed amused.

"He tried..." I began to laugh; I couldn't help it. "...from my garter," I sputtered.

"You mean this one?"

He dramatically pulled the red satin "Sexy Gramma" garter from a pocket of his jeans and swung it from the rearview mirror of his pickup.

Part Three

"Summer will end soon enough,
and childhood as well."

—George R. R. Martin, *Game of Thrones*

Fifteen

Cynthia was in Chicago but said Ada's cottage was nearly finished. Ada wanted me to see it before it was put on the market. "You won't recognize the place," Cynthia added. "It smells good, too! I can't wait to show you around; the transformation's pretty remarkable. I'm here to source a few last-minute furnishings, and I'll see you in a couple of days."

The boys informed me that Ginger had returned from her Door County visit. With that klutzy boot, I couldn't drive, so I had to take a boat to get to Lilypad. Dash jumped on board and kept getting his nose in my way when I tried to start the motor—a lot more difficult using only my left hand. Once we took off, I admired the way he proudly stood in the bow, facing the wind. In almost two months, he had grown from being an adorable, huggable puppy to gaining the bearing of a regal black Labrador retriever.

We took our time wandering across Star Lake and then over to Sundog. No sign of Ginger when we buzzed her dock; I should have called ahead. Since we were on the water, we journeyed up the crooked Lost Arrow River to Sickle Moon, where I almost killed the motor. Three young girls were lounging on lawn chairs on what I'd assumed was an unoccupied island. It was on this side of the peninsula from Maus Haus. I swung closer and made out the vague form of a large cottage behind them, but it receded into the setting, camouflaged by clusters of trees and leafy vines.

I waved at the girls. They turned away. Maybe they were new to

Northwoods conventions since it's common practice to give a friendly wave back when hailed by someone in a boat.

When I returned from viewing the Maus Haus, the girls were gone. And my viewing of Ada's cottage was restricted since I'd remembered my crutch but didn't have a key for the new door. It took me a long time to climb the improved stairway. I persisted, and the sturdy new railing helped. Then I limped around the cottage's exterior to admire the fresh siding. I peered in the windows and rested briefly on the attractive new deck.

Dash and I stopped at Lilypad on our way back to the resort. This time Ginger ran outside when I hollered, and she fussed over Dash. We made our way to her porch. I lagged due to my infirmities and, frankly, exhaustion. Finally seated, with a stack of magazines on which to rest my foot, Ginger gave me a good looking over and remarked, "Well, aren't we looking as sharp as a marble today!"

"It's a long story," I sighed.

"Don't I know it," she smiled and slapped her knee. "I know it all down to every pitiful particular. Stump came by to help with a little plumbing issue after you got back. Brought the Ironwood paper with him. And I have to say," she stifled a chuckle, "I wish I could've seen Mitzi in all her glory, that sexy getup, doing her shimmy on the poles. My goodness, those tattoos are something, aren't they?"

I let the mistaken "Mitzi" reference slide and assumed the boys had eavesdropped on my solemn confession to Brian. I explained that Ruby, a friend of our waitress at the Nip 'n' Nudge, was responsible for the tattoos. "The decision to go out on stage—that was my own recklessness. Although," I added, "if you recall, you advised me to give it a try."

Somehow, my confession to Ginger felt okay. She wasn't exactly commiserating, but she wasn't hooting with laughter, either.

"I got some stuff that'll take care of those tatts." She disappeared and returned with a plastic bag of cotton balls and a can of WD-40. While she wiped the "art" from my skin, I explained my altered insights on Lotta.

"The thing is," I said, "in the Victorian era, which is the period we're talking about, women essentially didn't have any freedoms. Wives belonged to their husbands. They were expected to marry, raise plenty of children, and keep house. That's it. If you were a widow and had to earn an income, tough luck. You'd probably have to take in sewing or mending or do some other kind of menial task.

"For an unmarried woman like Lotta who appeared on stage—well, that probably caused a moral panic among the locals. Actresses were supposed to have dubious scruples, anyway. Although they were enjoyed as entertainment on the stage, when they were offstage, they were considered sinful. In Hurley, no doubt there was a virtuous, maybe church-led campaign to intimidate women entertainers and shame them. So, of course, Lotta would naturally have been characterized as loose, debauched, and depraved. A fallen woman. Even though she may not have slept with every man in town. In fact, she'd have had to work hard to do that because she'd only lived in Hurley for four years before she was murdered, and for three of those, she was the partner of John F. Sullivan, one of the town's leading citizens, a member of the town board and a wealthy businessman, besides."

Ginger added that being an actress and living with a man outside of marriage may have led to a false impression of Lotta's ethics. "Could be she wasn't actually a prostitute; she just shacked up with a rich boyfriend who owned half the place."

I admitted, "I didn't need to try out the stage at The Dancing Bare to get a feeling of what it must have been like—"

"Stop!" Ginger abruptly interrupted. "I don't want to hear another dang word about what happened to you up in Hurley, and neither does anybody else, so forget it. It's in the past, and that's water over the bridge. Now you go wash that oily gunk from your arm with soap and water, and don't forget to give your leg a good scrub, too. Then I have an important announcement to make! Hurry up and get back here!"

I limped to the bathroom, admired the lack of my faux tatts, and washed off the smeared remains as instructed. Then I sat across from Ginger so she could make the enthusiastic announcement that she'd nearly forgotten about.

While Ginger was in Door County, Jeff Draper had left a message on her answering machine and said he couldn't reach me. Would she please inquire if I would be interested in posing as Lotta Morgan at their upcoming historical festival?

My response was swift and adamant.

"Call him back and tell him absolutely not."

Ginger replied that she wasn't going to make excuses for me. "You can't blame poor Lotta for the shitstorm you caused, kiddo! You're the one who's going to have to explain why you're not grateful for Mr. Draper's help. Look how much time he took to talk with us, to help you out, and all the materials he found! I figure you're considerably obliged to him for that."

Then she offered several more justifications for why I should accept: Who knew more about Lotta Morgan than I did? Who had all that research at hand? Didn't people need to realize she wasn't really "the most viciously depraved woman in Northern Wisconsin," like one newspaper called her after the woman had her head bashed in with an axe?

"Bearing in mind what we just decided about her and why she might have got the nasty reputation that she did, Jenny, you could almost say it's a public service for you to tell Lotta's story and clear her good name. Think of that, why don't you? Besides," she argued, "you might as well salvage something from your colorful adventures besides a bum ankle, a busted hand, and a bungled opinion of your sorry self."

"Give me a break, Ginger," I pleaded. "I'm still in pain."

⁂

The invitation gnawed at me for the remainder of the day. Back in my room, I studied Lotta's portraits and imagined her encouraging me to agree. Transforming my "adventures" (as Ginger called them) was certainly tempting. And surely no one in Hurley—besides Fawn and Ruby—would have a clue that I was (past tense) Misty Dawn. Or Mitzi, either.

I told Ginger I'd go ahead and "be" Lotta.

She was relieved because she'd already told Jeff Draper that I would.

Then I gave him a call.

Draper said he'd acquired a horse and carriage and driver so I could ride in the parade in character. They had found a dark dress resembling Lotta's that I could wear and a fancy hat like hers with a partial veil. And if I'd compose a brief essay, they'd print a proper account of Lotta's story to distribute to the crowd.

That was all fine with me. However, as absolution for my blundering indiscretions and using her stage experience as a misguided excuse for The Dancing Bare, I felt I needed to do more for Lotta than politely wave a gloved hand at the crowd. I needed to pay reparations and erase my guilty conscience. Instead of a printed page about Lotta, I asked Draper if he could arrange for me to present a performance. Do an impersonation of her. Tell her story in first person.

He was surprisingly enthusiastic and said he'd take care of the details and reserve a venue.

I also owed it to Misty Dawn, wherever she was. Or Mitzi.

The next day I explained my inspiration to Ginger. She claimed that as my "manager," she would offer comments on what "Lotta" would say. She also reminded me that I had yet to show her the Maus Haus, as promised.

⁂

Cynthia was back, and my boot came off after wearing it for a week. I asked the boys if I could get a ride to the Maus Haus the next afternoon, where Cynthia would be waiting to give me the grand tour. Toad hadn't seen the new cottage and was glad to drive.

Since she'd worked on the putrid version, Rosie wanted to come along and see the finished product. In addition, we picked up Ginger, and we all managed to squeeze into the Bug with Toad at the wheel. At the last minute, Dash insisted on sitting on my lap. He now weighed more than twenty-five pounds.

Once at Maus Haus, Cynthia greeted us with obvious pride. Toad inspected the exterior while Ginger, Rosie, and I were free to look around. It was clean, smelled new, and we assured Cynthia that her creative touch with staging would quickly attract eager buyers when it was ready to be shown. I loved every bit of it. Ginger opened cabinets and kitchen cupboards, checked out the bathroom, and flushed the toilet. She told Rosie to try all the faucets and turn all the lights on and off.

The deck now held new patio chairs and an umbrella table. Cynthia suggested we all relax and enjoy the vista since the brush and trees had been cleared, and we could admire the scenic view of the lake.

I hadn't seen Cynthia since she'd had dinner with Brian, and I was dying to inquire about that Saturday night. I'd have to wait until I was alone with her to learn whether she'd slept with him, bought him out, or both. Or maybe not. Brian certainly hadn't given me a clue. On the other hand (my bandaged left hand or my right?), it wasn't my business. I also wanted to know how my condo was coming along and if I should make a deposit.

Dash had been a good boy and stayed right at Toad's side. Then, suddenly, he tore into the woods and was gone. Toad volunteered to look for the dog, but after a few minutes of searching, he said we'd need to use the car to try and find him. Cynthia stayed at the Maus Haus to close the windows and lock up; the rest of us again squeezed inside the Bug. We rolled the windows down and called the dog's name.

At the end of the driveway, Toad turned right toward a set of tire tracks that led through the grass from the turnaround out toward the furthest point of land. I had not been out there, never noticed the tracks. They led to a small clearing where we could see the island and more of the concealed cottage where, I swore, I had viewed three girls the day before.

A dusty black SUV was parked in the clearing. Dash was there, sniffing the tires. He peed on one.

Toad was puzzled. "What the heck? I fished this lake hundreds of times. I knew about that broken-down building; to my knowledge, it's always been empty. And where in the hell did this new boat landing come from? Looks to me like it was built by a guy in a hurry with his head up his ass."

We lured the dog into the car and then waited a while to see if there might be movement on the island. Maybe the girls would reappear. Dash fell asleep in the back seat, on Ginger's lap this time.

Out of the uncomfortable silence, Ginger bluntly asked Rosie, "How come your dad did away with his Klavern and quit the Klan?"

All three of us were curious to know the answer, but we lacked Ginger's chutzpah.

"You don't have to tell us if you don't want to," I assured the girl.

Rosie took a deep, quivering breath.

"Okay, I haven't confessed this stuff to anybody else, so you guys have to all promise to keep it a secret. My dad would be so pissed off if he knew."

We each made a solemn pledge.

"The thing is," she said, "I never liked my dad making those awful proclamations about 'white power.' I didn't think it was fair, and I didn't agree with him. My mom didn't, either; that's one of the reasons she left him. There are nice, smart Native American kids in my school, and they get bullied a lot by white guys who think they're tough. I got bullied, too. How'd you like to be known as the daughter of the Grand Dragon? They made up little nicknames for me, like Dragonette or Klannie. It was awful. I wanted to disappear.

"My history teacher took me aside one day and encouraged me to write a paper on the origins of the Klan so I could see how it changed through the years. That was a stupid assignment, and I got sick to my stomach. Literally. I never handed in the paper. My father promised they'd never do anything really vicious, but still, the reputation was there. We argued a lot about it.

"Finally, for Father's Day this summer, I gave him one of those DNA kits. You know, like 23andMe. I challenged him to prove to me that 'white was right.' He had no trouble with that and spit in the test tube right away. He said 'White Power' and grinned when he handed it over to me to mail."

"Let me guess," I interrupted. "This way, you won't be betraying your father's trust. If I guess correctly, you didn't tell me. Okay?"

Rosie nodded.

"Your dad's DNA showed some African ancestry."

"Four percent," Rosie admitted. "*African hunter-gatherer.* He was mad at first and said he'd sue the company. Then he said the test was a hoax. So he got another kind of DNA test and tried it on his own. The analysis results were the same, and that was all the proof he needed to give up his Klan and his Klavern."

It must have been a serious blow to Larry Boone's pride. We waited for Rosie's reaction before we shared our own.

"I was so grateful, you guys," she said. "You have no idea how much I hated all that Klan stuff. I never told my dad about the bullying. Since his Klavern disbanded, I feel more like a regular person. I tried to be invisible and wore really frumpy clothes. No boy would date the daughter of Larry Boone. I cried a lot."

There wasn't much room in the VW for displays of affection, but I reached toward the back seat to give her an awkward hug. "I'm happy for you," I said. "And for your dad."

"I always thought you were one smart cookie," Ginger added, "and brave and gutsy, too. I admire you for what you did."

"Me, too," said Toad. "Way to go, kid. You should be proud of yourself."

Just then, a couple of men and a woman exited the building on the island.

"Hide," I suggested. "Back the car into the trees."

Toad shifted into reverse and slowly backed over shrubs and bracken until the car was well concealed. Then he, Rosie, and I got out and hid beside the car. We swatted mosquitoes and deerflies that swarmed out of the dense woods. Thankfully, Dash was still asleep.

There were no girls to be seen, and the boat motored across the lake toward us with a woman in the stern. The two men climbed out of the boat, and the driver aimed the SUV down the path past the Maus Haus.

"Pictures, Jenny," Rosie urged. "Get out your phone."

She already had one of the Florida license plates and each of the men. I got a close-up of the woman turning the boat and returning it to the island.

"Beats the dickens outa me," Toad said when everything settled, and we climbed back in the car. "What in the heck's going on?"

Ginger said, "There's something mighty curious about a man and a woman with three teenage daughters squatting in the heat of summer in a dilapidated shanty with no power or plumbing on an island in the middle of a lake in the middle of nowhere. Who in the heck owns that broken-down place, I wonder. Can't believe they asked permission to rent it."

"I'd be bored to death if I had to stay there," Rosie added. "Like, no Wi-Fi for sure. No TV, either. No car to go into town. What do they do all day?"

We were all in agreement. It was very unusual.

I didn't share my thoughts—I had suspicions.

I recognized that tall, black-haired woman. I had seen her before, at The Dancing Bare.

She was the one in charge of Cherry Delite.

Sixteen

Welcome to a representation
of Lotta Morgan (1861–1890)
as portrayed by Jenny Burgess.

Good afternoon. You may know me as Lotta Morgan, but my legal name is Laura Whitley. Accounts of my life and death have circulated for well over a century with an array of erroneous particulars. Thus I will now reveal my true history for your edification and purposes of veracity.

I was born in Milwaukee, Wisconsin, on the eleventh of April 1861. My uncle managed a variety theater in Chicago, which impressed me deeply; I wanted nothing more than to join a theatrical company and travel from place to place. I especially liked to sing, and upon occasion, when I was in that city, visiting artists would teach me little ditties and allow me to don their costumes.

As a young woman considering the theater, I thought it wise to adopt the name Lotta Morgan after Lotta Crabtree, the highest-paid actress in America at that time. Lotta's name often appeared on marquees simply as

"Lotta." I shamefully confess that by sharing her identity, I hoped I would achieve celebrity as well.

Before I adopted "Lotta," I appeared on the stage as a seriocomic singer at a Halstead Street Theater in Chicago, where I was occasionally referred to as "the Jersey Lily" on account of a fancied resemblance to the actress and socialite Lily Langtry who originally embraced that name.

I married a sergeant of police in Chicago and foolishly became the mistress of "Charley" Simpson, a once-famous poker player who died in penury in the county prison. My second husband was a veterinary surgeon whose practice was located on the city's south side. This was not a satisfactory match, and after our final separation, I followed my dream by joining a company of actors that eventually drifted toward the piney woods of Wisconsin, where lumber and mining towns were enjoying a boom time. Variety theaters were experiencing substantial and enthusiastic crowds at the Alcazar, the Hurley Opera House, and the Temple Theater in Hurley; the Alhambra in Ironwood, the Pierce Opera House, and the Empress Theater.

Unfortunately, much of the more recent disinformation regarding my life was fomented by Miss Edna Ferber, an authoress from Appleton, Wisconsin, who penned a novel in the 1930s entitled *Come and Get It*, which you may have read. Hurley still boasts of her brief presence in that city, but those who peruse her words will find her portrayal was neither accurate nor well-disposed.

In Ferber's novel, Lotta Morgan was tiny with golden hair, a "pretty little thing."

You can see that I am neither little nor golden-haired! She also referred to me as 'the bravest little girl in the north country," whose husband caused me "to be tattooed between the breasts with a likeness of Christ on the cross so that no other man should have [me]."

Why Miss Ferber chose to adorn my albeit fictional body with such a blemish is confounding, as such a tattoo neither furthers the story nor in any way represents fact. Only my sense of decorum before this wholesome assembly prevents me from undoing the buttons of my bodice to reveal the complete absence of such an astonishing representation.

Ferber also implied that I was a "famous beauty of the old stockade." This testimony should put to bed all rumors of my having been kidnapped and imprisoned such as those poor girls kidnapped by the villainous Maud Cassidy and her chief confederate, Dunk Beveridge. The two were brought to trial in 1888 for snatching innocent young Chicago girls off the street, plying them with liquor, and transporting them against their will by railroad to the Pineries, where they became unwilling victims of lust and avarice.

In truth, the rumor of my leaping a forty-foot wall to escape such vile confinement was birthed by that author and many who were unable to—or did not wish to—separate truth from fiction and readily clung to her lurid description of a blood-curdling poster that depicted a girl poised for a death-defying dive from the top of a high wall. The girl's face was cruelly distorted with fear. Behind her, fangs bared, eyes rolling, bounded a pack of slavering bloodhounds.

Yes, brutal stockades did exist in this vicinity. One such was described in another book as "a log pen with a single entrance guarded by savage dogs; inside the pen was a house consisting of a single large room, its floor covered with close-spaced pallets, or workbenches. Here a dozen girls labored, and the dogs trained to prevent them from escaping but *not* to prevent customers from entering."

In her pretended portrayal, I was the blonde daughter of a Portuguese woman and a Finnish man. Further, I had attempted to enter a convent but had been refused (presumably due to my immorality), and when I was introduced on stage—seated on a tree stump in a woodland scene—I wore a shanty boy's mackinaw, pants, and cap, with high-heeled boots that laced up over the calf. In an unintentional gaffe, I believe, the author depicted me standing by a fallen log with an *axe* resting on my shoulder as I sang a drinking song in a not-very-good voice while swinging a tin cup. When a melee broke out among the gentlemen in the audience, the manager's wife shouted, "I told you you'd have no luck with that slut, that hussy, that limping bitch!"

For the record, I have never heard myself referred to as a hussy or bitch. I may have been referred to as "vivacious, sprightly, well informed," a "sporting woman" or "the beauteous Lotta Morgan," a "high-class girl." And you may have noticed that I do not have a limp. But I am getting ahead of my story by quoting the Reverend Mr. Todd of the First Presbyterian Church in Hurley, who said at my funeral that I was "no ordinary woman. [I] was ladylike, [I] was courteous, and not only that, [I] had a woman's heart, [I] had aspirations for something better, [I] could adorn a social position."

(pause)

Miss Ferber's injurious fable now dismissed, I will proceed.

Perhaps due to the failure of my marriages, and surely attendant to my connection with the theater—an occupation considered sinful for a single woman at that time—I developed a reputation for being a "loose woman." By convention, "private women" were those who remained in the home and upheld values associated with the cult of "true womanhood." Conversely, "public women" were often identified as prostitutes or soiled doves. Since theater is understood to be an endeavor that depends upon the use of one's body as a vehicle for self-expression, any self-conscious display of the female body must therefore be disreputable. Indeed, I know of only a handful of stage performers, such as the Swedish Nightingale Jenny Lind, who were able to maintain the appearance of womanly virtue while enjoying lucrative careers.

It was extremely challenging for an actress to navigate the daunting space between the private and the public, respectability and notoriety, wealth and poverty.

The Alcazar Theater was a favorite venue for my own performances and for attending prizefights, wrestling matches, and vaudeville shows by visiting troupes. There I saw and participated in *The Black Crook* and many popular pantomimes. Our audiences of miners and lumberjacks preferred simplicity to sophistication, so minstrel shows were well-attended, especially Gorton's *Night of Minstrelsy*, which featured an unusual sextet clog dance. The comic opera *Erminie* was performed to much applause at Pierce's Opera House, and in July 1886, an athlete from the Alcazar brazenly crossed Silver Street on a tight rope above a large group of spectators.

Charles Dickens was then lecturing at a theater in Chicago, but he could not be induced to make an appearance in the Pineries, even though the editor of *The Montreal River Miner*, published in Hurley, bemoaned that fact and "regretted that the great novelist never saw the great Northwest—the region bordering the great lakes," since the caliber of Dickens' mind, "the matchless novelist, could comprehend fully the magnificence of this country and the enterprise of its people." Another local paper, *The Weekly Wisconsin*, offered a one-year subscription for two dollars plus a fifteen-volume set of Dickens' complete works, which proves, it seems to me, that the famed British author would have found favorable reception here.

When the Alcazar was destroyed by fire in 1887, I lost many of my dearest friends who were either consumed by flames or who frantically jumped to their deaths. I determined at this time to retire from acting and took up residence with Mr. John F. Sullivan, one of the town's leading citizens, a wealthy bachelor and town chairman, who owned several buildings and operated a jewelry store, a pharmacy, and a respectable new saloon on Silver Street between First and Second Avenues. The Sample Room featured both billiard and pool tables and an excellent orchestrion that employed revolving cylinders to replicate the music of a wind orchestra, including drums, cymbals, tambourine, and even a triangle. We did not conceal our intimate association. Mr. Sullivan and I frequently journeyed together to Chicago by train. He presented me with diamond jewelry and other gems, and while in the city, he encouraged me to visit dressmakers that I might be furnished with the latest fashions of the day.

You will note, in photographs accompanying my talk, that my hair was swept up with my bangs curled and frizzled. This was the modish hairstyle in 1887. The bustle, not evident in this picture, had reached its maximum size the year before. This particular dress was comprised of several shades of burgundy satin and lavish ornamentation on my jet-trimmed jacket up to the tight collar at my neck, where I'm displaying a gold bar pin. I have a timepiece attached to a buttonhole on my bosom and large diamond earbobs suspended by gold wires. These details will soon become relevant.

By April 1890, I had resided in Hurley for a total of four years. On the seventh of that month, the Hurley Opera House was sold out for a performance of *Uncle Tom's Cabin* performed by a traveling troupe that featured the "first and only trick alligator ever introduced on stage," Jerry, a trick donkey, and a forty-thousand-gallon tank of water—a feat in itself.

There was much entertainment to be had that month, and it so happened that on April 10, only a few days shy of my twenty-ninth birthday, I attended a performance of the popular pantomime *Humpty Dumpty* at the Alcazar with a lady friend. After bidding her goodnight, I stopped by Mr. Sullivan's saloon, where I was pleased to enjoy a small nightcap. Near half past eleven, I took my leave by the saloon's back door. I started up the alleyway toward my rooms only to realize I was missing one of my kid gloves. Anxious that it was not trodden upon in the grime and last vestiges of dirty snow in the alley, I turned and retraced my steps toward Sullivan's saloon.

It was then I realized someone was lying in wait.

With apologies, I must again digress to append necessary details:

The rooms of my second-floor apartment were furnished with many windows, several of which were located so that, if I wished, I was able to view activities at the nearby Iron Exchange Bank located on the north side of Silver Street between Third and Fourth Avenues. On September 21 of the previous year, 1889, that bank was robbed of $40,000. It was the largest robbery Wisconsin had ever known. Certain aspects of the theft were later reported in the weekly *Montreal River Miner*. Because the robbery is salient to my story, I will quote abridgments from their report:

Last Saturday was the regular monthly payday at the Ashland and Germania mines. They always pay in currency that comes here by express from the Ashland National Bank. On Friday evening, the money, about $41,000, arrived by U.S. Express on the 9 o'clock train and was taken in charge by G. A. Alexander, the company's agent here.

A good many thousands of it being in gold and silver coin, it was quite bulky and heavy, so it was loaded on a wheel-barrow and taken to the Iron Exchange Bank for safekeeping until the morning, as the mining companies would not receive so large an amount of money after the vaults had been closed for the night.

It was too late to get it into the inner safe at the bank, which had been closed with the time lock, but Cashier Reynolds allowed Mr. Alexander to place the treasure inside the vault, which is secured by a heavy outside iron or steel door, which locks with a combination, and inside of that is another heavy door secured by a Yale lock, so it was placed behind two seemingly strong barriers, though they proved to be not strong enough.

Not long after the money had been stowed away, or about 10:30, Mr. Reynolds left the bank, where he slept and was absent until about midnight. Before retiring, he made his usual tour of inspection to see that everything was all right for the night when he made the startling discovery that the vault had been opened, and all the money except a bag of silver, containing about $1,100, was gone. The bank funds were inside the steel chest behind the time lock, and they were, of course, untouched. He immediately gave the alarm, but no clue could be obtained to the mystery, and no clue has yet been obtained, to our knowledge.

The thief or thieves entered the bank building by climbing through the transom over the back door, and no doubt escaped in the same way... On Saturday morning, a coat and hat belonging to Mr. Reynolds, which the bold robber undoubtedly wore while he was working at the vault door (which is right in full view of the street) so that anyone passing the bank and looking in would think it was Reynolds...

There you have it, and a week later, the September 26 edition of that same paper remarked, "Every strange man on the street this week is pointed out either as a bank robber or a detective." Arrests were made, but no one was jailed. The mines lost nothing, nor did the mine owners or the Hurley or Ashland banks. The big loser was the United States Express Company, which was responsible for covering the full amount, and they dispatched a detective to solve the heinous crime. Three suspects subsequently appeared in court.

The trial lasted thirty-four days, and the jury was out for ninety hours before they cited a disagreement. The deputy sheriff was charged with bribing two members of the jury. Newspapers called the trial, which closed on March 19, "a grand fiasco." It was expected to be taken up again on April 14.

Remember that date.

Due to the location of my windows and the possibility that I may have witnessed the robbery, I was served with a subpoena to testify for the defense in the March trial. Mr. Sullivan suggested it might be expedient for us to visit Chicago during that week. Thus, I did not appear in court, and we did not return to Hurley until after the initial trial had been adjourned.

Let us now return to the night of April 10 as I searched for my lost glove. The moon was half full and shed only feeble light in the dark alley behind the saloons where I walked, my gaze toward my feet. Because it was a rough area, I carried a small pistol in the pocket of my dress. It was a .38, which had not been fired in a very long time and was doubtless full of lint.

A noise caused me to glance back for a moment before I was struck by an axe in my forehead above my right eye. A second blow was delivered after I fell—a deep and yawning gash, so the newspapers reported. That blow crushed my skull and pulled back my scalp.

I lay there in blood and filth for nearly six hours until my body was discovered early Friday morning by a random passerby. My small revolver, unfired, was at my feet. The diamond rings, diamond earbobs, and other jewelry on my body were undisturbed, as was the twenty dollars in cash that I had tucked in my purse.

A group of men moved my body to Ragan's undertaking rooms, where a jury viewed my pitiful remains. An inquest was scheduled for Saturday morning, April 15. An old axe, its broken bit matted with blood and hair, was found in a neighboring woodshed with the door propped shut. Not so ironically, the blade perfectly matched my wound. According to the inquest, I had also been shot.

Terry Day, who also used the surname "Riley," was arrested four days later on suspicion of my murder and for seemingly good reason, as his bloodstained coat had been discovered near where I lay. He was currently employed as a cook in a Hurley restaurant, but he possessed a shady background and had previously been suspected of murder in Bessemer, Michigan, a few years before. Mr. Day, a.k.a. Riley, was examined before Judge Blackburn, and Hurley's *Gogebic Iron Tribune* stated, "Every effort is being made to sift the affair and to arrive at some starting point or clue which shall unearth the perpetrators of the crime."

The Oshkosh Northwestern claimed Riley was "a hanger-on at some low dive near the scene of the murder and has acted strangely since, starting violently at any unusual sound or when spoken to unexpectedly. It was this that aroused the suspicions of the police" and when they came for him, "he seemed to know what was coming and surrendered without saying a word." The accused claimed an alibi, although he had blood on his shirt front and right sleeve. Detectives promised at least one more sensational arrest would be forthcoming involving prominent persons.

However, no further arrests were made, although a "leading businessman" was quoted as saying, "The slayer of Lotta Morgan could easily be found if the authorities would make an effort... There seems to be a disposition on their part to have the matter hushed up. The reason is patent to many of us, and something should be done at once to ferret out the murderer. A feeling prevails here that parties who were indirectly instrumental in the arresting of Day, all of whom are well-known in the city, know more about the case than has yet been developed."

Terry Day, a.k.a. Riley, was thenceforth released from custody to the alarm of both the prosecuting attorney and the chief of police. Judge Blackburn claimed there was insufficient evidence for Day to be tried.

Various reasons for my murder circulated, ranging from a jealous lover (ridiculous) to a jealous woman (even more preposterous) to suspicions that the quarters which I occupied on the night of the bank robbery were such as to enable me to look directly into the bank and to identify who entered and left. Perhaps I "knew some of the secrets of the men who had plundered the bank," it was surmised, and that party wished to keep me from talking. An Oshkosh paper called it "A Jack the Ripper" case.

The St. Paul Globe erroneously reported that my body had been found in Mr. Sullivan's saloon, which caused Mr. Sullivan to issue a special dispatch to *The Evening Wisconsin* in Milwaukee, where it was picked up by the Associated Press, the United Press, and forwarded to St. Paul. He wrote of "the horrible murder at this place of a young woman named Lotta Morgan" and remarked, "As a citizen of Hurley, I deeply deplore the death of this unfortunate woman. The facts are the body was found in the backyard of another saloon." He added that "No citizen of Hurley will be more persistent than myself to aid the officers of the law in bringing the perpetrators of this horrible murder to justice..."

At least I was given an extraordinary funeral. My body lay in state at the Hurley Opera House for four days and was viewed by thousands of inquisitive spectators. Handbills announcing my funeral were distributed; the service was held at the Opera House at three o'clock on Monday. A large crowd had gathered long before three.

Many newspapers covered the event with scornful hyperbole (a reporter for *The Detroit Journal* referred to me as "the most viciously depraved woman in Northern Wisconsin.") Still, the gathering, in general, was solemn and mostly respectful except for anticipated taunts shouted by unruly hooligans.

In addition to a prayer by Rev. F. A. McGraw of Ironwood, and short addresses by Reverend C. C. Todd (Presbyterian), Reverend W. P. Burrows (Methodist), and Father Gilbert (Catholic), beautiful singing was interspersed. I had been especially moved by a hymn sung at the funerals of the girls who'd perished in the Alcazar fire, so Mrs. Keenan rendered that in addition to "Asleep in Jesus" and "Where is My Wandering Girl Tonight," with touching effect.

Reverend Todd's homily was especially kind. "Here we come to drop a tear over her who has fallen at the hands of a midnight assassin, cruelly and inhumanely killed...how different the circumstances under which we assemble here today from those usually attended by the people of Hurley."

After the benediction by Reverend Burrows, a goodly number of carriages followed my mortal remains to the new Hurley Cemetery, where my body was the first to be interred. One newspaper observed, "It was a sad cortege, a sad ceremony—one that has undoubtedly left its lesson on the large number of fallen women who were in attendance."

It was my twenty-ninth birthday.

The following Sunday, the townspeople of Hurley, on their way to church, were given printed handbills that announced the death of Curly, a dog. "Funeral at the Opera House, 4:30 o'clock next week. Preaching by celebrated sky-pilots from abroad. Mrs. McGinty will sing Curly's favorite hymn entitled, 'Asleep in the Montreal River,' composed by one of our police. Everybody Invited. Refreshments may be had at the saloon. P.S. Any raffle pays 180 for 1."

A month later, my companion John F. Sullivan leased his buildings and left the saloon business. The newspaper said, "John has sufficient of this world's goods to meet his wants and is glad to get out of a business so foreign to his tastes and ambition.

Nearly six years after my death, in December 1895, a grand jury attempted a crackdown on Hurley with indictments of sixty-seven persons for malfeasance in office, being keepers of houses of ill-fame or gambling halls. In addition, several of the keepers of the houses of ill-fame on the outskirts of town were indicted for keeping women, sometimes in connection with saloons, right on the principal streets of the city.

In conjunction with the grand jury, a $500 reward was recommended for the apprehension "of the murderers of Lotta Morgan, a murder which has gone almost unnoticed till now."

The Ironwood Times boldly commented that the grand jury at Hurley *"would not make any attempt to clear up the mystery surrounding the murder of Lotta Morgan, which occurred in that burg a number of years ago, and, in fact, they lack the nerve necessary to indict anyone of the crime. The Times is reliably informed that a number, if not all, of the gentlemen who were conducting newspapers on the range at the time the crime was committed, could tell a thing or two about it, or at least about the parties who were interested in keeping it quiet, if they desired."*

If you were to search, you would not find my grave in the Hurley Cemetery today, as my family had my body disinterred and moved to the family plot in the southern part of the state.

My murder could still be opened as it continues to be an unsolved case. But for what purpose? The murderer long ago met his final destiny, and I gained more fame by my death than I ever could have during my life. My only wish is to have my story truthfully conveyed. You have my word.

⁂

Where is my wandering girl tonight
The girl of my tenderest care
The girl that was once my joy and light
The child of my love and prayer.
Once she was pure as morning dew
As she knelt at her mother's knee
No face was so bright no heart more true
And none was so sweet as she.
Go for my wand'ring girl tonight
Go search for her where you will
But bring her to me with all her blight
And tell her I love her still.
—Robert Lowry, 1875, "Where Is My Wandering Boy Tonight?"

Seventeen

"Lotta" drew an impressive audience at the Hurley Festival. I spoke at the local library, a modern brick building, where Jeff Draper gave a flowery introduction about my exhaustive research. He had no idea how truly exhausting it had been!

Ginger insisted on planting herself near the door, where she took names and email addresses to contact upon publication of *The Northwoods Nobody Knows*. She guaranteed the book would feature a chapter on "The Notorious Lotta Morgan: A Woman of the Demi-Monde." It didn't seem to matter that I still had to contact my editor about the concept, sign a contract, write the book, have the manuscript approved and revised, then copyedited and printed. Ruby and Fawn were the first names on the list; Myrna was third.

※

After the excitement of Lotta's performance the day before, I was drained and felt a little down on Sunday morning. That was predictable. We were now a week into August. I lingered on the porch and refilled my coffee twice until Brian asked, "Don't you have pizza crusts to make?"

I pulled my apron from the hook in the kitchen, dreading the laborious process since I was limited to working with only one hand. Rosie would ordinarily be helping, but she was spending the weekend with her mother.

Then I turned toward the table and saw a brand new bright red KitchenAid mixer with a tilt-back head and a six-quart bowl.

Yowza! I screamed for Brian. He was hiding just around the corner, wearing what might rightly be termed a shit-eating grin. That called for a spontaneous hug and numerous smoochy kisses on his cheek.

"Don't get too excited," Brian said softly in my ear, "I can declare it a business deduction."

"Um...the pizzas," I mumbled, pulling myself together. "Let's see what this big girl can do!"

The mixer, of course, was heroic. It handled my task swiftly and easily. The reputation of *Jenny's Last Pizzas* had multiplied so that it was nothing to prepare and serve at least fifty pizzas on a weekend. We weren't advertising; it was all word-of-mouth (not meant as a pun), and the bar business had picked up as well. So, yes, the KitchenAid was a business expense. But it was also a generous gift for our kitchen.

I'd just put the second batch of dough aside to rise when I thought I recognized Cynthia's voice. Then I thought I heard Ada Vogel! I glanced out toward the porch.

It *was* Ada Vogel, dressed very sporty in khaki slacks with white running shoes, a red polo shirt, and a floral scarf tied fashionably around her neck. She set aside her cane, and her arms enfolded me. Cynthia brought her north to see the reformation of the Maus Haus. She'd cried when she recognized the sign at Hazelhurst that said "North of the Tension Line." It was a long drive from Madison. Riding in the silver convertible was a special treat.

"We stopped for chocolate milkshakes in Stevens Point so I could use the little girl's room," she recounted. "I couldn't wait to get back on the road again. I told Cindy to go ahead and *floor it*. And she did!"

Cynthia, all smiles, said they would spend a couple of nights at her condo and head back to Madison later in the week. First, they wanted to have one of my pizzas for lunch, and then Ada would tour her new cottage with us.

Brian graciously welcomed Ada and advised her that I'd been a great addition to the resort. The three of them sat on the porch to chat while I fired up the pizza oven and threw lunch together.

Ada declared her pizza the very best she'd ever had. I didn't believe for a moment she was a pizza aficionado, but she may have been. Brian had minimized the bandage on my hand before my performance as Lotta, so I could now use the gearshift and work the clutch in the Bug. Ada was so impressed with Toad and Stumpy's resurrection of the car that she wanted to congratulate them before we left. Then she rode over to the Maus Haus with me.

Cynthia had a good eye, wasn't afraid to work hard, and I'd found pairing with her surprisingly enjoyable. Mostly, I approved of her well-informed decisions, but I'd helped with the staging. Dealing with Larry Boone after I'd backed away hadn't been a problem for her. "We're doing a renovation, Jenny, and that's what matters to me."

The place looked even more welcoming than it had during my recent visit; now I was seeing it through Ada's eyes, and it had been furnished. The cabin, with its new reddish-brown siding, had forest green shutters to match the new shingles on the roof. The railing around the edge of the deck was topped with pots of red geraniums. And next to the front door was a life-sized black wooden bear carved by a local craftsman, holding a "WELCOME" sign.

Ada was speechless. Her eyes glossed with tears.

Inside, Cynthia pointed out all the new additions—the stainless-steel refrigerator in the compact kitchen, the new stove, the beige quartz countertop and matching backsplash, the stainless-steel sink, oak cabinets, and extended peninsula with three upholstered stools. Against the front wall, just below the big window where we'd hung plaid café curtains, there was a small maple dining table from Goodwill with four matching chairs. The fieldstone fireplace had been scrubbed and looked handsome. The chimney had been swept, and the floors were now covered with practical laminate flooring. A new sofa with a matching loveseat provided sleeping space for three more guests in addition to a leather recliner for reading or enjoying the fire. There were new beds, each embellished with handmade quilts made by women from an Antler church. Dark paneling had been replaced with creamy beige walls. Jaunty curtains in the bedrooms matched the colors in the quilt squares.

We'd displayed the place as if a happy family occupied it. A couple of fishing rods were propped up next to the front door, and a dog bone and chew toy waited on a fluffy rug by the hearth.

"The whole shebang," Ada remarked as she tossed her cane and fell into the leather recliner, "It's perfectly wonderful!" She pulled the lever to raise the footrest and settled back, closing her eyes with a smile. "I could rest right here for hours. See you gals later!"

Best of all, the cottage was move-in ready. The realtor wanted photos ASAP for several potential buyers. I sent off a bunch of new pictures while Ada rested her eyes.

"Oh, I wish Gus could see what you girls have done," she mused sleepily. "We enjoyed so many family summers here!" Then she added, "I'll bet if my daughter saw it now, she wouldn't want me to sell."

Then Ada was snoring. The busy day had taken a toll.

Cynthia motioned to me. There was a bottle of prosecco in the refrigerator, and she grabbed a couple of glasses. We headed out to the deck while Ada napped. We lifted our glasses as Cynthia said, "Let's celebrate!"

"You and Boone did most of the work," I added. "Cheers!"

My reaction toward Cynthia had changed dramatically since we'd met. She honestly was a generous and caring person. Following my concussion, she'd looked after me daily, and with our work on the Maus Haus, we'd formed a strong alliance.

We reminisced about our initial visit to the decrepit dead critter-infested cottage and how we'd laughed until we'd cried on an earlier version of this very deck. I apologized again for sidestepping Larry Boone. I wanted to pass along the news of his resurrection, but Rosie had shared his DNA results in confidence.

The sun was warm on our faces. We sat in silence, savoring the wine and our accomplishment.

"So," I said casually, as if an afterthought, "how was your dinner at Bonfire?"

I didn't want to seem intrusive, but I'd been dying to know.

She topped off her glass and offered me more to me. I declined.

"The meal was incredible, of course. I had the grilled lamb, and Brian had the walleye. We had a nice evening. I haven't made much progress with him, though," she admitted. "I haven't given up."

Wow. I gulped the dregs of my wine. I hoped the extent of my relief wasn't obvious. I mumbled something about thinking about Bonfire while I nibbled my Ritz crackers and cheese at Myrna's B&B.

"How *was* your visit to Hurley? Did you find the courage to visit a strip club?"

Oh boy, did I ever. She'd be traumatized by a description of my Dancing Bare behavior! I wondered if Brian still had my red satin Sexy Gramma garter hanging from his rear-view mirror.

Instead, I painted a vivid picture of Ruby's gyrations at the Silverpalooza on Saturday night and revealed what I'd learned during brunch with her and Fawn the following morning.

"I heard there was a huge fire at a strip club up there that weekend," Cynthia mentioned. "Were you aware of that?"

Ada appeared at the front door just then and apologized for drifting off. Good timing, old girl! It was time to leave.

She eventually joined Cynthia in the Porsche. I followed. Cynthia paused where the driveway joined the road at the turnaround. I had to stop as well and got out to see what stalled their progress.

"Ada wants to know who created this lane." Cynthia indicated the tire tracks on the right that parted the tall grass and ferns.

"You two should know I still own all the land from here to the end of the point," Ada remarked. "Gus was always going to divide it into separate lots, and, typically, he never got around to it."

She insisted on following the tracks, although I knew Cynthia would be reluctant to drive her car through there. Thankfully, no boats or dusty SUVs waited at the landing. I joined the women as they stood near the water's edge and shared Cynthia's shock when Ada revealed that, besides Maus Haus, she also owned the decaying cottage on the island.

Three girls slipped out the front door, noticed us, and quickly turned back.

"Oh, for Pete's sake! Squatters are in Crow's Nest!" Ada exclaimed. "Who are those people, and what the heck are they doing there? How did they get permission? I sure didn't give it to them!"

I had never seen Ada so agitated.

"I'd like to row right across and give them a great big piece of my mind. That place isn't fit to live in, never was, even before Gus took ownership."

I gave Cynthia a fleeting look. She raised her eyebrows and returned my nod. "Kick them out! They shouldn't be there! Call the sheriff!"

"We'll take care of it, dear," Cynthia comforted Ada. "Jenny and I will take care of it. You can calm down. They'll be gone before you know it."

I slid my arm around Ada's shoulder. She was trembling.

"I forgot about Crow's Nest. Should have sold it off a long time ago. It's always been a wreck. The kids thought it was spooky. They liked to play there, but only during the day. It was a doggone mess even then."

Cynthia helped a still-indignant Ada back to her car. They were headed for Cynthia's condo for a short nap and then a stop to see the realtor in Antler. We'd agreed to meet later at The Star Lake Saloon.

After they left, I kicked my front tire in frustration. It wouldn't be long before Ada came up with the solution that Cynthia and I had already deduced with our swift glance.

I backed the Bug into the hideaway we'd used before, sprayed myself liberally with OFF, and returned to the pocket in the trees where I'd surveyed Crow's Nest with Rosie and Toad. My phone had a camera with a close-up feature I'd never tried. I rested it against the fork of a branch and aimed at the front door. After maybe ten minutes, the girls cautiously exited, scanned the landscape, and slipped out to lie in the sun. I snapped a photo whenever a face was revealed. A slender girl with auburn hair got up to wrap her body around a birch sapling and demonstrate a familiar lithesome position. That was certainly Cherry; her cell phone was on my bedside table.

Finally, the tall woman with long black hair waved the girls inside. She stared in my direction while I got some excellent shots. When she went back in and closed the door, I left.

On my way out, after I'd passed the Maus Haus's driveway, I met the black SUV heading back toward the landing. There were two male passengers with the same driver as before.

⁂

I explained Ada's concern to Toad and Stumpy. I showed them my pictures, and they offered to set up trail cams at inconspicuous locations so we could ascertain what was happening at Crow's Nest day and night. We agreed we needed more information to achieve a firm conclusion. Evicting the squatters might not be as easy as I'd hoped.

Cherry's phone needed charging, so I plugged it in with plans to check it later that evening. Internet reception at The Last Resort had improved with a new router and modem. Brian made changes that he said were necessary for business. I found the updates helpful with reading vintage newspapers and examining historical sites online. It was also easier to Facetime my daughters.

⁂

When I arrived at the Saloon, Cynthia and Ada had already scored a table on the porch. Ada was sipping a glass of Chablis and appeared much more cheerful. She was giddy about her escape from The Laurel Lodge and overjoyed to have Maus Haus on the market. She reviewed every little detail that she'd found so appealing.

"When the realtor viewed your photos of Maus Haus, she became orgasmic," Ada said. "I'm not kidding! You should have heard her squeal!"

Multiple showings for Saturday and Sunday had already been scheduled.

Cynthia asked how the Vogels came to own Crow's Nest. "The isolated location is unusual."

"Gus claimed he won it due to a gambling debt," Ada replied. "I never questioned him because, to be honest, I didn't want to know the truth. But I was curious since it was so close to our own place."

There was a pause, during which our waitress delivered my beer.

Ada took another sip of wine. "Jenny, you've already spent most of your summer here, and an old Volkswagen isn't enough compensation for your unfortunate turn of events. Cynthia, of course you'll be reimbursed for your expertise. I couldn't be more grateful for your vitality and, even more than that, for your friendship. You girls have been an incredible gift to me. Having said that, I'm reluctant to ask you to do any more."

Again, I caught Cynthia's eye.

"Forgive an old lady if this seems presumptuous. You two have become an exceptional team."

Before I could respond, Ada continued racing toward her objective. "I mentioned Crow's Nest to the realtor, and she said she couldn't wait to see it."

She spilled the words like she was pouring hot tea.

Cynthia was quick to explain. "I had to take a phone call, and Ada found a few moments to speak with the realtor on her own."

The interruption didn't slow Ada down.

"Now, we can go ahead with the same contractor! I told the realtor she couldn't even have a peek at what we'll be working with until those criminal squatters are kicked out," Ada continued. "Even if they hadn't moved in, I'm certain that we'd be facing major, major repairs. But with what I clear on Maus Haus, the realtor says I can anticipate overhauling Crow's Nest to be equally appealing and maybe even better. It'll need a well and septic system, for one thing. What do you girls think about a hot tub? Wouldn't that be fun?

"It was always a curious place," Ada continued.

I couldn't believe she was still so energized after her active day.

"On Sunday afternoons, Gus and I would take the children over to the island for a picnic, and they'd pretend to be gangsters. He'd told the kids bootleggers in the 1930s used it, so the children gave each other names like 'Bullet Bobby' and...oh, let's see, I think Susie was 'Shotgun Susie.' They found secret places to hide.

"I remember one time we were there, and a thunderstorm blew in. Gus didn't want to try rowing back with whitecaps on the lake, so we were stranded at Crow's Nest much longer than we'd reckoned. We were restless, and the kids got rambunctious, and I realized how lonely it would be to live in such a remote spot. I believe that's when Gus told the children there might be a hidden tunnel somewhere to give them something to keep them busy."

Hidden tunnel? That was intriguing.

"I thought it was just another tall tale. The children loved it when Gus made up stories about gangsters, like John Dillinger and Baby Face Nelson and the rest. We'd heard that downtown Hurley had underground tunnels where bootleggers took refuge when the revenuers or the FBI conducted a raid, so Gus's anecdote about a tunnel had a ring of truth. It kept the kids searching for a long time."

I was about to ask if they'd found a tunnel when Ginger appeared at our table.

"Oh, for the love, is that *Adabagel*?" she exclaimed.

"*Gingersnap!*" Mrs. Vogel was equally ecstatic.

The women reached across the table for an awkward hug that upset the wine and toppled my beer. Cynthia and I mopped the liquid as we signaled our waitress for more napkins. She also provided dry placemats and more drinks.

The women knew each other from the days when Gus and Ada came by boat to the Saloon, and Ginger was tending bar.

Stumpy and Toad accompanied Ginger tonight as a "thank you" for helping her clear Lily's things from her attic. She insisted that another table be pulled next to ours so we could all eat, drink, and visit together.

After the expanded group was seated, Ginger grabbed my arm and claimed she'd been trying to get in touch with me all afternoon: a woman from Antler who'd attended my *Lotta* presentation in Hurley wanted to know if I would repeat my performance for the Antler Women's Club.

Ginger had already agreed. She maintained she was still my "agent" and that I would get paid $150 for the night. "Of course, I'll get a cut of that," she grinned. "Think of the publicity for your book!"

The date for my appearance in Antler had not been set but "soon" seemed to be in consideration. I'd probably comply since it wouldn't take much effort. I hadn't yet hung up the costume I'd worn, and I could recycle the same script.

Ada and Cynthia insisted on being enlightened about Lotta Morgan. I let Ginger recite her version of Lotta's fame, of Skipper moving the bloody body, discoveries of further sordid affairs we'd gleaned from his clippings, our trip to Hurley where we'd had lunch at the Nip 'n' Nudge, and my subsequent research where I interrupted Ginger just in time to mention the Hurley Historical Festival, where I became a Lotta "impersonator."

"She did it yesterday, and that's what they want her to do again for the Antler Women's Club," Ginger said. "Perform as Lotta Morgan."

Cynthia expressed definite interest.

"Too bad you won't be here to see it, Ada," Ginger sighed. "You could go with us."

Ada had nodded with pleasure throughout Ginger's monologue. "What the heck," she said. "I'll make arrangements to stay."

"You'll stay with me!" Ginger didn't miss a beat with her response and slapped the table. She was jubilant. The matter was settled in minutes. Cynthia would move Ada's things over to *Lilypad*, and Ada would extend her escape for several weeks.

"I can help evict those nasty intruders from Crow's Nest," she added. "It will give me profound pleasure to participate!"

Throughout this entire exchange, Stumpy and Toad watched with amusement. I was anxious to hear their final impressions.

⁂

When I returned to The Last Resort, I texted my newest photos to Fawn and asked if she or her friends recognized the tall woman with long black hair. I also forwarded pictures from Cherry's phone with each of the girls in a seductive pose. Viewing those made me queasy.

I baked and served pizzas to the last few customers, then helped Brian close the bar. He was unaware of the cottage on the island or anyone who vaguely resembled the people I described.

"I forgot to mention," I said, as he grabbed a cold slab of pizza, "the cottage where they're staying—where they're staying without permission—it's called Crow's Nest. Ada Vogel owns that, too. And she wants Cynthia and me to fix it up to sell. When she said she owned it, we knew that was coming; it was just a matter of time."

"Larry Boone again, huh? Any more leftover pizza?"

Brian sat at the table.

"Wait a minute," I chastised him. "This is serious. Here. Take a look."

I showed him the pictures on my phone. "This girl with her leg around the tree was dancing up at Hurley when I did my, you know, my *thing*. She's just a kid. And she was crying when she came off stage."

He studied my photos and then viewed the unsettling ones on Cherry's phone. "You're thinking there might be trafficking over there?"

I took a deep breath and took a seat before I replied. "Every one of Wisconsin's seventy-two counties has experienced child trafficking for sex. I know that seems unreal, but it's true. Toad and Stumpy set up trail cams to record any activity going on. We need to learn more and get proof, then figure out if there's something we can do about it.

"According to the state, the average age of sex-trafficked kids is only thirteen," I continued. "They've found thirteen-year-old girls working in strip clubs. So, I guess it wasn't so unusual for me to find this girl at The Dancing Bare."

I was choking up as I spoke. He closely viewed the photos again. We considered the implications and wondered where the clients were coming from. How did they know where to meet the guy in the black SUV? How was this access advertised?

"They say the way to crack down on the crime is to destroy the demand, stop the men who are paying for it," I said. "I suppose I could try to follow the black van when it leaves."

Brian said the muffler on the Bug would give me away.

"And the girls—and sometimes young boys—aren't like regular crime victims because of the manipulation they're undergoing. It breaks my heart."

My phone dinged as Fawn's reply appeared. After reading it, I showed her message to Brian. Friends and other dancers agreed that the auburn-haired teen *was* Cherry Delite, the girl who'd danced before me. One dancer who had been "in the life" for a while said the tall, black-haired woman seemed familiar.

"We've been discussing this, and you should be very careful," Fawn said. "These people can be dangerous. Please watch out."

Brian read the remainder of her message aloud: "The Dancing Bare tapes all dancers on A.Nite. If that 1 didn't burn, I'll get so we know 4 sure it's Cherry. I'll hafta be sneaky 'cause they're in deep shit if she's underage."

"That would be excellent evidence," I said.

I thought that maybe her friend Billy owed her a favor. After all, he certainly knew why there'd been a fire, and she hadn't implicated him, had she?

"Do you suppose videos from your Amateur Night will include footage of Mitzi Dawn?" Brian gave me a crooked grin.

"It was *Misty* Dawn," I replied. "And I'm certain that any footage of Misty's less-than-graceful gyrations has been severely damaged. Or will be."

Eighteen

I went to Ginger's Monday morning to have coffee and discuss the Crow's Nest situation. Ada was there, too, and Cynthia, but she had to leave in an hour. I shared my pictures and told them of my qualms. I withheld the fact that I'd seen the youngest girl at The Dancing Bare because I was not ready to share my ridiculous disgrace with Cynthia or Ada now, if ever.

Ginger volunteered information we'd gathered on stockades in the Pineries and regaled them both with wretched Maud Cassidy tales. Maud's yellowed clippings were spread on the kitchen table in front of Ada, like a hand of solitaire.

"It looks like Maud's exploits were splashed all over the country," Ada remarked, passing the clippings over to Cynthia. "Here you can read about a woman who was '*an alleged decoyer of young girls to dens of vice at Hurley.*' And here you have her deeds described in the *Black Hills Daily Times, Quad-City Times, The Wichita Star, Detroit Free Press, Omaha Daily Bee, Nashville Banner*, and even in *The New York Sun*. One calls Maud 'The Notorious Hag' or a 'Human Vulture.' *The Philadelphia Times* comes right out and calls her '*Wicked Maud Cassidy.*' "

"She was wicked, all right. A rotten woman," Ginger said. "Her husband and another guy were in on the foul antics, too. I don't know what happened to them, but Maudie spent well-deserved time in the penitentiary."

"Listen to this," Cynthia added. "*Chicago Tribune. November 1887.*" A seventeen-year-old girl who was kidnapped from that city, and delivered to one of those Hurley dens, was introduced by the man who'd met her at the train as 'More fresh fish.' "

Ada gathered the clippings together and shook her head. "*Fresh Fish.* Just imagine. That poor girl."

I had made several copies of Wisconsin's most recent sex trafficking report for each of us. It defined how business was conducted these days with children under eighteen. "Unfortunately, you'll see the situation has not changed a lot since Maud's day."

Ginger was silent for a few minutes and then remarked, "The girls Maud brought up north had to turn tricks to pay for their train ticket. This says today's kids often have to do the same thing; only it's called 'debt bondage.' They're told they owe money for transportation and living expenses and have to pledge their *personal services* to pay off that balance. I'll be damned. *Personal services.* You know what that means."

Ada, still studying the fact sheet, asked, "How can we find out if this is what's transpiring at Crow's Nest? What do we have to go on besides the activities we've witnessed? And if it is, do we call the sheriff, the State Department of Justice, or one of these helplines?"

"Before we do anything," Cynthia warned, "we need to gather more evidence."

⁂

For my Wednesday night appearance as Lotta at the Antler Library, Toad and Stumpy arranged a spacious platform at the rear of the community room. They spread an old oriental rug over the surface (a remnant from Lily's collection) and placed a carved Victorian chair in one corner next to a fake potted palm. That allowed me to stand or be seated, whichever I found most comfortable. The microphone pinned to my dress could be adjusted.

To further entice my editor with the subject, I asked Rosie to capture my presentation on video. The library allowed us to borrow their video camera.

As I had in Hurley, I impersonated Lotta for the entire program and abstained from removing my disguise before my portrayal was complete. Afterward, there was an informal Q&A while the audience helped themselves to cookies, punch, or coffee supplied by the Friends of Antler Library. I was tired by then and ready to say good night.

Naturally, the first queries concerned who I thought murdered Lotta and why. And "How come the guy with the bloody shirt and coat wasn't charged?"

I replied that although it seemed obvious Terry Day was the guilty party, someone exerted pressure on the judge not to prosecute. In later years, even as recently as 1990, the hundredth anniversary of Lotta's death, questions were raised about Day's bloodstained coat that had been left behind. Newspapers had described him as a "poor half-witted fool" who worked as a paperhanger, a painter, and a restaurant cook.

"The Express Company, who'd suffered the biggest loss, did hire a detective to scope it out," I said. "One possibility is that the detective paid Terry Day to murder Lotta. Or Day's coat may have been purposely spattered with Lotta's blood and planted. Other arrests were said to be imminent. Unfortunately, they never materialized. That was a very long time before the availability of DNA analysis."

In closing, I reviewed the tales of Irish Annie and Piano Mary and repeated Toad's tale of Lumberjack Ida and her girls Tootsie and Big Florence, who kept a house of ill repute near the railroad depot, which wasn't far from where we were sitting. The audience was highly amused by that local anecdote.

"I hope you enjoyed learning about Lotta Morgan this evening," I said. "It's been a pleasure to tell her story."

I nodded farewell to the crowd and began to fuss with my microphone. People gathered their things and started for the door.

"Those stockades you talked about," one woman challenged before I could turn off my mic. "How do you know for sure houses like that were around here back then? And if they were, how do you know for sure they're not still all over the place today, in one form or another?"

I paused just a moment too long, and during that brief time, Ginger took advantage of the commotion to come forward and climb up on the stage. She unpinned my mic and blew into it. Folks who were getting ready to leave immediately resumed their seats. They all knew Ginger.

"Wait just a minute, everybody. This here is important." She held one of Skipper's old newspapers and flapped it above her head.

"This is *The Chicago Tribune* from March of 1888 and I want to read an example of what it says happened. Let me elucidate."

Ginger paused to dig her reading glasses from a capacious purse that she carried with her. She cleared her throat.

"'*In the deep gloom of Judge Horton's courtroom in the Criminal Court building sat Maud Cassidy, the procuress, yesterday morning. She was receptively dressed except for an aggressive green feather in her hat and had small eyes and repulsive features. She made a picture that was not pleasant to look upon.* The judge warned if there were any women in the courtroom, they should retire because *this is a filthy case.*' "

I took a few steps back, adjusted my bustle, and collapsed in the Victorian chair behind me. I had lost control of Lotta's evening.

Ginger continued, merging an extemporaneous summary with quotes from the article while the audience sat, enrapt. "Eventually, a young woman named Blanche, whose mother was dead, was put on the stand. Her father was a painter who also repaired tugboats and things like that. She testified that a woman stopped by her house in Chicago when she was only thirteen and asked where she could buy some milk. Blanche showed her where to find milk, and the woman asked if Blanche would like a job for twelve dollars an hour plus board at a Green Bay hotel. The girl got permission from her father. But instead of Green Bay, the poor girl ended up in the Pinery Dens, in a vile brothel. Just like that. She was expected to join a crowd of girls in the parlor and to wear scandalous dresses that exposed much of her body including her legs and her bosom. She was ordered to *dance, drink, and entertain the miners and lumbermen* to pay for her trip north.

"Maud was given twenty-five dollars for each girl she kidnapped.

The girls were usually raped right away by the proprietor when they got there, so the girls became *soiled doves*. That's what they called them, *soiled doves*. Isn't that the saddest thing? I can show you any number of newspapers just like this from all over the United States where young girls like Blanche testified to the same sort of activity happening in our area. In Wisconsin's Northwoods! The girls were imprisoned and forced to entertain grown men, mostly loggers and miners, until they earned enough to pay for the railroad tickets that got them here in the first place. And after that, the poor girls had nowhere else to go because they were 'ruined,' except to Hurley, where they had to become prostitutes.

"Jenny—I mean Lotta—told you that Governor Rusk, our 'genius' governor at the time, declared that he'd conduct an official investigation on the stockades, but it was reported that the women—" Ginger consulted further notes in her hand. "*The women, so my agent was informed*—that's Governor Rusk speaking—*were wont to be about the grounds during the summer in the most loose attire, and their conduct at times incensed passersby to such a degree that the keepers of the houses thought best to erect the fences to prevent the arousal of public indignation.*"

The audience chuckled.

"I thought you said these stockades were miles from anywhere," someone addressed me.

I removed my black lace gloves and checked my watch. It was time to wrap this up.

Ginger held out the microphone for me to speak. I stood to respond.

"Sex sold newspapers then, the same as it does now. And reporters tended to embellish their stories to increase the length of their report, which would then warrant more remuneration. Governor Rusk was eager to sweep everything under the rug. According to my research, Wisconsin's early sex trade was more vigorous right here in the Northwoods than anywhere else in the nation. It's fair to say the original roots of sex trafficking run more deeply in our state than in any other.

"Now, thank you all for coming this evening—"

But Ginger had not finished her proclamation.

"Hang on, Jenny—I mean Lotta—and every single one of you. I'm not done yet."

Ginger waved me back to my chair.

"I want you to listen to this very important fact which I wish to *elucidate, loud and clear*: There's evidence that each and every one of Wisconsin's counties has evidence of sex trafficking." Her voice rose with vehemence. "That's seventy-two counties! What do you think about that?"

"And it's right here in Lakeland County!" Ada Vogel stood and shouted, her fist in the air.

Ada's outburst silenced my audience. They stared at her, a stranger in their midst, then buzzed with asides and private commentary. Ada sat again and covered her face, embarrassed by her outburst. Ginger nodded to her with reassurance. Cynthia, next to Ada, reached over to give her a hug.

"Folks, allow me to introduce my old pal, Ada Vogel," Ginger indicated the flustered woman. "Ada and her husband, Gus Vogel, owned property up here for a very long time, and Ada still does, out on Sickle Moon. They were regulars every Friday at The Star Lake Saloon, where, as you all know, I presided over the bar for forty-odd years. Ada and I got to be good friends, as it happens."

This caused Ginger to smile briefly and take a brief bow. Then she became solemn.

"I have to agree with Ada, because what she said is accurate. It's a damn shame that we risk having revolting places nearby like the stockades we had back in Lotta's time. Now, don't you think for one minute I'm going to tell you where I've got a hunch one of those horrible locations might be, because we still need to check out a few particulars before we're one hundred percent sure. But if it's what we suspect it is, something radical needs to be carried out."

Why hadn't I warned them not to mention Crow's Nest? We were far from being able to verify anything, and if rumors reached the squatters, they could hit the road overnight.

Now Ginger had to shout above the murmurs that were building.

"Most of us here tonight are daughters, mothers, sisters, and some of us are grandmothers. We are all strong women. Matter of fact, I know most of you personally, and I know for sure we've all gone through our share of hardships over the years. Now it's time for us to dig deep and work hard again. Who's with me?

"The average age of a child being trafficked for sex is *thirteen.* I can't get over that, and it makes me sick to my stomach. Folks, that's like a kid in eighth grade, and it's the average, which means they can be even younger! Not just girls, but little boys, too. Because trafficked kids are said to 'hide in plain sight,' we might come in contact with them and never even know it. So here's what we should do to keep an eye out to identify possible victims."

She read from the sex trafficking information I'd found.

"They avoid eye contact. They are heavily guarded by someone who is always with them and speaks for them. They might seem confused or hesitant. They might have bruises or show other signs of being physically abused or appear very nervous. They could even seem like they've been drugged. Something might seem 'just off.' If you've been around kids at all, you'll recognize what that looks like.

"So, keep your wits about you, folks, and if you're up for it, let me know how to get in touch. My email is Ginger@Lilypad.com. If there's something going on, we're going to have to band together to destroy this evil behavior. Let's show how ruthless we Northwoods women can be."

Nineteen

Thursday night was always slow, and we had few patrons at the bar except for Moe and Curly, my private names for the two garrulous widowers who took their customary seats at the corner table by the window on Tuesday and Thursday evenings. They drank two beers apiece, shared a sausage pizza with onions at six o'clock, and played cribbage until eight thirty so they could get home in time to go to bed promptly at nine.

When Brian wanted to attend the monthly town board meeting on Thursday, August 20, to discuss further road repairs, I assured him I could handle the bar and pizzas by myself. He'd already asked Rosie to help since my right hand still had a mild agility problem.

Rosie wanted to know if I thought the girls in Crow's Nest were being held like those in the stockades we'd discussed at the library. "Like, I just have a bad feeling about it," she said. "Like those men coming and going all the time and the girls scared to be outside and stuff, and hiding? Maybe they're scared. Like, I don't think they're happy out there. I sure wouldn't be. And like you said yourself, they're staying there illegally. Isn't that enough to call the sheriff and get him to kick them out? Why can't you just do that?"

I handed her the hot pizza I had ready for Curly and Moe, which she delivered to their table, along with paper plates, napkins, and plastic forks. We weren't known for our gracious accouterments; they're not green, but they're easy for cleanup. I was thinking about ordering bamboo flatware.

"Okay, the people over at Crow's Nest look iffy, but maybe they can't afford more than a camping vacation in an abandoned cabin."

That was such a limp excuse that Rosie shook her head and moaned, "Oh, Jenny. C'mon. That sucks."

I knew it was ridiculous, yet I was reluctant to accept what it might mean to become directly involved. Such an operation would call for serious legal measures, and unlike Ginger and Ada, I secretly loathed to take part. If you asked me why, I wouldn't have been able to give a good answer. Perhaps I'd had enough excitement in my life for a while, and since Ginger was the one who'd brought it up, interrupting my lecture, maybe she should be the one to figure out what to do. Honestly, I was tired.

Rosie continued. "The thing is, after I got home last night, I told my dad all the stuff about the stockades and girls and Hurley. He said he didn't know anything about what happened up here a hundred years ago with kidnapped girls from Chicago, but he didn't like the sound of it. Also, Cynthia contacted him yesterday to think about renovating Crow's Nest, and he told her—and he said to tell you—that he knows that old place inside and out."

She explained that her father's Klavern had used the island and the cottage for their meetings when he'd initially formed his group. Then they needed more room, so they didn't go back there again. Larry had chosen the location because it was so remote.

"He said you're supposed to call him and set up a time to talk."

I made a mental note to call Boone the next day, and Rosie got busy preparing pizza toppings to freeze while I wiped down the bar.

Around eight o'clock, the screen door opened, and a party of five arrived: a man, a woman, and three teenage girls—one of whom was Cherry Delite. They pushed a couple of tables together and brought over an extra chair.

My heart began to gallop, and I felt lightheaded. I had to back away from the bar and move into the kitchen so I could lean against the wall. I willed myself to breathe.

Oh. My. God.

"Rosie," I called softly, "you have to help me."

She asked if I was okay because my face was pale.

"It's the Crow's Nest squatters. They just came in. We have to pretend we don't suspect anything, okay?"

She glanced at the table and squeezed my arm.

"Be yourself. Be calm," I told her. "You take their drink order, and I'll ask about the pizza."

I kept an eye on Rosie as she waited on them. The man did all the talking. The adults would have beers, and the girls, Diet Cokes.

"Good evening," I greeted them shortly after Rosie took their beverage request. My voice sounded alien, so unlike my own, even Curly and Moe turned to look. I pressed my face in my elbow, faked a deep sneeze as if I had a pollen allergy, and cleared my throat.

"Excuse me! Are you folks ready for your pizzas?"

The man, the one I recognized as driving the black SUV at the boat landing, removed his mesh trucker's cap and brushed back his greasy hair before settling it again. The cap was so stained I couldn't read the logo. Everyone in the group deferred to him. He hadn't shaved in quite a while and wore a faded T-shirt with a Harley insignia.

The tall woman with long black hair scooted her chair back and walked closer to squint at the pizza menu on the wall. Even though it was evening and not especially bright inside the bar, she didn't discard her dark glasses, which was weird. In contrast to her sweatshirt, jeans, and tall leather boots (which must have been hot and smelly), the girls wore cut-off jean shorts and skimpy ruffled tops. The girls (one blonde, one auburn, and one brunette) had ponytails. Cherry appeared to be the youngest. The girls were barefoot. One had a large bruise on her thigh.

The man ordered one plain cheese pizza and two more with sausage and pepperoni. Back in the kitchen, my hands trembled as I threw the pizza toppings together. I could barely carry a tray with two beers and three Cokes without spilling everything, but Rosie did it well. Compared to me, she seemed incredibly calm.

During the brief time the pizzas were baking, Rosie shared a brilliant inspiration. We switched places. I had to rush while she tended to the hot oven outdoors.

Brian's desk is in the laundry room attached to the kitchen. I found a pad of small pale pink Post-it notes in the top drawer, wrote HELP on three of them with a Sharpie, and then went into the ladies' room.

By anyone's standards, it's not a very fancy restroom. It's functional, and I check it often to make sure it's always clean. Like most of the Northwoods bars, we have a vending machine for condoms in the ladies' room as well as the men's and one for tampons that's only in the ladies'. We also post warnings about washing hands, no flushing of sanitary products, and (believe it or not) "Please Flush After Using." I'd also insisted on posting a bright red sign from the National Domestic Abuse Hotline that states "You Are Not Alone," with pull-off tabs and numbers to call if you are a victim. I added the pink Post-its to that red sign, just in case.

Rosie sliced and delivered the pizzas. I barricaded myself behind the bar, pretending to page through my phone and keeping a casual watch on the "family" as they ate. When it was convenient, I snapped a few covert photos.

Later, I delivered Moe's and Curly's second beers. Moe was winning at cribbage. Curly gave my butt a gentle tap of thanks like he always did. It was not a sexual move, and I didn't mind. While he did that, Moe opened the nearby window. That seemed odd because it was raining outdoors, but the entire evening had been thrown off-kilter.

"Can I get you anything else?" I then asked the gang of five. The man said no and handed me cash to cover their bill. No tip. They appeared to be in a hurry to leave.

I was aware that the girls had not looked up since they'd entered, nor had they made eye contact with Rosie or me, spoken to one another, or anyone else. Rosie said she'd done her best to engage them in conversation. Most distressing to me were their matching tattoos: a small heart with swirling wings inked in the middle of their chests. It reminded me of

Edna Ferber's contrivance of Lotta's tattoo, which the author claimed had been placed there by Lotta's husband "so no other man would have her."

"Thanks for coming," I said. "I hope the pizzas were okay."

No response.

They pushed their chairs back and prepared to leave. As luck would have it (or because I'd willed it to happen) Cherry Delite lingered behind to use the ladies' room. The older woman waited outside the door as if she were standing guard.

As it turned out, the woman didn't use the restroom after Cherry, and when the girl emerged, the entire group departed together. I watched them get into the black SUV. Rosie and I lingered a few more minutes after they drove away, then checked the restroom. All the pale pink Post-its were gone. We were not sure what that meant, but at least they'd been observed.

Rosie gathered the empty beer bottles, Coke cans, and glasses and placed the tables and chairs where they belonged while I wiped everything down. Killing time. Lost in thought.

I was anxious for Brian to return. The garbage pail in the kitchen was nearly full, so I pulled out the plastic bag for Rosie to add the paper plates before hauling the bag to the dumpster. That's when she noticed a pink Post-it stuck to the bottom of one of them: HELP.

Rosie's initiative worked. Before I could stop her, she was on the phone with Ginger.

Curly and Moe wanted to pay their bill. They were wrapping up much later than usual.

"You girls all right?" Curly wanted to know. "Something peculiar about those folks who just left."

Moe added, "Got a whiff of them at one point and had to open a window to bring in some fresh air."

"If you recall, I was winning at that point," Moe argued. "If we'd moved to another table, it might've jinxed my luck. All I can say is it's a damn good thing we had our pizza before they came in! And it was excellent as usual, by the way."

Behind me, I could hear Rosie recounting the events of the evening and replying to Ginger's response.

Brian appeared just as Curly and Moe were heading out. The men engaged in the usual small talk, how the latest crop of mosquitoes was carrying off the wolves. Brian swung the "closed" sign on the door, shut the corner window, and switched off the neon light advertising The Last Resort. He began to tell me about the town meeting, but when he came behind the bar, he could see Rosie was in tears, and my arms were shaking as we comforted each other.

I told him who'd been there and how dubious it seemed.

"We've got to do something," Rosie told him, sobbing. "Cherry asked us for help."

Twenty

The chilly August morning was a warning of autumn on the horizon. I had not slept well. Brian and I had our coffee on the porch despite the morning fog. It was Saturday, so there'd be plenty of pizzas to make, and I knew I should get busy, but the clasp of a hot mug was as welcome as my heaviest hoodie, and I had more on my mind than pizza: One of these days I had to run back to Madison to sort things out. Cynthia said it was time for me to select the final finishes for my condo. Any day I'd hear back from my editor about the book proposal that I'd sent him, and if he liked it, that would lead to a manuscript deadline ahead. Did Toad and Stumpy pick up anything of interest on their trail cams? What would we do about it if they had? And if Ada didn't want Crow's Next fixed up ASAP, I'd be extremely surprised, given her delight over the Maus Haus *rebirth*.

Add to the above, Ginger's plea for a meeting this morning. Rosie and I could mix the dough, then stick it in the refrigerator before heading over to Lilypad—I knew she'd want to be there. But I didn't feel I had much to contribute regarding the problem with the girls on the island; it was one of the reasons I couldn't sleep.

"I'll call the sheriff if you don't want your name on record," Brian offered. "I can tell him to run a check on the place. They can be arrested for illegal occupancy."

I demurred since alerting the sheriff might risk having the girls detained or cited for prostitution and jailed.

"You'll need more proof of sex trafficking than a guy with a van and a boat delivering men back and forth," he said. "Sure, it looks dodgy, but it could be drugs, stolen property, or gambling. Who knows what. Federal law enforcement might have to investigate. One thing you do know for sure is those people are trespassing, and for that, they can be apprehended right away."

He was right, but I was convinced that the men were pursuing sex with three young girls. How to prove that charge was a daunting challenge.

"The men in the boat are not dropping in for tea and crumpets, Brian."

He was trying to be helpful, but washing my hands of the situation was not a solution I could accept. "I told you, the youngest girl was at The Dancing Bare where I—fuck. It's not that I'm afraid to speak up; that would be simple. I'm wrestling with this. I feel a personal responsibility, and it's scary. If I contact the sheriff, he'll almost certainly discover other issues. I don't want to see those kids get arrested or subjected to all kinds of red tape and psychological distress in addition to whatever kind of torture they've already been forced to undergo."

Brian finished his coffee. He'd had enough.

"Do whatever you want to do, Jenny. Whatever you need to do," he claimed. "Ginger's no doubt cooked up some half-assed scheme already. Just be careful, okay? Your Hurley girls said those people are dangerous. Let me know if I can help."

He went inside, and I sat there for a few minutes, clutching my now-cold mug while listening to the birds, voices of fishermen that carried eerily well over water, and early morning rustlings in the woods. I was trying to craft a sense of calm from a slow simmer that had roiled up to medium-high and threatened to erupt.

Dash nudged my elbow, always eager to play fetch.

Brian hadn't seen Cherry Delite on stage like I had. Or the way the "family" interacted (or didn't interact) when they were here on Thursday night. He hadn't studied my research closely. He hadn't seen the boat or the wreck of a place they were living in and the traffic. Or the Post-it note that asked for help.

He hadn't seen Cherry's pubescent body exposed on stage, paraded naked in front of a crowd of loud, lustful men, and heard them shout. He hadn't felt the urge to wipe her tears afterward.

I hoped Ginger and Ada had come up with some kind of plan, half-assed or not, because my ingenuity was depleted. It was tempting to go back to bed and pull my soft comforter over my head. Being with crowds of people these last few weeks had depleted my energy. I was worn out.

⁂

I felt better after I arrived at Ginger's. Rosie had shown up on her bike to help with the pizza dough, and we drove over there with Dash, where we discovered that a fresh batch of chocolate chip cookies had been secured in a plastic container. Ginger thought that Rosie should canoe over to Crow's Nest with cookies for the girls and attempt to bond. I didn't think that was the worst idea, but I wasn't convinced it was worthwhile. It was a long way to paddle and would take a lot of time. Besides, approaching the girls could be treacherous.

Fear not. Ginger had already organized the paddling portion. I was to use a neighbor's new boat to meander through the potentially dangerous Lost Arrow River with its boulders and crooked path, skimming underwater stumps and logs and submerged pilings from a long-ago railroad bridge (which was okay for the crummy motors that belonged to *The Last Resort* but this one was brand spanking new) and tow Rosie to Lake Sickle Moon. When we reached a sheltered place on the lake, Rosie would untie the line and paddle the canoe to the island with her offering.

"If you shear a pin on that danged river, my ass is in a sling," Ginger warned. "That boat's not like those rusty contraptions you've been using, but you need the power. I had to promise to hand over my firstborn son to borrow it."

Rosie was game and eager. The impressive boat was already tied to Ginger's dock. I used the bathroom to pee, grabbed a few cookies for myself, and we left with Ginger's and Ada's blessings. Dash was content to stay behind and gnaw on one of his old bones.

After a slow and cautious trip, we made it to Crow's Nest. The delivery of the cookies was simple. The watchdogs were either tied up or indoors, and the adults were not around. As she pulled up to shore and secured the canoe, Rosie waved the box of cookies at a girl who happened to be exiting the outhouse.

The girl quickly warned her. "You can't come here!"

Rosie climbed out of the canoe anyway and handed over the cookies, which the girl grabbed and stuffed beneath her shirt before scurrying into the woods.

We made it back down the river at a languid pace. Occasionally, I pointed out a maple sporting a scarlet branch, tamaracks turning yellow, and a birch tree beginning to glow. Sumac along the shore flagged bold red leaves.

Ada said, "We've been conferring back and forth, so we'll lay out the bare bones of our exploratory plan." The women had already called a meeting of volunteers for the next day, Sunday, since many who'd attended my Antler presentation had signed up to be involved. Rosie reminded me to call her dad.

The "bare bones" were woefully bare: someone would get access to the girls while the adults were preoccupied. That was it. At least others were taking the initiative so those bones could be fleshed out the next day, voted down, or drastically revised by a gathering of rational minds. I wouldn't have to be essentially involved. Despite his ridicule, I was not completely immune to Brian's warnings or Fawn's and Ruby's. In fact, Ada suggested we invite my exotic dancing friends to our Sunday morning meeting because they might have knowledge that would fortify the scheme. Since they recognized our problem, I knew Fawn and Ruby would be willing to assist.

Ginger was in her element. She had discovered a cause and dubbed Ada her deputy.

"I told you I needed something to occupy my time," Ginger said, "and now here we are!"

I was fading in and out; I needed a nap before the evening's pizza rush. We were on the porch, and I was in the rocking chair.

Ada suddenly perked up with news of the sale of Maus Haus. There'd been a bidding war that brought in twice the price she was asking, so Cynthia and I could include even more big-ticket items to Crow's Nest with our makeover. As soon as that place was free of its occupants, Cynthia and I could get to work.

I nodded agreeably and fought the urge to close my eyes.

Then, suddenly inspired, I asked Ada, "Is there really a hidden tunnel?"

"We found out there was supposed to be one, all right; it wasn't just some fly-by-night rumor that Gus invented, after all. Bootleggers used the cottage to hide liquor they brought down from Canada during Prohibition. The tunnel was a means for them to escape if they had to.

"I was told they always had a boat at the ready, hidden in the brush along the shore, behind the cottage. Probably near where you landed your canoe, Rosie. That way, if the Feds were on their trail, the gangsters could make a quick getaway.

"Gus loved to spin those tall tales," Ginger interrupted.

"You're right," Ada smiled. "He could be very convincing. That's the reason I wasn't sure he was being truthful with the kids. But you know what? Bobby and Susie searched every crumbling nook and cranny. It kept them occupied.

"Years ago, parents didn't worry about their offspring being protected all the time," Ada explained to Rosie. "We were cooped up in that pile during a storm, and the kids were rambunctious. Eventually, the winds died down, and we were able to get back to Maus Haus. They called their game Mobster Hideout. We visited several times a week after that. I preferred to sit outdoors, where the air was fresh. They made machine guns out of branches and sticks. Not just Bobby; Susie did, too. Bobby always loved guns, and after he was killed, I wondered if that's why he volunteered to go to Vietnam. We didn't let him have toy guns when he was a child. It was after President Kennedy had been murdered, you see, and following that, lots of parents didn't let their kids play with toy guns.

All my kids had were those sticks and branches to pretend with. I worried about that, but Gus said just let them play."

Rosie, impatient, asked if the kids ever discovered the tunnel.

"Yes! They found the tunnel. Even Gus was surprised. They also found a cache of empty old bottles and had a grand time exploring."

"And it's located...where?" I asked, now wide awake.

Ginger wanted to know if it could be accessed from inside the cottage.

Ada said she thought the tunnel led from a closet or maybe the kitchen sink. Or a trapdoor, or maybe there was a false panel in a wall. She had no idea.

"And where did the tunnel lead?" I asked. "Where was its terminus?"

"Out in the woods. I don't remember that part, either. I'm sorry."

It was all she had. I couldn't disguise my excitement as a brainstorm began to brew.

"*Under the woodpile!*" she shouted so suddenly that we all jumped. "There was a stack of wood next to the outhouse, wood for the fireplace. I think I recall Bobby exiting there and remarking he was glad the escape wasn't *through* the privy!" She laughed at the memory.

"If Bobby were here, he'd be happy to show you the tunnel and tell you everything about it. Susie might remember. I don't know what time it is in Paris right now. Let's give her a jingle."

Ada went ahead and placed the call. It wasn't as late at night as I'd thought, only ten in Paris. Susie and her husband had just finished serving dinner to their Saturday evening guests and were enjoying after-dinner liqueurs on their balcony. I could not conceive a more vast contrast in locales unless Ada had placed the call from Crow's Nest.

Mobster Hideout was recalled, and Ada related our situation to her daughter with impassioned details. When the phone was handed to me, I expressed my apologies, but Susie knew her mother and was remarkably patient. She said the island was mostly rock, and indeed the tunnel exited beneath a woodpile *beside* the outhouse. They'd only discovered it when Bobby entered an opening beneath the kitchen sink and then came up against a blocked exit in the dark. He pounded and yelled while Susie searched for the source of his fury, then removed chunks of firewood and uncovered a square of cement set into the ground. The slab had a chain attached to a ring and was very heavy. She had to call her father to help free her brother.

My wild idea could be the key to resolving a major hurdle in the plans for escape put forth earlier by the women. It would depend on good luck and guardian angels, but I'd weigh the details and share them the following day.

I gave Rosie a ride back into town and told her I'd deal with the pizzas myself that night. We were fairly busy until midnight when I told Brian I was heading up to bed because the only patrons left were the usual beer-drinking neighbors who'd be leaving soon, and they'd already purchased an extra pizza to take home.

With so much already on my mind, I now needed to figure out how to escape by using the tunnel at Crow's Nest. My mind flipped from one crazy scenario to another, taking into consideration everything that could go wrong.

I took a warm bath and tried to continue reading a murder mystery I'd begun, but I didn't get anywhere. Maybe I'd feel better if I made a list of everything I needed to accomplish; sometimes making a list helped to free my mind of the fear of forgetting details, which kept me awake.

The list was long. I didn't feel better. I added "ask Ada about tunnel" and then crossed it out.

By that time, it was nearly two in the morning.

I felt as if I needed to cry, but I couldn't make it happen.

At last, I got out of bed and gazed out the window of the flouncy bedroom Cynthia had designed. I had memorized that view long ago when my head hurt and I'd had trouble falling asleep. Still leaning in the window and breathing deeply of the fragrant night air, I heard Brian close the bar, heard the doors slam on the cars in the parking lot, and heard them drive away. Brian locked the door, switched off the lights, and wearily climbed the stairs.

He took a shower, walked into his bedroom, and I could see when his light went off beneath my closed door. I waited.

Dash was snoring with his head on my pillow. He'd given up waiting for me to join him.

The smooth wood of the hallway floor was warm beneath my bare feet. I shuffled silently over to Brian's door, which had not been closed all the way. I pushed it open.

"I could use a back rub," I whispered.

"Come here," he said softly.

I burrowed my head into the space between his chest and neck, savoring the warmth of his body, his clean, soapy smell—at one with his solid heartbeat and the steady rhythm of his breathing that matched my own. Finally, he pulled his quilt over both of us.

There was something I wanted to say, but he was whispering my name, softly stroking my back.

Then it was morning.

Twenty-One

I overslept on Sunday and woke in Brian's bed alone, reluctant to get up. When I did, Dash, confused, ran to greet me as if I'd been lost. And I had been in a dreamlike reverie that I didn't want to lose. I smiled while showering and felt renewed with the recollection of my soothing massage.

Then I was racing to leave for the big meeting at Ginger's, when my editor called to say he'd watched my Lotta Morgan video and was intrigued by *The Northwoods Nobody Knows*. He wanted to discuss the book idea. "When could I have a sample chapter?"

So, before I left for Ginger's, I got out my list from the night before and crossed off "discuss book idea with editor"—one thing at a time.

One task at a time. One step at a time. One pleasure...

I was confident we had enough pizza crusts in the freezer to handle tonight, and I was already an hour late. I needed coffee!

Ginger's driveway was clogged with cars; I had to park the Bug on the side of the road.

The crowd overflowed her kitchen and trailed out onto the porch. I recognized a few people, although I hadn't often gone into town. There was the woman from the Antler post office, another who clerked at the pharmacy, and the library director who smiled and nodded in my direction as I squeezed through the door. Larry Boone was leaning against the refrigerator with Rosie seated nearby.

Cynthia, well-groomed as always, stood at the kitchen table speaking, so I sought an inconspicuous corner.

"Men purchasing sex generally don't tell their friends about what they're doing," she said. "And survivors are not like most crime victims because they've been brainwashed and traumatized and are usually so terrified that they won't come forward of their own volition."

Cynthia paused, took a sip from a glass of water, and then took a deep breath. She explained that when she was thirteen, she was approached by a well-dressed couple in Mayfair, an upscale shopping mall near Milwaukee where she was hanging out with her pals. The couple took her aside and asked if she'd ever considered being a model because she was tall for her age and remarkably beautiful, they claimed. The man gave her a card that said they were modeling agents from Hollywood, and he asked if she'd agree to be photographed for their portfolio. She was so flattered that she left her friends and went along with them right away. They took her to a motel where she had a room with an adjoining door, and the next morning there was a salon appointment to have her hair styled and her nails and makeup done in preparation for the "photo shoot." She was excited.

After that, they returned to the motel. She was asked to pose on her bed, wearing lingerie. Cynthia was now apprehensive and became even more so when she noticed the man's camera was just a cheap Polaroid. He assured her that they'd be utilizing specialized, high-tech equipment once they got to California. Professional makeup artists would work with her, and shooting locations would be stunning. She might even meet some movie stars!

Flying to California was exhilarating, as she'd never flown before. Since she'd been having problems with her parents, spending the night at a friend's wasn't unusual. But traveling to California was a big step; she wanted to call her mother and tell her where she'd be.

"You call your parents, and they might as well be dead," the woman warned.

Cynthia explained to the group, "I was lucky because, at first, my girlfriends were excited for me. They waited a couple of hours, and when I didn't come back, they got worried. They talked it over, decided to call my mom, and described the couple. The police told my folks at least twenty other girls had been approached by that same duo that day at the mall with the goal of recruitment. I was the only one who was naive enough to go along."

Cynthia stared down at Ginger's kitchen table and was unable to continue.

"But you escaped, honey," Ginger said, patting her arm to encourage her.

"Yes, I got away. After a time," Cynthia said. "I'm sorry—I can't disclose the rest of what I was subjected to. I'm sorry."

I had not known this about my friend. What a shock! Cynthia took a deep, shaky breath, and I wanted to give her a hug. I heard Larry Boone rumbling behind me. It sounded like, "Those fucking bastards."

Cynthia collected herself and continued. "It's not just slick con artists haunting the malls that young girls should be wary of; it's also the friendly lady at the Stop & Go who asks, 'Honey, what are you doing here at eleven o'clock at night? Is something wrong? Can I help?' Recruiters are everywhere. Especially online, where girls can be groomed. This makes it problematic to hunt down predators. Craigslist is notoriously dangerous.

"Think back to what you were doing in eighth grade." Cynthia directed a firm gaze at each one of us. Children account for twenty-seven percent of all the human trafficking victims worldwide, and two out of every three child victims are girls."

She collapsed onto a kitchen chair and covered her eyes.

Ada stood up and noted, "I just want to say, Cynthia, your story breaks the hearts of everyone here. What you had to go through, well, it's nothing more than modern-day slavery. Evidently, it's a belowground business all over Wisconsin and the rest of our country. As the mother of a daughter, it makes me sick to the very depths of my soul."

Ginger introduced Fawn and Ruby as "special friends of Jenny's who are entertainers in the Hurley area and have helpful experiences that they want to share."

"Sex trafficking isn't something that happens only in big cities like Cynthia here talked about," Fawn said quietly. Obviously, she was nervous speaking in front of this crowd. Ginger gave her a glass of water. She took a sip and continued. "You might not realize it, but it's right here under your nose. Amber, Ruby, and I have seen proof of it. You've no doubt spotted these girls someplace, not having the slightest idea of who they were with or what they were up against. Some posters say, 'It's Happening Right in Front of You,' and I can tell you for sure that's a true fact. These kids are deprived of sleep and food and are physically tortured to boot. They might be told, like Cynthia was, that their families will be harmed or even murdered if they try to escape or tell anybody. Believe it or not, we've seen little girls forced to strip in front of grown men who are leering at them and cheering them on. You have no idea. The average age of girls who are sex trafficked is between twelve and fourteen. Men like 'em young."

"Fresh fish," Ada muttered to Ginger.

"My story is a little different," Ruby said when it was her turn. "When I was a little girl, I asked my mother where my daddy was because all of my friends had fathers. Finally, she admitted I was 'born of the boats.' When I got older, she explained to me what that meant. It's not exactly like what might be happening on the island, but I want to tell you because it's still going on, so you should be aware of it because, well, because we're Native Americans, nobody does much about it.

"When my mom was in her early teens, she ran away with her best friend, a Native American girl from Thunder Bay. They went to Duluth, and right away, they were trafficked to work on the ore boats. That's gone on for generations, especially with Indian girls. Mom said the average age of the girls was about fourteen. One girl was only ten, and most were from reservations. Because Duluth is an international port, there are a lot of seamen from all over the world looking for sex.

"To make money for her pimp, my mom was forced to move from bunk to bunk on the ore boat, selling sex to sailors. She traveled all over the Great Lakes for months at a time. She suffered physical injuries like black eyes and fat lips from pimps and johns. Once, she said, she was sexually assaulted with a crowbar. I cried when she told me about this, and she said, 'You wonder how could you let yourself do this, and why do these men want to do this to you? Eventually, you become in your mind what these people do and say you are. You begin to believe it.'

"My mom was able to get away when the boat docked in Cleveland, but she was already pregnant with me. I have no idea who my daddy is. No idea of his origin or ethnicity or where he might be, or if he's even alive. All I know is I was 'born of the boats.' My mother said she'd rather die than have me live like that."

"What happened to your girlfriend?" someone asked.

"She disappeared. That happens. Every year Indian girls just disappear. Nobody makes a fuss. I mean, it's upsetting to their families—what can they do about it? Minnesota has a terrible sex trafficking problem. Minneapolis is really bad."

That's when Ginger beckoned me to come out of hiding back there in the corner and reveal what I thought might be happening at Crow's Nest.

I shared what I had gathered and expressed what I felt were relevant details to support my suspicions so far. I began by relating Ada's denial that the cottage had been rented to the "family" we saw there.

Ada popped up. "That cottage has been vacant since Hector was a pup!"

Larry Boone added, "I'll vouch for that." His deep voice silenced the crowd. He blushed and issued a crooked smile as he muttered, "Not sure who Hector was, but I know it's been a helluva long time."

After a few moments, with Rosie's assistance, we added the bit about the "help" Post-it note stuck to the paper plate. I shared images I'd shot with my phone that evening in the bar of the group sitting at a table and eating pizza. Then Rosie and I passed around pictures we'd taken of the boat and SUV, the different men being transported back and forth to the island, shots of the girls outside on the lawn, and the two big curs who slept near the front steps. I played videos from the trail cams Toad and Stumpy had strategically placed that revealed the regularity of male traffic.

One woman remarked, "I'm ready to say those girls are captives, kept there to service the men. Like in those stockades."

I nodded in response. "Except there isn't a fence keeping them in."

"Hell, there's water. It's like a moat," Larry offered. "They can't escape; it's a pretty fair swim."

After that, Fawn showed stills of Cherry Delite from the video of Amateur Night at The Dancing Bare and compared them to a close-up I'd taken of her at the bar.

"The same girl. She was crying all the time she was performing on stage," Ruby admitted. "That little girl whose body, as you can see, is still that of a child. Fawn and I noticed bruises on her arms and legs. The big woman in charge of her, our friend Amber recognizes her from when she was on the circuit, too. The woman's name is Brandy, and Amber knew Brandy when she was a teenager, starting out as a dancer ten years ago."

They introduced Amber—plump, gray hair, wearing jeans and a chambray shirt. She had volunteered to help because she had also been a sex trafficking victim. "I've gained a few pounds since then and let my hair go natural, so Brandy didn't recognize me. In the sex trade, someone like Brandy is called the 'Bottom,' a woman who's in charge of supervising the girls. She collects the money, books motel rooms, and inflicts punishment. I kept out of her way when I saw her managing her victim at The Dancing Bare. She was always nice enough to me years ago and was a good dancer, but she aged out like I did. I never dreamed Brandy would end up doing something awful like this."

"What about the guy running the boat?" someone asked. "Does anybody have any idea who he is?"

"The girls would call him 'Daddy,' " Amber offered.

"He's not from around here," Ginger added. "Drives an old black SUV with a Florida tag; you can see that in Jenny's pictures. I called in a favor from Deputy Craig and had him run a check on his plate. Guy's name is Vernon Roscoe, and he has a history in the sex trade down south, served time in the good old Sunshine State."

The group became animated with talk of immediately turning the couple into the sheriff. Ginger called for quiet and expressed our concern about the well-being of the girls. She outlined, in general, the proposal she and Ada had devised.

"Ladies, we are going to free those girls ourselves."

Talking died down, and everyone was silent. Waiting.

"The thing is," Ginger explained again, "we don't want them to be arrested. We figure they should be treated with kindness and not punished for what they've been forced to do."

"That's where the rest of us come in," Ada said.

Hands were raised. Everyone had questions.

"Fawn and Amber and I came up with a plan last night that we merged with the rescue procedure drawn up by these two." Ruby indicated Ginger and Ada. "It's not perfect, but having had some experience in this field, so to speak, I think we will be able to gain some ground. You folks have already done a lot, coming together like this, and we are sincerely willing to help as much as we can to give whatever comfort to these kids that we can. After they've been freed and feel confident that they're safe, we're going to take good care of them and see that they get plenty of affection and counseling so they can go back to their families if they want."

"These girls are not criminals," Fawn added. "I can promise you they probably feel like they are, like Ruby's mom did. It's been beaten into them. So their rescue has to be sympathetic."

"That's why we need your help," Ginger declared to the group.

Larry Boone's deep voice was heard once again.

"Okay, most of you know me as the Grand Dragon around here, and I could say a lot more about that—mostly that I'm sorry. I'm done with all that Klan bullshit, and I apologize if we hurt any of you with the hijinks we raised. It's time I got involved with more positive actions instead, like this one. I want to help.

"My daughter, Rosie, told me about Crow's Nest and what she's seen happening there. She's about the same age as those girls in that cabin. I promise you right now that I'm committing myself to do whatever I can to help free those girls and look after them after that. Just tell me what you want me to pull off. I'll do anything. Go ahead and put me to work."

"We have to apprehend this man Vernon Roscoe and this woman Brandy," Ginger said, "to put a stop to what they're doing and make them pay a hefty price."

Ginger was finally at a loss for words. Her face was red, and she seemed flustered. The morning had been exhausting for her. It was time for Cynthia to take over.

"What we want to do now is break into smaller groups and discuss the details of how we'll proceed. We've made handouts that relate a variety of responsibilities, and you can check off what you're willing to do."

This was my opportunity to amend the basic plan with my bright idea regarding the tunnel. It wasn't a work of genius, though it realized a system with potential. There was unanimous approval.

Since I'd come up with the suggestion, however, it was universally assumed by all present that I'd carry out the dirty work myself. That's not what I'd intended!

It would seem cowardly to back out now.

"If you prefer not to be physically involved, that's all right; there are other roles you can take," Cynthia said. "Keep in mind that we have to keep our plan confidential. Feel free to leave if you'd rather not participate. No one's going to think less of you. We realize everyone has their priorities, their strengths, and I thank you from the bottom of my heart for coming out this morning for your support."

No one left.

The game was on.

Twenty-Two

Brian had a meeting in Chicago and flew out of Rhinelander early Tuesday morning. He had an appointment with his insurance company, and there were other business matters he didn't divulge, but he promised me he would be back in time on Thursday to help with the release of the girls that night.

Stumpy, Toad, and I oversaw the bar while he was gone. Rosie handled most of the pizza preparation. She would start school soon, and tourist crowds would increase with the arrival of leaf peepers for Colorama, but she thought she could help on Saturday nights. That was a relief.

Meanwhile, I repeatedly met with Ginger, Ada, and Cynthia to meticulously review the strategy for our "raid" (as Ginger liked to refer to it). We went over my tunnel concept to be sure it was physically possible, although we wouldn't know until the time came, and we were as convinced as we *could* be that the getaway plan was solidly in place. Thursday's forecast was for a cloudy night with the likelihood of rain, which meant the moon would be undercover.

Brian texted me Thursday at noon to let me know he was back.

Our staging area was at Lilypad, where we all met early for snacks and to re-examine each teammate's detailed instructions, which reminded me of something I'd overlooked—the watchdogs. I had no idea how ferocious they were, but howls of the old stockades' "bloodthirsty bloodhounds" still echoed, even though the long-deceased dogs may not have been bloodhounds or bloodthirsty. Ginger resolved this by digging in her freezer and bringing out two enormous blocks of venison. "Throw these at 'em," she said. "They're not thawed, so the meat should keep 'em out of the way for the time you need."

Eleven women from the Antler Women's Club had volunteered, plus Larry Boone, Amber, Ruby, and Fawn. We all wore our normal street clothes to Ginger's because we didn't want to look suspicious if we were seen before the raid. At the appointed hour, everyone (except for Larry, Ginger, and Ada) pulled on black sweatpants or jeans, black hoodies, or black T-shirts with long sleeves. And we had black gloves as well as black caps if needed. Yes, we were very warm. And before leaving, we sprayed ourselves with liberal doses of mosquito repellant, although our faces were the only flesh exposed.

Ginger and Ada would remain at Lilypad. We'd depart from there, where the girls would be delivered after their release to meet with Brian. He'd give them a brief examination and drive, along with Rosie, whose presence would hopefully help calm the girls, to meet Dr. Singh in Cedar Springs. The hospital staff had already been advised of the need for discretion, and we'd been assured that the girls would receive sensitive examinations.

Larry had a "dramatic" assignment.

To reiterate: to reach Crow's Nest on Lake Sickle Moon from Lilypad, one had to launch on Sundog from Ginger's dock and then maneuver up the Lost Arrow River for about a mile. It was a winding route on the chain of lakes I had taken many times. When Rosie and I made the trip nearly a week ago, we'd timed it as forty-five minutes one way, but that was with a powerful boat.

Toad drove my Bug to the secluded hideaway at the point of land just beyond the Maus Haus, where he would have a good view of Crow's Nest, as distinct as it could be in the dark. He was dressed in black, too, and would send me a signal when the time was right. The maneuvers were complex, and we'd tried to envision anything that might go wrong. Cellphone coverage was nonexistent, so we were compelled to depend on timing.

⁂

Lightning flashed on the horizon as night fell, and I could hear the distant rumble of thunder when Stumpy took Cynthia, Rosie, and me upriver in a Chris-Craft. The inboard motor was muffled compared to the big outboards some sportsmen favored. This allowed us to sneak up to the back side of the island, where the rear of Crow's Nest was barely apparent on a sunny day. Behind us, the others had boats with regular motors, but they'd kill them and row when they got close. We had work to do before they landed, anyway.

Without using our flashlights, we depended on the lambent glow from oil lamps in the cabin windows and brief flashes ahead of the approaching storm.

Almost at once, we faced the menacing dogs. They were not bloodhounds, but they were big, and remarkably, their barks were muted and hoarse. Perhaps their vocal cords had been cut? The venison weighing down my backpack piqued their interest, as Ginger had foreseen. I felt their paws on my shoulders as they clawed at the fabric.

I swung the backpack around, and Rosie unzipped it while they snorted and drooled. Then she dug in with her gloved hands and flung a hunk to each beast who jumped upon the meat with zeal. They were starving, and only later would we realize how pronounced their ribs had been.

Rosie and I wedged our way through saplings and undergrowth to stealthily reach the rear of the cottage while Stumpy and Cynthia headed left, toward the outhouse. We saw movement in the main room where, of course, there were no curtains or shades. Vernon (the daddy) and Brandy (his bottom) were already showing a burly man to the front door. We had to hurry.

I peered around the side of the cottage as the three of them went down the path to the dock and climbed into the boat, where its motor came alive.

When they'd advanced far enough, Toad's signal from across the water, a good imitation of an agitated loon, encouraged us to enter. Rosie tried the back door, but it was padlocked. That had been foreseen.

Cynthia and Stumpy were swiftly dismantling the pile of decomposed wood. Under it should be a square concrete slab with a chain attached to provide access to the tunnel. Rosie and I helped remove the remains of the woodpile and threw the crumbled bits of moldy bark aside.

The chain at the bottom of the rubble had not, as I had feared, completely rusted away. Stumpy grabbed it and began to pull until a narrow passageway beneath the concrete slab was exposed. A rank cloud of decay, damp earth, and rot rose to greet us.

"Good luck," Stumpy whispered as he and Cynthia went down to the shore to help the Women's Club ladies clamber out of their boats.

My job, now, was to enter the fetid tunnel while Rosie deftly aimed her flashlight inside to guide my access. I tied a bandana over my nose and mouth and got on my knees. The beam revealed a rocky route tangled with roots and cobwebs and little animal skulls. Susie had promised it led toward an egress in the kitchen. The rest of the crew had duties, each depending on this ambitious role.

I took a deep breath of fresh air and slid inside, feet first, shoving myself backward on my belly with my gloved hands. The damp ground crumbled beneath my body, and stones and broken glass impeded my progress, but I rammed it all aside with my shoes.

At last, even though I was backward, a soft gleam of light came over my shoulder. According to Susan Vogel, that would be coming from the exit beneath the kitchen sink. Be aware, she said, that the sink was known to drain gray water into a large plastic pail. Of course, that was many years ago.

I'd have felt more comfortable if I could emerge head first and see where I was going, but that was impossible, and the closer I grew, the more distinctly I heard girls' voices. Finally, the tunnel became more spacious, and I could turn my head. My backward advance was blocked by empty bottles that had been stuffed into the opening.

Breathing in that enclosed space was difficult, and I accidentally inhaled a bit of debris that caused me to cough. I had no choice but to kick at the bottles. A few of them broke and caused a major commotion.

As Susan had correctly recalled, a curtain still hid the access to the cupboard beneath the sink, where a pipe from a hand pump extended down into a well. I pushed a plastic jug of bleach aside with my foot and gave myself one last shove so I could squeeze my body out onto the worn linoleum. It was a tight fit, like being born, and there was plenty of water broken because I spilled the pail that the sink drained into when I emerged.

With all the clatter I'd caused, the voices were silenced. A flickering oil lamp stood on a counter that partially screened the kitchen and served as a peninsula.

Larry Boone had provided me with a detailed sketch of the interior, so I knew where I was. A sink and a small counter were along the wall. The kitchen area formed a kind of "L." Two doors opened toward the rear, most likely bedrooms. Nearby, the enclosure was lined with gallon bottles of fresh water, cans of Spam, tuna, Dinty Moore beef stew, and bags of rice and beans. The interior was crowded—maybe 24' x 24' if one included the other rooms.

I hoisted myself up as quickly as I could, which wasn't very fast and involved a groan on my part. The jug of bleach fell over. I grabbed it before it spilled much; the plastic cap was loose.

A girl appeared in a nearby bedroom doorway and began to scream when she saw me.

"Quiet," I said. I tore off my bandana and fumbled forward to grasp her. "I want to help you escape."

But she pulled away shrieking and clung to her friends.

"The pizza lady," she shouted. "The pizza lady's here!"

The bedroom, probably the larger of the two, held three foam mattresses squeezed beside one another on the floor. They were so closely aligned that they nearly touched, but a crudely arranged series of shower curtains strung on wires separated them into individual enclosures, like stanchions. The old log walls had been painted over with sickly bubblegum pink, and posters of pop stars and ads for beauty products futilely mimicked a teenager's bedroom. A battery-operated lantern illuminated the disturbing scene that included a variety of stuffed animals.

Cherry and the other girls huddled together on the middle bed. They wore skimpy short pajamas made of flimsy material and were not very clean.

"Where'd you come from?" one of them asked me. "Vernon and Brandy always lock the doors when they leave."

"There's a secret tunnel, and we're going to use it while they're gone. I want to help you get away. But we have to be fast!"

The girls didn't seem to grasp my urgency. Instead, they latched onto one another, trembling and sniffling, unable to budge.

"That girl from the pizza place brought us cookies. Do you have cookies?"

"There will be cookies," I promised. "Now, if you want to get out of here, we have to go *right now.*"

Still, they remained, cowering.

I sat beside them on the scrunched-up sheets and sheltered them with my arms, like wings. "Listen," I said slowly, touching each of them gently. "I know why you're here. I know you've each been hurt. One of you asked for help, but maybe you're scared to break away. I'm scared, too. But if we don't hurry up and get out, we'll *all* be in danger."

"What are we supposed to do, anyway?" the oldest asked dully.

They didn't flinch when a loud crack of thunder shook the cabin and seemed to rip open a seam of rain that pummeled the roof. I suspected they'd been drugged with anti-anxiety meds. Poor Cherry could barely keep her eyes open; she was limp and wilting.

"Do you have sweatpants or jeans?"

Nope," one girl laughed. "We're not supposed to cover up for visitors, even if we're cold. We just had a visitor."

"Sweatshirts? I know you have hoodies. I saw you wearing them."

The oldest girl sorted through a pile of dirty laundry on the floor and pulled out three of them, one at a time.

"Put them on, and each of you bring a towel. Now! I mean it. This is your chance, and if you don't take it, you'll be left behind."

"Brandy's going to be so pissed off."

"Fucking pissed off," the oldest girl laughed.

"She'll beat us up again," Cherry sobbed softly. "Vernon, too!"

We were running late.

"Get some towels. *Please!*"

"What about Cherry? Can't you see she's out of it?"

"I'll take care of Cherry," I assured them. "Just get moving. I'll meet you by the kitchen sink."

Two of them ran off, and I was left with Cherry, who was nearly comatose.

"Cherry," I whispered, "can you stand up?"

The storm was on top of us, the roof was leaking, and I could no longer hear Toad's yodeled warnings because of the heavy rain and thunder. Instead, I heard Rosie's voice outside the bedroom window.

"Jenny, the boat turned back! Get 'em out now!"

I helped Cherry with her hoodie, then grabbed her under her arms. She tried her best to walk while I dragged her into the kitchen. The floor was a mess, but I bent over in front of the sink and pointed to the beam of Rosie's flashlight that extended down the rocky shaft.

"See that? It's the entrance to a secret, old-fashioned tunnel where kids used to play. You don't need to be scared because that's how I got in. Now, one of you must be brave and be the first to climb up and out. You'll have to crawl with your elbows and your knees. Put the towel in front of you for your elbows, then kneel on that, then take a towel from the girl behind and put it in front again. Got it? The idea is to pass the towels along for the others to use."

"I'll go first," the oldest of the girls volunteered. "Show me how to get inside that stinking rat hole."

We swept away all the bottles with our arms, and two of the girls crept into the cavity beneath the sink. The second wriggled to pass a towel to the girl ahead so they would crawl on thin terry cloth instead of dirt and broken glass. With their bodies in the way, Rosie's flashlight was barely visible above, yet I could hear her welcoming voice urging them on. They were barefoot, and I hoped they wouldn't incur any injuries; there hadn't been time to hunt for their shoes.

Cherry was the last, and I had to plead with her to focus. Just as I pushed Cherry far enough to shut the fabric closure behind my butt, the front door opened.

"Jesus Christ, you guys want to get me struck by lightning? Only a horse's ass takes a boat out in a thunderstorm. Holy shit."

"Quiet!" I urged Cherry. "Don't move. Don't make a sound."

"Goddamn phone," the deep voice growled. "Probably dropped it when I shucked my pants. Let me go have a look around, okay?"

That was Larry's voice; he was playing the "john" for the night, although he would never have touched the girls.

There were stomping noises, frantic voices, and mattresses shoved around. Much cluttering and confusion in the girls' room. Larry was doing his best to detract any attention to the kitchen area and kill time.

"Now move!" I urged the girls. "Faster! You're safe. It's okay. Just keep going."

"I need my stuff," one of the girls called back. "My makeup, my earrings."

"I want my backpack," Cherry sobbed.

I promised that once they were safely out, I'd go back and recover all their belongings.

Then, another male voice. "What the hell's happened to the girls? Where'd my little pussies disappear to?"

"They're not here?"

"Brandy, check the back door. Make it quick."

"It's still locked."

I called softly up to the girls, "You're almost there."

"They must be hiding somewheres. What the fuck's going on?"

Her foot hit my face and dislodged my glasses as Cherry squirmed backward. "My backpack's got my stuff..."

"I'll get it, sweetheart," I assured her, more loudly than necessary. "I promise. Just try to climb faster. Please! Your friends are up there, waiting."

I pushed back and shoved myself into the kitchen again. That seemed to convince Cherry, for she scrabbled ahead as hastily as she was able.

"Go!" I shouted, leaning toward her, no longer caring if anyone else heard. Rosie's beam was brighter now, and I could see Cherry as she emerged into the night. My job was done.

"Okay, whose goddamn fat ass is this?" Daddy Vernon stood behind me. He kicked my leg with his boot. He aimed and struck again, much harder this time. "What's going on, bitch? What'd you do with my little girls?"

"Hey...wait a minute," I heard Larry try to hold Vernon back from hurting me as I crouched on the floor.

Despite the rain, I hoped everything was progressing as we'd planned. Amber, Fawn, and Ruby should be welcoming each girl as she surfaced from the tunnel, and then Rosie would be wrapping them in soft blankets.

"It's that slut from the bar," Brandy said as she bent over to look at me, then glanced under the sink. "There's a tunnel here, Vern. I think she smuggled them out!"

When she backed up next to Vernon, Brandy flashed a switchblade from a pocket of her jeans.

"Goddamn, she let my little girls escape," Vernon explained, turning to Larry. "We need to catch 'em before they get away! Hurry!"

Vernon started for the door, but Brandy lunged toward me with her knife. "This is for letting 'em go," she snarled. Larry tried to grab her.

I was now on my knees on broken glass, with one hand grasping the nearly full jug of Clorox. The cap flew off as I swung it toward her, knocking the knife away. Bleach splashed onto Brandy's face and in her eyes. She screamed and then fumbled to follow her partner into the storm.

Larry helped me to my feet. "Good job," he said before going after the couple.

The woods would now be coming alive with women dressed in black who'd emerge from the shadows to ambush the two of them. Larry would help bind their legs and arms with electrical tape and seal their mouths with tape, too.

Meanwhile, the girls would be guided to waiting boats where more

Women's Club ladies waited with comforting hugs. They would all be taken to the boat landing near Maus Haus, where vans would deliver everyone to Ginger's. And from there, Brian would take the girls to the hospital at Cedar Springs. I leaned against the wall to catch my breath.

Cynthia came in the front door and cried, "I'm here, Jenny."

Together, we filled pillowslips with everything we could find that might belong to the kids. The rain was diminishing when we finished and located Stumpy with his Chris-Craft. I paused a moment to remove my backpack from the entrance to the tunnel and glanced over at the lone figures bound and writhing on the grass. I hastily delivered a solid kick to Vernon's hip and would have given him another if Larry had not pulled me away.

"That's enough, Jenny. You can let 'em alone."

The dogs continued to gnaw the frozen meat.

Stumpy guided the Chris-Craft to the boat landing near Maus Haus, where Cynthia and I found Toad.

I'd hooked up a landline at the Maus Haus that afternoon. Toad had been instructed to use it a few minutes ago to telephone 911 and play a recording of my voice saying there was an alarming disturbance on the island on Sickle Moon that frightened me.

"All set," Toad assured us. "Sheriff's on his way, so go ahead."

The men took off, heading for Ginger's by Chris-Craft with the girls' belongings. Cynthia and I drove the Bug over to Maus Haus, where we waited for the sheriff, who appeared in about fifteen minutes in response to "my" 911 call.

The storm had moved on.

"We saw lights and heard noises, and there were girls screaming over there," Cynthia told the officers, pointing toward Crow's Nest.

"Mrs. Ada Vogel, who owns this place," I referred to Maus Haus, "also owns the vacant cottage on the island. No one's supposed to be there, so that's why we called. "Maybe it's kids having a beer party," I suggested with a casual nod.

"Or doing drugs and stuff," Cynthia added with incredible sincerity.

"You really should check it out, just in case. You never know these days."

The sheriff was no longer paying attention to us. He and his deputy had no way to reach the island without a boat of their own. I recalled the dented canoe and paddles in the shed, and after calling for aid, they'd have to employ that.

We thanked them for coming and headed back to Ginger's in my Bug. During our few private moments in the car, I praised Cynthia for her bravery in sharing her abduction experience. I was curious to know how she'd gotten away, but I resisted that query. The fact that she'd been able to escape was knowledge enough.

"It's a part of my life I've been repressing," she said. "Every once in a while, I wake up at night, and that torment reappears. I only disclosed it the other day because I wanted to emphasize it could happen to anyone. And to let everyone know their courageous efforts could have rewards."

We were both exhausted, but we decided to get together the next afternoon to visit the newly vacant Crow's Nest, check with Larry, and assess what could be done. Might as well get started right away.

At Lilypad, the women had removed their rain-sodden black clothing and changed into the clothes in which they'd left home. Seeing these mothers and aunts and grandmothers high-fiving one another and recounting the adventure was gratifying. Ada was pouring mugs of hot cider to ward off a wet chill and to accompany a huge platter of what else, chocolate chip cookies. The girls had already enjoyed their share and were on their way to the hospital with Brian and Rosie. The Hurley girls—as they were now being referred to—had followed closely behind.

There were many smiles but still unease about the girls' future welfare. I said I'd keep in touch with everyone so we could follow their progress.

Ginger welcomed us warmly, but after a short time, she encouraged everyone to go home. "We've all done enough for one night, and I know you must be pooped. I am, anyway."

Brian called from Cedar Springs and said the girls had been bathed and were resting. They would remain at the hospital for several days for further medical and psychological review.

"We'll have to wait and see what tomorrow brings," Ginger added. "But before you all take off, I've got something I want to elucidate."

She led me into the center of the kitchen and pressed her cheek onto mine. The room was silent as everyone strained to listen.

"As all of you know, Jenny, here, came up north to learn about the 'Northwoods nobody knows.' That turned out to be digging up information about Lotta Morgan's murder and the 'soiled dove' children who were kidnapped by Maud Cassidy and trapped in stockades.

Now, it's because of those poor forgotten girls that Jenny discovered with me, that we all came together and did what we did tonight. Grandmothers, mothers, aunts, sisters, and fathers—we mounted our own rescue.

"We freed Crow's Nest from evil. We were a success. We are all heroes. Every single one of us. We stepped up and dammit, we were tough. We can be proud of that."

Twenty-Three

Bluegill is still my favorite retreat, and I'm diligently working on my new book at its scarred kitchen table. This is the calmest place at the resort right now, with the entire place under construction. Bluegill's days are numbered, and sadly, it will soon be razed. By then, I'll hopefully be settled in my lovely new condo at Aspen Glen, planning an over-the-top Thanksgiving dinner for my family and friends.

Much has happened since our dramatic rescue of the girls at Crow's Nest in late summer. For example, one chilly Monday night, as our weekly neighborhood bonfire drew to a close, northern lights illuminated the sky with greenish opalescent sheets of color that danced in a peculiar rhythm. Some folks were convinced strange sounds could be heard. I had never seen the aurora borealis, and the sight stirred me to tears.

On another memorable evening, I was invited to accompany a group of tourists on a Wolf Howl. After dark, we traveled into the Chequamegon-Nicolet National Forest in an old school bus and hiked to a known wolf rendezvous site. I learned to howl, and eventually, my feeble attempts were answered by a lonely cry that rose into the night like a brilliant tendril of smoke. It was my own personal link to the wild world. The memory of that moment still gives me goosebumps.

Happy news also about the girls we saved from Crow's Nest. Following tender nurturing by Fawn, Amber, and Ruby, in addition to healing treatment with experienced counselors, each girl managed to adjust to a new kind of normal. One could not hope for more than that. Lakeland County Social Services praised the Hurley women for their caring custody and supervision, and the women from the Antler Women's Club were honored for their resolve.

Cherry, whose real name is Katie, had to be held at the hospital for nearly a week due to internal injuries and medical treatment for numerous STDs. The other two had less serious sexually transmitted diseases and were released after several days in the custody of their "guardians," Amber and Ruby. All three needed multiple antibiotics, supplemental nourishment, and sessions of cognitive processing therapy, which they received as outpatients.

Katie was eventually sent home with Fawn, but before leaving the hospital, she asked to see Rosie and me to express her tearful gratitude for noticing the Post-it note. We all became tearful and had a good cry and a group hug.

The "blood-curdling" dogs, big old starving curs, were held at the Lakeland County Humane Society and eventually adopted, to my relief.

Brandy Collins and Vernon Roscoe made court appearances where they were convicted of child sex trafficking and each sentenced to twenty-five years in federal prison. Vernon was also ordered to pay $50,000 to each of his victims. The assistant U.S. attorney argued in the government's sentencing memorandum: "The victims will carry the emotional scars of the defendants' actions for the rest of their lives."

Similar situations in other, probably urban, locations may require more stringent government and legal obligations. But we are a small, sparsely populated northern county where nearly everyone knows one another, and trust is paramount. That's why the unlawful occupancy of Crow's Nest was conspicuous.

Last Sunday's Milwaukee paper carried an interview with the director of an anti-trafficking group, who said, "Everyone's feeling like this is overtaking the northern, quiet area of Wisconsin." He described a circuit from Milwaukee to Madison, up through the Wausau area, and then northward to Minocqua and Mercer, where pimps move their "product" from place to place. Their alliance places bars of soap printed with a hotline for victims to call for help in motels and truck stops where sex trafficking occurs.

⋇

Cynthia and I began working again with Larry Boone, and even before we tore it down, the Antler realtor offered the new Crow's Nest as an exclusive property. "Own your own private island," she exclaimed. The glossy periodical *Lake Homes of the Midwest* featured plans for a timber-frame home with environmentally appropriate landscaping and a heated in-ground pool. We're going all out with the most luxe conveniences. By utilizing her plentiful proceeds from the Maus Haus sale, Ada is relishing her involvement. Quite honestly, it's fun to team up with Cynthia again.

Here at The Last Resort, changes are taking place that had their genesis in the wake of the Crow's Nest escapade. A simple summary will not be sufficient, so a recapitulation of events is in order:

⋇

I was so drained when I got back from Ginger's the night of the rescue that I collapsed on the scruffy loveseat, unable to marshal the energy to shower and scrub away nasty organisms I could imagine swarming around in my hair and underwear. Now freed from emotional and physical exertion, there was a vast release of adrenaline. We were all home and safe. The girls were safe. Brandy and Vernon were in custody. Crow's Nest had been evacuated. It had been a very long day. Another item to cross off my list of things to do.

Brian's steps on the stairs sounded equally tired, but he still managed a teasing gibe.

"I'll get the iodine and bandages, Jenny."

He nudged Dash aside and collapsed next to me. "C'mon, let me have a look! You must have some wounds from crawling through that tunnel. The girls had cuts from broken glass and other trash, and their feet were a mess, too."

He lifted my filthy shirt. There were superficial abrasions but not a lot of blood. Tomorrow I'd have a hell of a bruise on my leg from Vernon Roscoe's boot, but I'd be damned before I'd mention that to Brian, and I told him I'd apply antibiotic salve on the scratches before I went to bed. Truthfully, I wouldn't have minded a hearty "Congratulations!"

"You did good," he said. There. That was nice. He cupped my chin in his hand and gave me a gentle kiss. "We need to talk."

I nudged Dash aside with my elbow and dragged myself into the shower. After scrambling through that squalid burrow, I was relieved not to find a cluster of little mouse bones, bat guano, or something worse.

What did that mean? *We need to talk*?

Brian was ready to take a shower when I got out.

"We need to talk," he said again when he passed me.

We need to talk. That phrase usually preceded something dire, like a breakup or an admission of infidelity. Whatever it was, I didn't want to hear it tonight or maybe ever. Yet I waited on the loveseat, still toweling my hair.

I tried to beg off. "I'm really tired, Brian," I protested when he joined me. "Can't this wait? Please?"

I knew he must be super exhausted, having flown back from Chicago early that morning—a surreptitious trip that intrigued me—but an explanation could be postponed. He slouched by my side in pajama bottoms while he dried his curly hair and beard.

"I have good news and better news," he said. "We *could* wait, but due to time constraints, it would be wise to have a discussion tonight.

"First," he said, reaching for my hand and bringing it to his lips, "I want to thank you for what you did. I know you had help from a lot of good people, but if you hadn't raised the alarm in the first place, those girls would still be getting raped every day. I admire you for that."

Still holding my hand, he leaned back against the sofa and closed his eyes for several minutes as if deliberating what he wanted to tell me next. It must have been momentous. Then he sighed deeply and muttered, "What the hell. Why don't we just go to bed?"

He led me to his bedroom, where we both fell asleep without a word.

※

Friday morning, the sheriff was there before breakfast and demanded to speak to Brian. The hospital had called about the girls and the circumstances prior to their admission. So, Brian was tied up with the police while I headed over to Ginger's to have coffee with her, Ada, and Cynthia, who brought fresh cinnamon rolls (could she be more perfect?). We sat on the porch to evaluate and bask in our success.

Before we met Larry Boone at Crow's Nest, Cynthia wanted to show me the progress that had been made on my Aspen Glen condo. The basic structure was now framed in, so it was fun to walk around and ascertain the actual size of each room. I'd already chosen my kitchen cabinets, asked that the study have built-in bookshelves on each wall, and looked at carpet samples. Hundreds of choices were yet to be made, but thank goodness, not right away. One thing at a time.

After that, the visit to Crow's Nest was brief yet consequential. All three of us agreed the place must be razed and burned.

When I returned, Rosie was loading pizzas with toppings, and the bar was getting busy. She was in good spirits now that the girls had been rescued. Of course, I shared her pleasure, but beneath my satisfaction, "We have to talk," stirred deviously. That remark, albeit suppressed, had grown more ominous as the day wore on.

I couldn't talk to Brian until the final customer left the bar, and by then, I had already changed into my customary sleeping gear. The night was growing cool, so I reached for a worn fleece throw on the porch that I knew was clean but nevertheless carried signs of Dash. I didn't mind. I am one of those goofy people who enjoys a sniff of her dog's paws.

Brian pulled up a chair, facing me. This was when he revealed that he'd checked in with Dr. Singh during the day and apprised me of the girls' recent status. I had a few questions about their continued treatment and whether their families had been informed, but he didn't yet have a definitive answer.

I was uneasy, knowing something else was coming, something I was certain I wouldn't be happy to hear. I pushed back my chair. I didn't mean to pace, but I did take a few steps because...well, I was frightened.

"That's not why we need to talk, is it? About the girls?"

"You're right." He stood. "It's not. Let's go for a walk."

The cool, dewy grass always felt good on my bare feet. I figured we wouldn't be going very far but kept the fleece around my shoulders. We paused by the fish cleaning shack. He took my left hand in his and gripped it so hard that it hurt, but I didn't want to pull it back. Due to the odor of fish guts, it was not the most romantic of settings. He pulled me close and wrapped me in an embrace that was so consuming I could feel his heart racing.

"I told you last night I had good news and better news," he said, softening his hug.

Now he seemed nervous and stammered. This was not typical behavior.

"I'm going to start with the good news. But you might not think it is. Good, I mean. I'll admit it's not exactly what I had in mind, either, but I had it checked out, and the proposition's solid. There'll be necessary approvals to get from the State of Wisconsin, agreements to be signed—"

"Brian, for God's sake," I interrupted. "Get on with it."

"While I was in Chicago, I met with a development enterprise that made a serious offer for this place. Very generous."

I was certain, now, that this was a disturbing disclosure. Yet I had no authority to express an opinion as it was described rather obliquely. Most likely on purpose.

Brian cleared his throat. He was terribly ill at ease.

"Be more specific," I said.

"Hospitality consulting for resorts," he replied. I met with them. They negotiate development, handle strategic planning, community relations, management—"

"This is bullshit, Brian. Who are these people, really?"

"They offer their services to tribal nations."

"In other words, they want to develop a tribal resort and gaming casino.

Right here? Where we're standing?"

"Here."

"What the hell?"

"Wait, it's not that *I* want to develop it; they'll be in charge. And it's a Native American company. They know what they're doing. They've been in existence for over thirty years."

"That's your *good news,*" I replied, roughly thrusting him away with both hands. The fleece fell on the grass, and the malice in my voice was unmistakable. I was so astonished I could barely speak.

"They take charge of everything from the ground up," he argued.

I was silent only because I was trying to temper my response. I turned aside.

"Brian, you know I have nothing against Native Americans."

"Okay, I understand you're not tickled pink."

"*I think you're out of your goddamn mind!*" I sputtered. "I can't come up with enough vile profanity to express how much I despise that idea and how much I hate you at this very moment for even *entertaining* such an egregious plan!"

"Calm down, calm down," he murmured, reaching for me and attempting to pull me back toward him again. "I'm not finished."

I fought his efforts. "You cannot allow that to happen! What in hell were you thinking?"

My gestures were wild as I flailed in disgust, and I wouldn't shut up.

"I'll fight you, Brian, and I'll get everyone in Lakeland County to join me in the battle. You know I can do it. Imagine the chaos if you go ahead with this! The enormous crowds! The drunken clamor carried across the water! Think of everyone else with a home on Star Lake! There's no link to the Northwoods in this offer and no special regard for this historical site. What about the peace and quiet everyone seeks up north? When did you turn from being a good guy into such a money-grubbing fuckup?"

"Calm down, Jenny," he urged. "I'm not finished."

"Oh, so now it's the *better* news. After that, is there going to be the best news?"

"You might agree that the *better* offer is the *best*."

"I don't—"

He interrupted my dismissal and finally caught my arm. "Hold on. Listen to me. There's another offer. It's personal. I need your authorization to go ahead."

That made no sense. I didn't have a stake in the resort nor any cash to provide. My only investment had been emotional, too deeply so, and my lengthy stay had clearly been more of a debit than an advantage.

I tried to shake off his grip as he patiently asked me, several times, to shush.

"Ginger came to me a few weeks ago with an initiative. It seems she realized a sizeable windfall several years ago, and Lily did, too, which she bequeathed to her. Ginger was guarded about the source, but she said she's always wanted to own a resort of her own where she could be the one to give the orders and make the rules. For most of her life, she's worked at resorts, made beds, scrubbed toilets, tended bars, and helped the owners get by. Done the grunt work. That's how she phrased it.

"So, she offered to buy out half of my interest in The Last Resort."

That took a few moments to register.

"Ginger? Only half? Why not buy the whole thing?"

"Because she's old, for God's sake! Because she wants my help running it," Brian replied. "She has her sights set on turning it into a retro resort with a 1940s vibe. 'The Last Resort: The Way Family Resorts Used to Be' is how she put it. She blamed you for putting this bug in her ear.

"And she insists on having you join us in the operation. Meanwhile, Ada's moving her things up from Madison to live at Lilypad."

I think I muttered, "Huh?"

"There hasn't been a good time to discuss it, with everything else going on. I should've mentioned it to you earlier because now it's almost too late."

The remainder of my response remains foggy. I know I must have expressed surprise, astonishment, alarm, and confusion—every entry in the thesaurus under shock. Dash, who'd set off for the lake to check things out, ran back up the hill to see what was going on with his freaked-out mom.

"All summer you've seemed fond of this place, Jenny. And I think you've been reasonably happy when you weren't banged up and bandaged. We all enjoy your friendship, and it feels like home with you and Dash around.

"Now that you'll be living within walking distance of the resort, it makes sense, doesn't it?"

"I don't know," I faltered. "This is crazy."

"The thing is, we don't have much time. The developers stopped in to look the place over that weekend when you were in Hurley. We discussed some details with their attorneys on Wednesday when I was in Chicago, and they're flying up tomorrow morning to discuss the final transaction. They're very determined. They're offering me a ridiculous amount of money."

"More than Cynthia offered?" I asked with what little composure I was able to generate. But I meant it. "Can't you be gracious and at least owe Cynthia first dibs?"

My mind was whirling—too much to think about and contemplate all at once.

With silent determination, I flung the throw around me and headed toward Bluegill with Dash at my heels. It was after midnight by then, and the landscape was hushed except for loons and random woodland rustlings. After a while, I heard Brian close and lock the door to the bar.

⁂

Yes, I had grown to savor this relative wilderness. At night, I experienced an altered awareness—unlike the city, where a woman walking alone required undeniable precautions.

I also enjoyed living here because of the friends I'd made. And, yes, because I was with a man I'd grown to love. There, I said it.

On the pier in front of Bluegill, I watched the bottomless cosmos above me melt into the lake. Memories of viewing the Pleiades meteors with Brian were poignant to recall.

I dropped the throw and stripped off my pajamas. Then I sat on the edge of the dock, dangled my feet in the warm water, and slid down into it, which felt like entering another world. I'd been here all summer and hadn't even gone swimming; how crazy was that? Among childhood friends back in my little hometown, skinny dipping at night was called a "chocolate dip." I'd only tried it a couple of times, but I enjoyed the fluid feeling on my body. It was slick and sensual.

Even though I was a strong swimmer, I loved to float with my arms and legs spread out and let the water support my body. It's kind of like the yoga *Savasana*, where you can gain access to a higher state of consciousness when you lie on your mat that way. While floating, it was fascinating to gaze at the brilliant stars on that clear, calm night. It seemed the immensity would swallow me if I stretched out my arms and let myself go.

Dash paddled around and bumped into me with his snout every so often.

More than three months ago, my stormy visit to this beautiful setting had been a painful misadventure. And when the Hurley girls brought me back from my Dancing Bare debacle, this *was the last resort* for me. I had nowhere else to go.

I tried to empty my mind, but waves washed onto the grassy shore, and in my reverie, I was swept back to childhood summers when these night sounds outside our little cottage at Birchwood Lodge were so comforting. "Think of a place that makes you happy," Mom used to say, bending over my bed when I was sick with an upset stomach. I always chose a site with the fragrance of pine and woodsmoke, the loons in the night with their tremulous calls.

I ached, then, for my childhood. I wanted to close my eyes, and when I opened them, magically be back again with my family: young, unblemished, with all my mistakes and blunders erased, all of life's possibilities lying wide open ahead of me. That profound sense of wonder—an inner child still vibrant, free, inspired, and full of joy.

I climbed back on the dock, where Dash licked salty tears that seeped from my eyelids when I bent down to gather my clothes. I swaddled the fleece around me and found the rickety metal bed in Bluegill, where I flopped, utterly depleted. Dash joined me and nestled with his warm, musky presence.

I had no idea how late it was; I didn't care.

⁂

The squeak of Bluegill's screen door woke me. Dash whimpered softly at the sound of Brian's voice: "Now, this was the only cottage left somewhat intact by the storm."

Heavy feet shuffled into Bluegill's kitchen. I could vaguely sense the bulk of strange men crowded together and smelled smoke from a cigar. There was laughter. I imagined them taking in the blue tarp over the ceiling, the old gas stove with the tin can labeled "grease," the rumbling refrigerator, and the warped knotty pine walls.

"Jesus, I haven't seen a Kelvinator icebox since we sold my great-grandma's place."

"Certainly, a gorgeous spot. Marvelous. Our dining room should overlook the water right here. Ambiance is significant; it's everything. We can carry this exquisite natural setting and spectacular view through all aspects of our design. Don't want to put the slots and tables up front with scenery like this. Add a nice flagstone terrace for relaxing with cocktails on the shore.

"The hotel, though. I want even more floor-to-ceiling fenestration in the rooms than we previously planned. I like the idea of competing with that Star Lake Inn up the road that calls itself 'eco-friendly.' "

They hooted and snorted. "Our crowd will have more lucrative things to do." Even heartier laughter. "We might even want to hire a stripper now and then, just to liven things up. Maybe during deer hunting season? Compete with those bawdy bars up the road."

Why was Brian so quiet during this discussion?

My bare feet hit the cold linoleum floor with a thud, and I burst from the bedroom like a freaking banshee, grabbing the fleece just in time to shield my naked body.

"No!" I shouted. "Get out of here. Go!"

"Jenny," Brian uttered, surprised,

Dash, at my side, began to growl.

"This little sweetheart your girlfriend, or what?" one of the men asked Brian.

"Out of this cabin and off this property," I screamed. "*Now!*"

"What gives this bitch the right to tell us what to do?" the tallest of them demanded. "Jesus Christ!"

"My sympathies," another man laughed.

I pulled the fleece tighter. "Things have changed since Brian met you in Chicago," I proclaimed.

"Oh, is that so?" The tall man queried disdainfully and grinned. I wanted to kick him in his junk, but I was too short to make that move.

Brian broke his silence.

"When we met earlier this week, I did mention that another possible option was on the table," Brian explained at last. He placed one arm around my shoulder and, with the other, adjusted the fleece that had slipped during my crazy gestures to reveal my left breast. Not a big deal. Both nipples had appeared rather boldly in public not long ago.

What the actual fuck is going on, Brian? You mean you let us haul our asses all the way up here from Chicago."

"How much longer did you intend to twiddle your thumbs before informing us you weren't going to entertain our proposition?" the tall man addressed Brian angrily.

"Jenny and I had unfinished business to discuss," he apologized. "But I think it's been resolved."

He hugged me closely.

"He means the answer is no," I stated bluntly, calmly. "No, you cannot build a resort and gambling casino on this property. And yes, Brian, I accept the offer you and Ginger made last night."

"Gentlemen," Brian gestured toward the door.

The men stood motionless, as if in shock. Then they nearly stumbled down the steps in their haste to escape. We watched from Bluegill's porch as they fumed and flapped in confusion. Their shiny Oxford shoes had slick soles, and they slipped while attempting to climb the damp grass on the hill. At last, the group scrambled into their rental car and drove off, presumably to the Rhinelander airport and their private jet.

Dash ran after them, barking. He thought it was a game until he was distracted by a squirrel.

"We woke you up," Brian said. It wasn't a question.

I was so excited. "*The Last Resort: The Way Family Resorts Used to Be.* I love it! Ginger and I already have snapshots set aside that we need to have enlarged and framed, and those postcards, too. There has to be a swimming beach," I was clutching him and speaking too fast. "We could bring in truckloads of fine, clean sand and put it over there, where the first cabin used to be. With comfortable Adirondack chairs so mothers can relax while watching their kids. And lots of picnic tables scattered among those trees.

"We can plant more trees to replace the ones that blew down. A fire pit, a big one built of fieldstones with a circular bench around the edge for seating. We can continue our sing-alongs and have potluck suppers that the guests can join.

"Could we add kayaks, canoes, rowboats, and inner tubes down here for everyone? No jet skis because they make too much noise but maybe water ski lessons? Duncan Sunderlast took his regulars for pontoon rides, according to Ginger, so getting one of those would be a nice nod to history. A paddleboat would be fun; we could name it *The Skipper.* And a raft with a diving board. A place to play shuffleboard. We have to have shuffleboard; it's a tradition."

Brian attempted to silence me with a kiss, but I kept going.

"And a badminton court. Beach volleyball would be popular with teens. Cane poles, hooks, and bobbers for kids to fish off the dock. Maybe a place to dig for worms; we could salt it with nightcrawlers. Board games and a special building for kids to play when it rains."

Another kiss.

"Ping pong tables in a large enclosed log building that serves as a shelter.

A jukebox there with nostalgic music and costs a nickel. Pinball—the old-fashioned kind, not with guns and shooting but one of those you can 'tilt.' A popcorn machine and one of those vending contraptions where you can roll out a bottle of pop with old-fashioned flavors like orange and cherry but not crème soda because I'm not a fan. A shelf of books with *Nancy Drew* and *Hardy Boys* mysteries, reading that harkens back to that period in time. I'll contribute my own copies.

"We would be pet-friendly, especially dogs, but cats are okay if they're kept indoors or on a leash. No Wi-Fi and no air conditioning, just rotating fans. No TVs, no hot tubs; it has to be rustic except for a laundry facility. We'd have to offer that, maybe near the shelter house.

"Over in that area where Bud Foster kept his dogs, there should be a playground. We can call it Bubba's Playground and move his little grave nearby. I can see a tennis court, a pickleball court, a basketball hoop!

"Every cabin must have a wood-burning fireplace, not gas. Cynthia and I can draw up the plans. And there should be hiking paths with markers and maybe brochures to identify the trees, ferns, birds, and woodland flowers.

"And somehow, we must provide deeded access to a boat launch for residents of Aspen Glen. I don't know how that's done legally, but I'm sure it can be. Cynthia deserves that, at least. Don't you agree?"

"Take a breath," Brian said, finally subduing my frenzied outburst. "There's no need to rush, Jenny. It'll all work out."

"*The Last Resort* will be the name for the new beginning, too. It's perfect," I added. "The Last Resort reincarnated, but like the resorts you remember."

"And each of the 'new' old log cabins," Brian said slowly, "will have an excellent new mattress."

He led me back inside Bluegill.

Dash jumped up on the squeaky iron bed, waiting.

"With handmade patchwork quilts..." I couldn't stop. "We'll still serve pizza."

Brian murmured, "We're going to have so much fun."

The End

Author's Note

In 1927, my grandfather and friends built our family cabin, Lindsay Lodge, four miles north of Mercer on Catherine Lake. It's a rustic retreat (no plumbing or electricity) and, until recently, was accessible only by water. Generations of family and friends continue to find solace and healing in this beloved Northwoods setting.

While reading our cabin journals, I realized that I have a bizarre (albeit distant) link to the gruesome murder of Lotta Morgan, which plays a significant role in this novel. Lotta's body was found in an alley in Hurley on April 11, 1890. Several men carried it to the nearby undertaker, including young Herb Mielke, who eventually owned Cedar Island Resort on Cedar Lake, which adjoins Catherine Lake. Years later, when my grandparents drove north from my hometown of Manawa, they parked at Mielke's resort so Herb could deliver them and their gear by boat to Lindsay Lodge. My dad said "Uncle Herb" enjoyed narrating his connection to Lotta's murder.

Hurley is less than a thirty-minute drive north from our cabin. Once widely renowned as the most depraved region of the country, today the city (population 1,560) still features seven strip clubs on Silver Street. I've always been fascinated by its notoriety, and research into Northwoods' corruption revealed the deplorable origins of Hurley's status. Now I'm even more intrigued by my curious connection to "The Notorious Lotta Morgan: A Woman of the Demimonde."

Acknowledgments

When I sent a very rough draft of this book to my then-editor, Raphael Kadushin, it held every enthralling concept about the Northwoods that I could dream up. Wisely, I followed his counsel to reduce it to a single story instead of an amalgamation. Thanks, Raphy, for persuading me that Jenny had an important narrative of her own.

Writing is a solitary and lonely task. I'm grateful to my River Valley Book Club, which has supported me for the past twenty years with their friendship and abiding patience. Judy Marcus, Patti Yentz, Peggy Radel, Pat Scofield, Jill McDermott, Linda Kettner, Patti Peltier, Susan Jannotta, Jane Peckham, and Jan McCormick—I love you all.

Jane Kivlin kindly utilized her genealogy expertise to track unfamiliar facts of Lotta Morgan's past. John Ostrom's Facebook accounts guided me toward further resources. Whenever I hit a wall, I could count on Mary Craig, an excellent sleuth and childhood pal.

Shannon Booth's keen edits enabled this story to come alive. I'm especially pleased with Kristin Mitchell's enthusiasm and the warm welcome from Little Creek Press.

And finally, much appreciation to Jeff Curtin for generously sharing your beautiful home on Catherine Lake while my husband and I listened to loons and immersed ourselves in a luxurious northern lifestyle with hot water, internet access and laundry facilities—all within sight of our modest little cabin yet a world away.

Fate intervened thirty-three years ago when I was seated next to a handsome man on a plane. Remarkably, it was the second time we'd found ourselves in that situation on Midwest Express. Del Lamont and I were married a year later, and the depth of his love for me and encouragement of my work has never wavered.

For readers who wish to learn more about the evidence and information from which the history of Wisconsin's decadent reputation was formed, I have compiled a bibliography of available resources.

NOTE: Photograph of Lotta Morgan from author's collection.

Bibliography

"About Edna Ferber." *Monthly Bulletin*. August 1936, 4–5.

"Accused of Abduction: A State Warrant Sworn Out for Mrs. Maud Cassidy." *Chicago Tribune*, October 30, 1887. https://www.newspapers.com.

Ahlgrim, Charles. *The Mercer Oxbow*. Self-published, Charles Ahlgrim, 1998.

"Arrested on Suspicion: One Day Alias Riley Arrested for Complicity in the Murder of Lotta Morgan." *Gogebic Iron Tribune*. April 19, 1890. https://www.newspapers.com.

"Axe Sunk in Her Brain: A Fallen Woman Murdered in Cold Blood at Hurley." *The Weekly Wisconsin*. April 19, 1890. https://www.newspapers.com.

"Badger State Infamy: Marinette's Awful Dens of Vice and Scenes Therein. Foul Blots on the 'Scutcheon of One of the Fairest Lake States." *The Nebraska State Journal*, November 16, 1887. https://www.newspapers.com.

"Bet on the Red: How a Detroit Paper Refers to the Funeral of Lotta Morgan." *Interstate News-Record*. May 3, 1890. https://www.newspapers.com.

Bishop, Hugh E. *Haunted Lake Superior: Ghostly Tales and Legends from the Mystical Inland Sea*. Duluth: Lake Superior Port Cities, 2003.

"Brained with an Ax: Mysterious Murder of a Courtesan at Ashland." *St. Paul Globe*. April 12, 1890. https://www.newspapers.com.

"But Partially True: The Stories of the Dives of Northern Wisconsin." *The Saint Paul Globe*. February 12, 1888. https://www.newspapers.com.

"Charles Dickens." *Montreal River Miner* and *Iron County Republican*. September 4, 1890. https://www.newspapers.com.

"Chicago Procuress: Officers Expect to Send Her to the Penitentiary for Ten Years." *Lincoln Evening Call*, October 29, 1887. https://www.newspapers.com.

"Circumstances of the Case: Deep Mystery Which Has Surrounded the Famous Bank Robbery." *Ashland Weekly News*. November 27, 1889. https://www.newspapers.com.

Cirilli, Armand. "Lottie Morgan Was 'Tame' Compared to Irish Annie." *Iron County Miner*. n.d

"Clearing the Case: Solution of the Hurley Bank Robbery at Hand." *Ashland Weekly News*. November 27, 1889. https://www.newspapers.com.

"Covering Up Crime: Hurley Police Officials Accused of Shirking Their Duty." *Interstate News-Record*. May 10, 1890. https://www.newspapers.com.

Davis, Emily. "NewsChannel 7 Investigates: Sex Trafficking in North Central Wis. It Can and Is Happening Here." Wausau, Wisconsin (WSAW). November 23, 2016. https://www.wsaw.com/content/news/NewsChannel-7-Investigates-Sex-Trafficking-401764295.html.

"The Dens Again: Dr. Bushnell's Address at Madison. She Tells the Legislators about Her Experience in the Woods: The Victims Mostly Young Girls – Cases of Cruelty Described." *Oshkosh Northwestern*. January 17, 1889. https://www.newspapers.com.

"Dens of Infamy: The Terrible Story of Life in Michigan Lumber Camps." *The St. Paul Globe*. January 24, 1887. https://www.newspapers.com.

Endrizzi, Gilbert. "Centennial Anniversary of Lotta Morgan's Murder This Week: Still No Answers." *The Mercer Oxbow, 1920–Today*. 1998.

"The Examination of Day Alias Riley, Charged with Implication in the Murder of Lotta Morgan..." *Gogebic Iron Tribune.* April 26, 1890. https://www.newspapers.com.

Ferber, Edna. *Come and Get It.* New York: Knopf Doubleday Publishing Group, 1934.

"Forty Thousand Dollars: A Bold Bank Robbery, The Iron Exchange Bank Visited and a Big Boodle Secured! The Largest Robbery Ever Committed in the State." *Montreal River Miner.* September 26, 1889. https://www.newspapers.com.

"Governor Rusk Determines to Clean Out the Infamous Dens at Marinette and Hurley." *Lincoln Evening Call,* October 29, 1887. https://www.newspapers.com.

Hawks, Howard, William Wyler, and Richard Rosson, directors. *Come and Get It,* Howard Productions, Inc. 1936. 1 hr., 39 min. https://www.amazon.com/gp/video/detail/amzn1.dv.gti.38b9955c-5641-2aff-6f01-7e876395755f?ref_=imdbref_tt_wbr_pvs_piv&tag=imdbtag_tt_wbr_pvs_piv-20.

Human Trafficking Search. "How Street Traffickers Recruit Young Girls." March 17, 2014. https://humantraffickingsearch.org/how-street-traffickers-recruit-young-girls/.

"The Hurley Bank Robbery: A Sensational Story That It Was Followed by a Murder." *St. Louis Republic.* May 14, 1890. https://www.newspapers.com.

"The Hurley Murder: Lottie Morgan Was Not Killed for Sake of Robbery, but She Had Many Lovers." *Bay City Times.* April 14, 1890. https://www.genealogybank.co

"Hurley, Wisconsin – We Are Truly One of a Kind. Home of the 'Silver Street Experience.'" *Hurley Chamber of Commerce.* 2017. https://www.hurleywi.com.

"'Irish Annie' Killed." *Ironwood Times*. June 12, 1897. https://www.newspapers.com.

"'Irish Annie' Murdered." *Montreal River Miner*. June 9, 1897. https://www.newspapers.com.

Jensen, Joan M. *Calling This Place Home: Women on the Wisconsin Frontier 1850–1925*. Minnesota Historical Society Press, 2006, 54–61, 210–30.

"J. F. Sullivan...Has Always Had the Best Interests of the Town at Heart." *Gogebic Iron Tribune*. December 27, 1890. https://www.newspapers.com.

LaToya, Dennis. "Sex Trafficking Happening in Every Wisconsin County." Milwaukee, Wisconsin (WUWM 88.7). January 23, 2018. https://www.wuwm.com/regional/2018-01-23/sex-trafficking-happening-in-every-wisconsin-county.

"Let's Have the Truth: An Alleged Reliable Citizen Makes Terrible Statements." *Sterling Daily Gazette,* February 7, 1888. https://www.newspapers.com.

"Lotta Morgan's Early Life: Industry of the Woman Who Was Murdered at Hurley Last March." *Milwaukee Daily Journal*. May 15, 1890. https://www.genealogybank.com/doc/newspapers/image/.

"Lotta Morgan's Fate: The Mystery of Her Awful Murder at Hurley May Yet Be Unveiled." *Chicago Herald*. May 15, 1890. https://www.newspapers.com.

"Lotta Morgan's Funeral." *Gogebic Iron Tribune*. April 19, 1890. https://www.newspapers.com.

"Lotta Morgan's Murder: Re: Grand Jury at Hurley." *Ironwood Times*. December 7, 1895. https://www.newspapers.com.

"Lottie Morgan Murdered." *Montreal River Miner* and *Iron County Republican*. April 10, 1890. https://www.newspapers.com.

"Lottie Morgan's Murder." *Ironwood Times*. December 7, 1895. https://www.newspapers.com.

Lowry, Robert. "Where Is My Girl Tonight?" (Companion to "Where Is My Boy," Robert Lowry). 1877. https://www.hymnary.org.

"Lust in Wisconsin Pineries." *Daily Inter Ocean*. October 28, 1887. https://www.newspapers.com.

Martin, John Barlow. *Call it North Country*. New York: Alfred A. Knopf, 1944, 141–49, 176–88.

"Mary Schuman's Experiences." *Chicago Tribune,* November 1, 1887. https://www.newspapers.com.

Mercer Area Historical Society. *Mercer Remembers,* 1998.

"Miss Bushnell's Stories Exaggerated—Many Charges Are Absolutely False." *Chicago Tribune*. January 11, 1889. https://www.newspapers.com.

Monaco-Wilcox, Rachel, and Daria Mueller. "The Perfect Storm." *Wisconsin Lawyer,* State Bar of Wisconsin. Volume 90, Number 9. 2017. https://www.wisbar.org/NewsPublications/WisconsinLawyer/.

"More Wisconsin Horrors." *Daily Inter Ocean*. October 27, 1887. https://www.newspapers.com.

"Murder at Hurley - A Woman Killed with an Ax: A Character of the Town Found Dead in the Rear of a Saloon with Her Head Chopped Open." *Oshkosh Daily Northwestern*. April 11, 1890. https://www.newspapers.com.

"Mystery Growing Darker: Detectives Promise a Big Sensation in the Murder Affair at Hurley." *Milwaukee Daily Journal*. April 15, 1890. https://www.genealogybank.com.

"Not as Bad as Some: What a Detective Thinks of Wisconsin Dives" *Ashland Weekly News*, November 9, 1887. https://www.newspapers.com.

Ostrom, John D. "The Death of Lottie Morgan." Miscellaneous *Facebook* posts, 2010.

"The Pinery Dens: Governor Rusk's Statements About Them." *The Oshkosh Northwestern*, November 26, 1887. https://www.newspapers.com.

"A Pretty Woman Murdered." *Wessington Springs Herald.* April 18, 1890. https://www.newspapers.com.

Probate Notice – Ashland County Court: "In the Matter of the Estate of Laura H. Whitley, Deceased." *Gogebic Iron Tribune.* May 31, 1890. https://www.newspapers.com.

"...A Reward of $500 for the Detection of the Murderer of Lottie Morgan, Here, Two Years Ago." *Montreal River Miner* and *Iron County Republican.* May 14, 1892. https://www.newspapers.com.

Ritscher, Adam. "The Ku Klux Klan and Racism in the Northland." Northland College, Ashland, Wisconsin. Re: KKK Rally in Ironwood, MI. September 16, 1997.

"Shame on Hurley: Billing a Woman's Funeral." *The Oshkosh Northwestern.* April 16, 1890. https://www.newspapers.com.

Shucha, Bonnie. "White Slavery in the Northwoods: Early U.S. Anti-Sex Trafficking and Its Continuing Relevance to Trafficking Reform." *Combating Human Trafficking Through Law and Social Policy, William and Mary Journal of Race, Gender and Social Justice.* Volume 23, 2016–2017 Issue 1. Article 6. November 2016. https://scholarship.law.wm.edu/cgi/viewcontent.cgi?referer=&httpsredir=1&article=1441&context=wmjowl.

Shucha, Bonita. "Badger State Infamy: Wisconsin Early Sex Trade." *Wisconsin Lawyer.* State Bar of Wisconsin. Volume 90, Number 9. October 2017. https://www.wisbar.org/NewsPublications/WisconsinLawyer/.

Smith, Linda, and Cindy Coloma. *Renting Lacy: A Story of America's Prostituted Children.* Shared Hope International, 2013.

"Some Monkey Work: Capture of the Notorious Procuress Maud Cassidy, Wanted at Chicago." *The Saint Paul Globe,* December 27, 1887. https://www.newspapers.com.

"Some Person Purporting to Be a Correspondent of the Milwaukee Evening Wisconsin at This Place Recently Caused to Be Published the Following Concerning the Lotta Morgan Murder." *Gogebic Iron Tribune.* May 10, 1890. https://www.newspapers.com.

"State of Wisconsin: In Circuit Court, Iron County – Grand Jury Report." *Iron County Republican.* November 22, 1895. https://www.newspapers.com.

Stonehouse, Frederick, and Konnie LeMay. "Unsolved Mysteries of the Lakes." *Lake Superior Magazine,* November 1, 2006.

Sullivan, John F., Letter to the editor, "Done an Injustice: Lotta Morgan Not Found Dead in John F. Sullivan's Place." *The St. Paul Globe.* April 17, 1890. https://www.newspapers.com.

"Teen Girls' Stories of Sex Trafficking in U.S." ABC News, February 9, 2006. https://abcnews.go.com/Primetime/story?id=1596778&page=1.

"A Terrible Deed: Lotta Morgan Killed by a Midnight Assassin. The Deed Thought to Have Been the Act of a Woman." *Gogebic Iron Tribune.* April 12, 1890. https://www.newspapers.com.

"'Tis a Tough Town: Investigation Shows That Old Hurley Is as Wicked as in the Boom Days of 1889." *Eau Claire Leader.* December 21, 1895. https://www.newspapers.com.

"Uncle Herb Leaves! Pioneer Resort Owner to Go to Alaska." *Ironwood Daily Globe.* January 8, 1937. https://www.newspapers.com. Herbert Mielke: "One of Mielke's favorite reminiscences concerns Lotta Morgan, whose mysterious slaying in Hurley in the early nineties is still unsolved. Mielke helped to carry the body of the slain woman into a nearby building. The killing was a topic of conversation for years after, and the question was often asked, who killed Lotta Morgan? Mielke's theory was that the woman had knowledge of who was implicated in the Hurley bank robbery and that she was killed to silence her."

Uthe, Dorothy. *From Soup to Mostly Nuts: Stories from the Jones Family*. Anundsen Publishing Company. 1990.

Vanderlinden, Wolf. "Carl Ferdinand Feigenbaum: An Old Suspect Resurfaces." Casebook. n.d. https://www.casebook.org/suspects/carl-feigenbaum.html.

"Who Killed Lottie Morgan? A Pretty Variety Actress Struck Down by Unknown Assassin. Jealousy the Probable Cause." *Detroit Free Press*. April 12, 1890. https://www.newspapers.com.

Wisconsin Department of Justice, "Human Trafficking in Wisconsin – It's Happening Here." January 22, 2016.

"Wisconsin's Bonanza – The Newly Developed Iron Region Near Hurley." *Chicago Tribune*, September 15, 1886. https://www.newspapers.com.

"Wisconsin's Disgrace: Mrs. Julia Howden Relates Her Experience in a Pinery Dive." *Daily Interocean*. October 28, 1887. https://www.newspapers.com.

WPA Guide: *Michigan: A Guide to the Wolverine State*. Oxford University Press. 1941.

Printed in the United States
by Baker & Taylor Publisher Services